THE SCOUNDREL OF DRURY LANE

THE ROGUES OF DEVIL'S SQUARE

1

LAUREN SMITH

LAUREN SMITH
BOOKS

England, 1810

Christopher "Kit" Hollingsworth was trapped in hell. His hands were bound with iron manacles, and he was in the belly of a transportation ship bound for Australia. His head throbbed from having been struck several times in the last few days. He groaned and tried to sit up. How long had he been unconscious? The sound of waves crashing rhythmically against the wooden hull reminded him that the ship was already far out to sea. England was fading farther and farther away.

He examined the manacles and then peered at the other prisoners around him. Men and women were seated close together, hip to hip and packed like animals. A heavy stench pervaded the air, making Kit's stomach roil.

A large, bulky man walked through the rows of prisoners. He wielded a thick wooden club the length of his forearm. Kit had taken that club to his stomach when he'd first been shoved belowdecks. Even the sight of that thick piece of wood caused a cold sweat to break out on Kit's brow. The man slapped the club restlessly into his meaty palm as he peered at the prisoners.

"Oi, which one of you is Hollingsworth?" he demanded.

Grimy, weary faces of broken men and women showed no reaction to the man's words. They weren't the one he was looking for. Kit didn't want to know what the man wanted from him, but he *wouldn't* hide. He was the son of the Earl of Kentwell, by God, and he would not hide or cower from his fate, no matter how grim.

"I am Hollingsworth," he said, but the sound was raspy from lack of use and lack of water. His lips were chapped, and it hurt to swallow. He raised his manacled hands a little, catching the man's attention.

"Stand up and come with me, the captain wants to see you" the man barked, and then he turned away.

Kit braced himself on the nearest wooden beam and stood. He shuffled behind the man with slow, painful steps. His entire body felt as though it were one raw wound. Thankfully, they'd left his feet unbound, and he was able to follow the man up the two decks to where the captain and his officers had their quarters.

They proceeded to a cabin at the stern of the vessel. Kit straightened his spine, readying himself for whatever came next. The man shot Kit a loathsome look before he curled his fingers into a fist and rapped his knuckles on the door.

"Enter," a hard voice called from within the cabin.

The burly man opened the door and shoved Kit into the cabin before he turned and stood in the hallway to wait, closing the door.

Kit's gaze darted around, taking in the bed, washstand,

sea chest, and table laden with maps and ship's logs. A man who Kit presumed to be the captain sat at the table, his back to Kit as he reviewed a stack of papers on the desk.

"Come around front so I may see you," the captain ordered.

After a moment's hesitation, Kit moved around the table to present himself to the captain. As he did so, he caught a glimpse of his own reflection in a tall, cheval glass mirror in the opposite corner of the room. His once fine clothes were damaged beyond repair. His white lawn shirt was torn, and the fine embroidery of his silk waistcoat was frayed and stained with blood, dirt, and other things. His hair hung in dark, limp tendrils on his head. Only his eyes, a dark fathomless brown, held any of the fire left within him.

"Christopher Hollingsworth, son of the Earl of Kentwell." The captain lifted a piece of paper to better read the information. Kit said nothing and waited for the man to continue speaking.

"You are nineteen years of age. Your crime, it seems . . . was grand larceny of goods from the *Wind Sprite*, a ship belonging to the East India Company. You were sentenced to death, but the sentence was commuted to seven years' transportation. No doubt your influential father had a hand in that." The captain didn't seem to expect an answer, and Kit didn't give him one.

Kit stared straight ahead, his gaze boring a hole into the wall behind the captain's head. Two months ago, Kit had been at his gentlemen's club, Berkley's, playing whist with his friends when he was seized and charged with stealing goods from the *Wind Sprite*. After spending four months in Newgate Prison, he'd faced a trial and sentencing. Mere days before his execution, he'd been informed that his father had used every bit of his power and money to buy Kit's life. A life that for the next seven years was not to be his own.

"That *is* you, isn't it, boy?" the captain inquired as he set his paper down on his desk and folded his hands in front of him.

Kit slowly lowered his gaze. The captain was perhaps in his late forties, with a sallow, pinched face and a thin but muscular form. He wore a finely embroidered waistcoat and well-tailored trousers. Kit assumed this man was the captain of the ship.

"Yes, but I am innocent." He had screamed those words so often in the last few months that he had lost his voice. Now when he spoke, he no longer expected anyone to believe him. The three men who had sealed his fate had planned their deception and betrayal so cleverly that most of England believed in his guilt.

"I'm sure you are," the captain said with a cold, ironic chuckle. "But it is far too late to change that. You are on my ship. Mind my rules, keep your mouth shut, and you might survive the journey."

Kit tried to wet his lips and cleared his throat. "May I ask where we are headed? I assume it is Australia?"

"We are bound for the colonial settlement at Sullivans Cove."

Kit asked no other questions, even though he wanted to.

"Most of the convicts on this ship will be sent to work gangs or stations outside of the settlement. If you do well at this, you may be free to work for money in the last few years of your sentence. You may also be sent to work for a private individual who may pay you for your labor at their discretion. Once your sentence is at an end, if you have behaved, you will be declared a free man. You will be free to stay in Australia or return to England. At that point, you may go wherever you wish, so long as you have the means to travel."

A dull ringing started in Kit's ears. *Seven years . . .* The number was slowly beginning to penetrate the shock that had kept him frozen the last several months. But as the shock faded, anger took its place, coiling around his heart and planting itself like a thornbush within his bones. His anger was so deep it blistered his very soul.

"Do we understand each other?" the captain asked. "I know you come from a bloodline that must date back to the days of Charlemagne, but aboard my ship you are no different than any other criminal. Remember that."

"I understand," Kit replied, the two words heavy as they left his lips.

"Good. You may return below with the others."

Kit wondered if his status as the son of an earl had caused him to be singled out or if the other prisoners would be similarly called. He joined his surly escort in the corridor outside the cabin and was escorted back to the dark belly of the ship where the sights, sounds, and smells of human despair threatened to drown him. He was defeated *for now*, but he'd begun to count down the days of those seven years. When he was a free man once again, he would return for revenge.

~

Captain James Murray stared thoughtfully at the papers that concerned the young lordling's crime. The boy was barely nineteen and would likely not survive the voyage. Despite the beatings he must have suffered at Newgate before he'd been put aboard James's ship, he was still a strong young lad, and that would make him a target.

James had been paid handsomely to see that Hollingsworth didn't survive the crossing. The terms were that he'd be killed and tossed overboard. Normally, James would see it done, but not with this boy.

Hollingsworth was an earl's son. That carried some weight, regardless of the boy's conviction. If the lad died while on the ship, James would have to give an accounting of the incident to the authorities, which was far more than he would do for the other convicts. It would put him in the path of powerful men like the boy's father, and he didn't want an earl out for his blood. Better to let the boy reach Sullivans Cove and allow the wild and untamed country and its criminal inhabitants handle the matter for him.

James tried to focus on the stack of papers on his desk, but his mind kept drifting back to Hollingsworth.

What bothered James the most was the boy's eyes. He'd never seen such a look in a man's eyes before, and he'd been taking some of England's worst criminals as prisoners to penal colonies for nearly ten years. The lad's eyes held such a fury that James had no doubt that, if given the chance, it would seal the doom of whoever stood in his way.

Those eyes held the promise of *death*.

1

A ship docked under the cover of darkness. The moon was shrouded by storm clouds, concealing the ship's entry as it slipped quietly into port just after midnight.

Kit Hollingsworth gripped the railing so tightly that the faint scars on his knuckles turned white. He scanned the docks, listening to the creak of the ship and the light wind rustling through the canvas sails as sailors rushed to the rigging to finish tacking them.

Seven years. He hadn't seen London in seven years . . . but those seven years felt like a century.

The young nineteen-year-old Christopher was long dead. Kit's body was hard from years of physical labor—breaking stones, building settlements, and working fields. His life in Sullivans Cove had driven out any weakness within him. He had grown another three inches, making him taller than most men, and the slender muscles of his body had become thick and tight. A roughly trimmed beard covered his jaw, and his dark hair was longer than he guessed was fashionable—not that he knew or cared what was in fashion in this part of the world. He doubted his own mother would have recognized him if she'd been alive.

As the crew ran a gangplank down to the dock, men began unloading crates of goods. An officer from the Thames River Police came aboard to oversee the proceedings and make sure the goods on the ship went where they belonged and were not stolen or dropped into the water to be collected later by thieves. It didn't escape Kit's notice that he had been framed for a crime that was now easily prevented. He'd lost seven years of his life because he'd been accused of hiring "scuffle-hunters" and "lumpers" to steal nearly an entire ship's transport of tobacco.

A tic worked in Kit's jaw as he slung the canvas bag that contained his meager belongings over his shoulder and descended the gangplank. His boots landed with the agile grace that he'd gained over the last two years, working in a house as an indentured servant. *Seen, not heard.* That was the most valuable thing he had learned: the ability to move quietly, quickly, and without being seen. He nodded at the ship's crew as he passed, then walked alone toward the distant smoke-hazed taverns that ringed the wharf.

As he passed old places that should have been familiar, he felt he was an outsider looking in on a place he no longer recognized. He dug in his purse for a few coins and flagged down a hackney once he reached a street with more traffic. The driver raised a brow at Kit's coarse clothing and rough appearance, but he took the money nonetheless.

"Where to, then?" the driver asked, punctuating his sentence with a yawn.

"Knightley Street," Kit said.

The man gave a little shudder. "The Devil's Square?"

"The what?"

The driver peered down at him. "Where ye been living? That's what it's called, innit?" the driver said in a hushed voice. "Devil's Square, on account of them lords that live in those fancy houses being dangerous. You sure you want to go there?"

"Dangerous, are they?" Kit's dark grin made the driver shut his mouth and settle into his perch. He doubted anyone in this city could frighten him anymore. Not after the things he'd seen . . . the things he'd done.

Kit opened the door to the hackney and climbed in. He eased back against the cushions of the coach, reflexively flinching, but no pain came. The whippings had stopped several years ago, but his body remembered every lash, every laceration, and he had gone for months without being able to lean back against anything. Old habits were hard to break.

He closed his eyes and drew in a deep, steadying breath. In some ways, London hadn't changed. The scents and sounds of a city full of people, industry and vice all tumbled together in the atmosphere, making his head throb. It was so different from Australia. He'd spent the past seven years in a wild land with dangerous creatures of all sizes and some of the most dangerous criminals who'd escaped the noose. But beyond that, the landscape had been open, with clear blue skies and clean winds that tasted only of freedom.

London was no less dangerous than the colonial settlements in its own way, but here, in this city, he was now one of the creatures to be feared in the dark. His innocence, his boyish charm, and his entitlement as a rich young lordling were gone forever. He honestly didn't know who he was anymore. Kit only knew what he *wasn't*.

When the carriage rolled to a stop, he leapt out onto the sidewalk.

"Good luck." The driver hastily tapped the reins against the backs of his horses, and the hackney pulled away, vanishing quickly into the darkened street.

Kit faced the row of houses on either side of the street as memories he had fiercely hidden in his heart, memories that had once been his only light, came back in wild flashes. He was a lad of fourteen, racing down the street, calling for his friends to catch him. At sixteen, he'd ridden his first fine gelding to the park with his father, his head held high. He'd climbed every tree in the garden behind his home and scaled every wall of his friends' homes. A thousand sunny adventures whispered to him from behind a wall of pain, shame, and regret.

His dearest friends had once lived here . . . Did they still? *Lionel, Darius, Felix, Vincent, Warren.*

Their names drifted back to him. They had been as thick as thieves, thought themselves to be handsome young devils who had only the world ahead of them. They'd run about London getting into good-natured mischief like all young bucks their age. Where were those boys now? They had defended him valiantly seven years ago; they'd cried out for justice and done what they could to help his father save him from the short drop and sudden stop of the noose.

Kit feared those boys who had been so loyal then would be changed now. Had any taken their titles? Were they living in the country with wives and children? He had a thousand questions, but he would have no answers tonight, save one. His father. He put aside all other concerns and focused on what he would say to his father when he saw him.

He moved silently down the street, avoiding the blossoms of light the oil lamps cast from the windows of the homes. At last, he was facing his father's townhouse. Kit's heart battered against his ribs as he rapped the knocker on the door. For a long moment, nothing happened. The hour was late, but surely someone would hear—

The door creaked open a few inches and a gray-haired butler peered at him from behind, a pair of spectacles perched on his nose.

"Yes?" the butler asked suspiciously.

Kit squinted back as he slowly recognized the man. "Good God, is that you, Palmer?"

"Yes, I'm Mr. Palmer."

Kit took an instinctive step toward the familiar man in relief, but Palmer drew back.

"Keep your distance, sir. I'll have no funny business here," the butler warned.

It was only then that Kit realized why Palmer didn't seem to know him. He was no longer the boy Palmer would remember.

"Palmer . . . it's me," he said, his voice still rusty from lack of use.

Palmer squinted even more. "Name yourself or I shall call for the constable."

Kit stepped slowly closer. "It's Christopher. I'm *home*."

"Mas—Master Kit?" the butler gasped. "Good God—"

Palmer disappeared from view, and Kit heard the distinctive thud of a falling body as the butler fainted dead away behind the partially closed door.

"Bloody hell." Kit pushed the door open and crouched over the fallen man. "Palmer, wake up." He shook the man's shoulders, and after a moment Palmer's eyelids fluttered.

"Master Kit?" the butler moaned as Kit helped him sit up. "Is it truly you?"

"Afraid so," Kit said dryly.

The butler stared at him in stunned silence.

"I know it's late, but I must see my father." He needed to see him, to see his father's face now that he was finally home. He'd dreamed about this moment so many nights and had longed for it more than anything in the world.

"Master Kit . . . your father . . . he's . . ." Palmer's face was ashen, his eyes wide in pain.

He didn't have to say more. Kit had been in the presence of death for so long that it had become an old friend whose presence he could sense easily.

"When did he die?" The words were bitter on Kit's tongue, and his bluntness seemed to stun the older man. The tactful, polite boy he'd been was gone.

"He passed just after Christmas last year. I remember because it snowed so fiercely that day and he kept asking why he was so cold, no matter how many fires I lit in the house."

His father was gone. Kit was too late. The strength he'd clung to for the last seven years, the hope as well, was all gone, along with his father. He'd hoped that the one and only letter he'd been able to send would have reached his father, telling him that he was coming home.

"Did he receive my letter?" Kit asked, his throat tight.

"No, Master Kit. We received nothing . . ."

He'd feared as much. "Where did you bury him?"

"We buried him beside your mother in the country."

Kit closed his eyes and let out a shallow breath as he fought off a wave of grief. His future held a so many uncertainties, but this was one he had never considered. When he had last seen his father, the old lion had been roaring against the injustice of the legal system that had allowed Kit to be falsely convicted. He had been neither ill nor frail then.

"How did it happen?" Kit asked.

"He was never the same after you were transported. He stopped taking care of himself. Mrs. Swanson drove herself mad trying to cook anything that would tempt him to eat. The young lads of the square did their best to watch over him. But a broken heart is a broken heart, and he feared you might never come home. He fought tirelessly to appeal your case, but he failed every time, and with each failure, he lost more and more hope."

Palmer clasped Kit's hands in his own, and his ancient eyes peered down at Kit's large, calloused hands as if he didn't recognize them.

Strangely ashamed, Kit nearly pulled away. He'd grown wary of anyone touching him. A touch usually came with pain. He'd had to fight more than one prisoner for food, water, or simply to defend his own life. He hadn't had a touch of comfort from anyone since he'd left London.

"My friends? They looked after him?"

"As best they could," Palmer said with quiet pride. "The lads never stopped waiting for you to come home or to hear news of you from the colonies."

Kit would have smiled, but he had no joy left within him.

"I wish I'd been able to write. I couldn't afford to, not until I was free to come home." He didn't dare tell the old man that he'd been too busy the first few years trying not to die from the elements, the other convicts, and the men in charge of his labor assignments.

"Help me up, Master Kit." Palmer paused, frowning. "I'm sorry, you're . . . *his lordship* now . . . I must remember."

"*Master Kit* will do for now, Palmer." He lifted the old man up to his feet and guided him to the drawing room, where Kit lit a lamp. He glanced around, noting that the house was clean, but much of the furniture was faded and the carpets were threadbare.

"How bad are things, Palmer?" he asked after a minute. "Did Father lose everything trying to buy my freedom?" When he'd been charged and convicted, his father had spent so much of his wealth trying to save him that Kit had feared his father wouldn't recover financially.

"No, he had plenty of money left at the end. His investments were managed well by his friends while you were away. They stepped in after your transportation and helped him recover much of what he lost."

"Then why the devil is the place in shambles?" Kit's tone was a little harsher than he intended it to be.

"'Twas your father's decision. He simply didn't want us to touch anything other than to clean it. I think he feared that if we changed anything in the house, it would mean you might never come home."

Kit dragged his palm over his beard, and this time the sigh he let out was long and left a hollow feeling in his chest.

"Who handled the house and the staff after he died?"

"Lord Tiverton, of course," Palmer said with pride.

"Ah," Kit sighed. Lord Tiverton was the Duke of Tiverton, Darius St. John's father. They'd lived across the street as families for more than thirty years, long before Kit or Darius had been born. Of course Tiverton would have watched over the house, hoping Kit would return to take over. If he hadn't, Kit may have been declared dead by a scheming distant relative, and then the estate would have passed to that relative before Kit returned from Australia. He owed Lord Tiverton a great debt.

"Why don't you go on back to bed, Palmer? I'll find my old room and settle in." His focus drifted to his canvas bag that sat in the corridor outside.

"Are you hungry, Master Kit? Mrs. Swanson still remembers all of your favorite dishes, and I'm sure she could cobble together a nice little meal for you before you retire for the night," the butler suggested.

"Hungry? No." He would find some food in the kitchens after Palmer was in bed. He didn't wish to trouble the old man any further tonight. "Go on to bed," Kit urged as he escorted the elderly man to the servants' stairs. "We'll sort out everything in the morning."

"Very well, my lord." Palmer entered the stairway, and Kit closed the door behind him.

Kit retrieved his bag and carried it to his room on the

first floor. The bed, the red coverlet, the writing desk, along with the dresser hadn't been touched in seven years. Two tall bookshelves were still filled with tomes adorned with gleaming gilt letters on their spines.

His fingers itched to touch them. He'd had no chance to read and no money to buy books until the last two years he'd been working in the colonies. Even then, he'd been saving every bit of coin to buy his passage back home. The only time he'd read books was when he had borrowed books from his employer to read after his work was done for the day, but usually by then he was exhausted and fell straight into sleep. When he woke, the nightmare of his life would start all over again.

He set the canvas bag down on his bed, knowing that he would have trouble sleeping on the feather tick mattress tonight. His last bedding had been only a few inches thick, and over the last seven years his body had grown accustomed to sleeping on hard surfaces.

Kit lit a lamp and set it on a side table near his window before he unpacked his belongings. His bag contained a spare shirt, a pair of sailor's trousers, one small broken-toothed comb, a pair of scissors, and a dull shaving razor. There was also another pair of boots and a tiny piece of carved ivory in the shape of an elephant. He held up the elephant, the cool ivory warming his palm.

His last master, a man named Anthony Lockwood, had given it to him one night after Kit had shared his story of how he'd ended up working in Sullivans Cove. Lockwood had actually *believed* he was innocent. He had passed the elephant to Kit as a gift and said, *"Elephants never forget. Neither should you."* He referred to the three men who had sent Kit to prison. Thomas Balfour, justice of the peace; Jackson Townsend, the shipping company clerk; and Maynard Walsh, Kit's business partner in the shipping company Kit had purchased half ownership in.

He hadn't known then that his investment had been a trap, that he was meant to be the fool they'd planned to pin the tobacco theft on once the theft was discovered.

Kit set the elephant down on the windowsill, then stilled as he heard something plinking against the window. He pressed close to the glass and stared down at the street below where a dark figure stood. The man bent to retrieve something from the ground and stood again. He wound his arm and threw something at Kit's window, which hit with another plink.

Bloody hell, the man was tossing stones at his window. Kit moved quickly and rushed down the stairs to the front door before the man smashed his window.

The instant he opened it, the figure from outside slipped into the foyer. It was a trick! The man wasn't trying to get his attention—he'd been trying to get someone to let him inside. Before the man could react, Kit grabbed him by the throat and slammed him against the wall, growling a warning in the dark.

"Move and I'll break your neck." He squeezed his fingers on the man's throat in emphasis. He didn't know what this man wanted, but Kit trusted *no one*. For all he knew, this man could have been hired by Balfour and Walsh to watch for his return and to kill him if possible.

"Might be hard to do . . . if your lung is punctured," the other man growled back.

The sharp prick of a blade against Kit's ribs made him

realize what a fool he'd been. Of course a thief would be armed if he was making such a bold attempt at robbery.

Knowing when he was beat, Kit let go of the other man and slowly stepped back. The man was close to him in height, with hair as black as a raven's wing, and his bight blue eyes glowed in the waning moonlight coming in from the open doorway. He recognized the man, but the shock of the face, as changed as his own, caught him off guard.

"Darius?" Kit said uncertainly. He would never forget those eyes, even if the face had changed from a boy's to a man's. It was Darius St. John.

"Good God . . ." Darius's face turned a stark white as he stared at Kit. "Kit," he breathed, his eyes softening with brotherly affection. "Christ . . . it's really you, isn't it?"

"It is," Kit replied. He was uncomfortable with the rush of emotions he felt at seeing his old friend. He wasn't ready to face the past, even the better parts, perhaps even those more so than the rest, because he could never go back to those good days before his world had burned around him.

Darius grabbed him in a tight embrace. "God, man, you have no idea how much we missed you." He slapped Kit on the back and then finally let go of him. Darius was grinning, but Kit remained frozen as he felt the burden of those missing years weigh heavily on his shoulders.

"Kit, are you all right?" Darius asked, then cursed under his breath. "Of course you aren't. That's a stupid question. No one would be all right after what you've been through."

Kit had no idea what to say to that, so he merely grunted in response. How was it that Darius could so easily read him and the situation he was in?

"I want to hear everything, of course, but we ought to wait for the others," Darius said quite seriously.

"The others?" Kit replied in confusion.

Darius walked into the drawing room and took the lamp over to the window. He stopped and passed the lamp in front of the window, then withdrew it from view five times in succession. Then he watched the street for a moment and repeated the odd motions. Only then did he finally set the lamp down and face Kit again.

"What on earth were you doing?" Kit asked.

"Summoning the others," Darius said with a grim smile. "They'll be on their way. We devised a simple method to send signals to each other when we have news. Ever since you were sent away, we haven't trusted anyone to not read the messages we send, at least not anything about you."

"Why would you be sending messages about me?" Kit asked, still confused and still baffled as to who Darius would be talking to.

"Because we've never stopped trying to prove your innocence. We've had to be careful about it."

"When you say *we*, you mean . . ." Kit waited for him to explain.

"The others . . . Lionel, Warren, Felix, Vincent. Good Lord, Kit, you can't think we'd have forgotten about you after all these years." Darius stared at him, clearly stunned at Kit thinking just that.

"We've spent the last seven years pretending to be scandalous aristocrats playing in the pleasure gardens and racing our curricles and all that nonsense. But in truth . . . we've changed, Kit, just as you have." Darius's eyes were filled with an old pain. "We've become a sort of . . . secret society. You remember that old joke they used to make about us when we were lads? The Rogues of Devil's Square? Well, I'm afraid it's become true—we're dangerous men, Kit, as dangerous as we could manage to make ourselves. We've trained in combat of all forms, we've practiced signals and writing in code and all manner of things, all while we kept watch on your enemies, because they became *our* enemies."

"You've been watching Walsh and Balfour all this time?"

"Walsh and Balfour are clever, and we don't wish to underestimate them. It's why I came to investigate when I saw you here. It was my night to stay on the street and keep watch," Darius declared as if that was quite obvious. "I saw the light on in the window and didn't know who'd be in your room. I thought I'd come to see and lure whoever it was to the door. I never imagined it might be you, but I'm deuced glad it was. It seems . . ." Darius paused as he glanced out the window again. "That we're fortunate. The others are coming now. They must have come home early from their evenings out and seen the signal."

Sure enough, a moment later, four figures were seen moving toward Kit's home. Darius left the drawing room to meet them at the front door. Kit stayed where he was, his mind racing as he realized who was about to come through that door.

For the first time in seven years, his friends, now *dangerous* gentlemen who lived in Devil's Square, were going to be together again.

2

Nothing could have prepared Kit to be in a room with his boyhood friends again. Certainly not like this. The golden-hued memories that surrounded their now hardened masculine faces were like faint auras, echoes of the past. His chest ached with an unexpected hollowness. He had lost something precious these last seven years.

Time.

Time was all a man truly had of value, and he'd had seven years stolen from him. Seven years of their friendship had been taken, just as his father had been, and neither could be reclaimed.

"I still can't believe it," Lionel Thistlewaite murmured after everyone had briefly greeted one another. Lionel stepped toward Kit. His old friend looked at him as if he was a ghost, and he was only slightly surprised the man didn't come over and poke his chest to make sure he was real.

His friends stood in a loose half ring facing him across

the other side of the drawing room. Only Darius dared to cross the chasm. Kit turned back to the window. He was unable to meet the curious and probing gazes of his friends. He wasn't used to being looked at, not with such intensity. He would have given almost anything to douse the lamplight and vanish into the dark. Coming home now felt like a mistake.

"Kit . . . ?" Warren Burville's green eyes sought out Kit's face, and Kit could feel the man's searching gaze upon him.

"Yes?" Kit asked after a moment's hesitation.

"What can we do? What do you need?" Warren kept his voice low, and Kit was grateful. He did not want Palmer or Mrs. Swanson woken by their late-night meeting.

Felix Hawkins, with his wild tangle of golden blond hair making him look like a roguish knight of King Arthur's court, leaned against the wall. "Yes, we *want* to help. Tell us what we can do." His gray eyes were earnest and sharp. Bittersweet memories of Felix as a boy made Kit's heart ache enough that he nearly fisted a hand over his chest. He remembered everything about these men . . . or at least, the boys they had once been. He knew nothing of the men they had become.

Kit cleared his throat, aware more than ever of the condition of his clothing and his wild appearance among these polished gentlemen. It left him feeling off-balance.

Vincent, always the quietest of their group, seemed to read Kit's mind. "Revenge . . . that's why you came back, isn't it?"

Kit answered with a slight nod.

"Then tell us what to do," Darius said. "We'll help in any way we can."

"No, I must do this alone," Kit said.

Lionel chuckled. "I don't think you understand. We weren't asking permission."

Kit blinked at Lionel's offhand remark.

"We've waited seven years to have you back, and we aren't about to let you have your revenge alone. We want it too. Those men need to pay for what they did." Lionel's hazel eyes were filled with all the cleverness he'd had as a child, and Kit sensed that Lionel had honed that ability into a dangerous skill.

Kit took the measure of each of his friends. None of them had become the leisurely, relaxed aristocrats he'd expected them to be. It seemed they had suffered from a restless need for justice, just as he had. He could see that now. Beneath their gentlemanly clothing, there was a hard edge to each of them that reminded him all too much of the feral animals and even more feral men he'd lived with in Australia. His friends had in some ways spent the last seven years in a battle here just as he had battled all the way on the other side of the earth. They carried a darkness that almost matched his own.

"You truly want to help me?" Kit asked, and his throat suddenly tightened with a flood of emotions as the men facing him all solemnly nodded.

"We're with you to the *last*. We always have been," Warren replied.

The confident words stung deep within Kit's chest. It felt like a lightning bolt had struck his dead heart, forcing it to beat again. He'd been dead for seven years, a ghost of a man . . . And now here he was, breathing, hurting all over again.

But he wasn't *alone*, not anymore.

"Where do we start?" Felix asked, still lounging against the wall, arms crossed over his chest.

"There are only three people I want," Kit said after a moment. "Thomas Balfour, Maynard Walsh, and Jackson Townsend, the shipping clerk who gave false witness against me."

Vincent took a chair at a reading table. The other men followed suit except for Kit, who kept near the window away from the others. He still wasn't used to being so close to his past.

"Well," Vincent began, "Balfour is now a chief magistrate, and he a partner with Walsh in your old shipping company. He did wait a full year after your transportation before he bought into Walsh's company. They handle almost all the major shipping out of London's ports now, except for those ships that Ashton Lennox hires for his cargo. He is the only one still giving them any competition."

"Lennox?" Kit wasn't familiar with the name.

"He's a baron," Lionel explained. "He's a ruthless businessman, but fair. If you need anyone investing your money, he's the man to trust, and likely a good ally if we ever need one. After you left England, he handled your father's financial affairs at my suggestion. We thought he wouldn't take advantage of your father during the period of his grief, and he didn't."

Kit tensed at the mention of his father. "Thank you for watching over him." He met the eyes of the men in the room, letting them all know he meant it.

"You would have done it for any of us," Warren replied.

That was certainly true, but Kit needed them to know

how grateful he was. "What of the clerk, Townsend?" Kit asked, forcing himself not to think of his father again. He would face that bleak emptiness when this was over.

"The man died last year, but . . . his daughter works at the Drury Lane theater," Vincent added, and the others shot him a look of surprise.

"How on earth do you know that?" Darius demanded, a little suspiciously.

"I always keep track of pretty women. And she's rather pretty," Vincent admitted. "I decided to follow her one night."

Kit listened to his friends, who all began to talk at once, arguing about who had watched whom, and it was in that moment Kit realized just how deeply invested his friends had been in keeping informed of his enemies' movements. Even after all this time, they'd really been watching out for his father and for him.

"How pretty is *rather pretty*?" asked Felix with a rakish grin.

"*Quite* pretty," Vincent replied seriously. He leaned back in his chair, pensively studying the card table in front of him, which held a few dusty books that hadn't been touched in months. "If she has any of her father's wealth from his payoff for betraying you, Kit, she's hiding it well. One of us should investigate her more thoroughly."

"I suppose you're volunteering?" Warren chuckled and rolled his eyes.

"I always volunteer when it comes to beautiful women," Vincent freely admitted. "I'd much rather watch her all day than I would Walsh or Balfour."

Kit envied their easy camaraderie. Once upon a time,

he'd fit in so well with them, but now he had only memories of the boys they'd been, and he didn't know where he fit in the group anymore. He struggled to regain his focus on what mattered in this moment.

His hands curled into fists. So Townsend's daughter was an actress on Drury Lane and living on blood money from his conviction?

"Let's start with her," Kit said. The teasing and bickering amongst his friends died away. "And I'll be the one to deal with her," he added.

Lionel cleared his throat. "Just to be clear . . . you aren't planning to *hurt* this woman, are you? She was only a child when you were convicted."

"If she's gained any advance from her father's betrayal of me, I will take it from her." He paused briefly, meeting Lionel's eyes. "But I do not hurt women. Vincent, is there a play on tonight?"

"Tonight? No, they will likely be working on the new play that debuts in a few weeks. They've been staying late each evening for rehearsals."

"Good. That gives me some time to develop a plan for her."

"Kit, you'll need to visit the shops to buy new clothes . . . and cut your hair. You look a tad . . . well, *frightening*," Darius offered with brotherly gentleness. "If you're to return to London, that means a return to society, even if only long enough to exact revenge."

Darius was right. The way Kit looked at the moment, he would terrify anyone he came across. His plan to exact revenge required fitting back into society. He would have to become a gentleman again. He had considered just killing the three men who'd destroyed his life, but that would have been too quick of a punishment for them. They needed to suffer, to have everything they cared about taken away, just as he had.

"Why don't we meet tomorrow evening at the club?" Warren suggested. "The Bombay Room at nine o'clock?"

Everyone murmured their assent, and Kit finally nodded as well. One by one, his friends took their leave until Kit was alone with Darius in the drawing room.

"I'll come over sometime around midday. We'll see about a new wardrobe and a haircut." Darius lightly slapped Kit on the back. "I'm glad you're back. It's been . . . not right here without you." He seemed like he wanted to say more, and the ghosts of old wounds gleamed once again in Darius's blue eyes.

Seeing his friend hurting like that pierced the wall that Kit had built around his dead heart years ago. Damn his friends for bringing his heart back to life. Each beat was heavy in his chest, and the depth of the feelings that tumbled around inside him grew impossible to ignore.

"Sleep well, Kit," Darius said, and then he too slipped out into the darkness, leaving Kit alone once more. The house felt empty, even though he knew more than a dozen servants slept within its walls.

Kit turned out the lamp and lingered between the shadows and moonlight as he listened to the quiet settling of the wood and stone of the house. Then, after a long moment of utter stillness, he collected his small coin purse and left. He took a route he remembered from years ago to reach Drury Lane. The theater house appeared empty of patrons, but a few lamps were lit in the windows.

So this was where Townsend's daughter worked as an actress? He had never met the girl. His few interactions with Townsend had been brief. He'd always greeted the man before going into Maynard Walsh's office. He'd exchanged pleasantries with the fellow, but that was it.

Kit frowned as he crept closer to the theater. He edged around the side of the building, where he caught a slender beam of faint candlelight slicing through the inky night. A door to the back of the theater was propped open with a sturdy rock.

A dark-haired man around Kit's age or perhaps a little older was emptying a bucket of dust into the street. A small cloud billowed up, causing the man to cough violently as he stepped back into the theater, carrying his broom and bucket with him.

Through the half-open doorway, Kit spotted a few actors adjusting elaborate costumes while they chatted. Beyond them, a woman was perched on a ladder, holding a paintbrush. The scenery she was painting looked unbelievably vivid. She'd created a dark forest background with motes of sunlight that pierced the gloom of the greenery. It was so lifelike that Kit blinked several times. He found himself drawn toward the exquisite quality of the background sets, and he'd just reached the half-open door when the dark-haired man stepped into his path.

"Oh, I beg your pardon." The man peered outside. "Are you one of our new theater staff?"

Kit glanced down at the bucket and broom the man held. "Yes," he said quickly. "I'm to clean . . . the theater." He laid on a slight Cornish accent, sounding like the sailors he'd traveled with back to London.

"Well, nice to meet you, old chap. I'm Florizel Holland, the stage manager." He thrust out a hand and smiled at Kit. "Everyone calls me Flory."

Kit shook his hand, taken aback at the man's friendliness. He certainly wasn't used to that.

"Come on in. We're finishing up for the night, but I could show you around." He beckoned for Kit to follow him into the theater's back entrance.

The space was shadowy and cramped with costumes, extra sets, and ropes and rigging to move things about on the stage. But his gaze kept drifting to the woman still on the ladder wielding the paintbrush. Her long blonde hair was pulled up in a messy but attractive style on top of her head, fastened with a green ribbon that was coiled between tumbles of gold strands. He had the sudden desire to pull on that ribbon and watch her hair cascade down. She was a petite creature, perhaps only just above five feet, and yet she still had a strange, enchanting presence that left Kit all too aware of her.

Flory talked about the play they were preparing and pointed out various things Kit would need to clean, but Kit couldn't tear his eyes away from the pretty little set painter. She seemed to be lost in the mastery of her work, and he imagined how her sets would look upon the stage when the fires were lit and the place glowed with merriment and warmth. They would look magnificent. She wiped at her face with the back of one hand and a smudge of dark green paint marred her cheek. Kit wanted to smile at the adorable imperfection of this little creature.

Something inside him went very still. His heart gave a wild sort of thump-thump in response. He *was* smiling.

He'd gone so long without a genuine smile that he'd forgotten what it felt like . . . how *good* it felt.

"Well, that's the tour. Would you care to report in tomorrow evening, around six?" Flory asked. "Even if we're rehearsing, we always have some tidying up to do. We tend to be a bit . . . well . . ." With a good-humored smile, Flory gestured to the trail of discarded costumes that led to changing screens in the wings off the stage.

"Six," Kit echoed, though he had no intention of returning, not like this. When he came back, he would be as Lord Kentwell, and Flory would likely not remember the shaggy, bearded man in sailor togs.

Kit walked with Flory to the back door, and with a polite nod at the stage manager, he stepped back into the street. The door closed, and yet Kit didn't leave. He lingered. He needed to focus, not on some pretty chit and her talents but on the clerk's daughter. She was the prey he needed to chase to ground. Vengeance was all that mattered to him. He couldn't let any other emotion take hold.

Suzannah Townsend carefully descended her short ladder and retrieved the glass bottle of water she kept on the floor next to her palette of paints. She swirled her paintbrush inside it, washing away the paint from the last touches she had made to the forest scene for their play. There were still some parts she wanted to deepen with more color, but they had so many sets still to do that she knew she couldn't focus too long on any single background setting.

The stage manager joined her by the ladder. "Are you done for the night?"

"Yes, I think so, Flory. It's not perfect, but it will do." She still stared at the forest scene. "Were you just talking to someone?" She vaguely remembered he'd been walking about the stage with another man a few minutes ago.

"Well, I was . . . It was rather odd, actually." Flory folded up the small ladder and carried it off stage. Suzannah walked alongside him, carrying her palette and jar of water. They both paused just off the stage, where Flory set his ladder against the wall, and she set her palette on a small writing desk.

She wiped the clean brush on a spare bit of cloth to dry it. "What was odd?"

"Well, some chap turned up at the back door. I thought he might be one of our new backstage hands. I showed him around, but he was quiet. Theater people are never quiet—except you." Flory shot her a teasing smile.

Suzannah poked him with the wooden handle of her paintbrush. "That's because I'm a painter. I'm supposed to be quiet and reflective, not noisy," she reminded him.

"Good point," he agreed with a laugh. "Are you ready to go home?"

"I think so. I've got to get some rest. We have so much work to do before the play opens."

"Give me a few minutes to finish up here and I shall walk you home," Flory offered with a slight bow. "You've got a bit of paint on your cheek, love."

Suzannah wiped the paint off and kissed his cheek. "Ever the gentleman. I shall be all right. It's only a short way."

Flory frowned. "I've seen that boardinghouse you live in, Suzannah. It's not exactly in the best part of town."

She didn't need reminding of that. A year ago, she and her father had lived in a nice suite of rooms in a much better part of London, but since he died she'd been on her own, and what little money she'd had after paying her father's final expenses had vanished quickly. Her landscape paintings that she sold to tourists who visited London paid for her food, but the money for her room at the boardinghouse came from the theater.

Wealthy patrons were recruited for each play, and they usually paid for decent set production and design. Thankfully, her wages were a part of that. But there were often lean weeks between plays while the producers searched for financiers for the next production.

"I'll be all right, Flory." She squeezed his shoulder. "You can't walk me home *every* night." With that, she collected her cloak and reticule before heading for the back door.

Admittedly, she did not like walking alone. She knew the dangers, but she had to learn to face them alone. Flory would not always be there to protect her.

The streets were empty of people, but rather than feel relieved, she had the eeriest sense that she was being followed. The hairs on the back of her neck rose in warning. She was almost at the street that led to her boardinghouse when the door of a nearby tavern burst open and a trio of drunken men stumbled out, laughing uproariously. The sudden sound of their laughter jarred her to a halt, which in turn caught the attention of the three men.

"Well now, there's a pretty dove," one man cooed.

Suzannah got her feet moving again and started to cross

the street toward the boardinghouse. The one who had called to her trailed behind, his companions with him, their laughter increasingly unsettling.

"Here, little dove, come home to roost with me," the second man jeered, and slapped his thigh. "I'll give you a good home."

Suzannah broke into a run. If she could just reach the boardinghouse—

Something caught in her cloak. She choked as her legs flew out from under her. She hit the ground with a sharp cry as the shadows of the three men blotted out the moonlight as they formed a ring around her.

"Why did you run?" one demanded. "We only wanted a kiss." The others laughed, the sound cruel and vicious. Men like these wanted more than just a kiss, and she was not about to give it to them.

"Leave me alone!" She swung her foot out, kicking the shin of the man nearest her legs. He fell over, cursing. Suzannah wore boots rather than slippers most days, and it paid off this evening. She got to her knees and tried to stand, but one of the men struck her with a backhanded blow. Stars streaked across her vision and the acrid taste of blood filled her mouth. She fell back onto the ground in a heap.

"You little—"

The man's words were cut short by a bellow of rage. Something lunged from the shadows like an animal. The other two men cursed and scrambled to flee as a new man arrived, towering above Suzannah. Half a dozen feet away lay the man who had struck her. He was moaning piteously on the ground, one of his arms set at an odd angle. He'd been thrown, it seemed.

The new man stood above her, his breathing rough as he stared at her.

When the man reached down for her, Suzannah threw up a hand to shield herself. "Please don't hurt me," she whispered as his hands grasped her arms.

He didn't hurt her. He simply lifted her to her feet. "Do you live nearby?" his low, gruff voice demanded.

"I . . . yes . . . just there." She nodded at the boarding-house up the street.

"Show me."

Suzannah would have argued, but there was something about his tone, the air of natural authority to it, not to mention he still had a hold of her arm, albeit a gentle one.

"Are you . . . are you going to . . . ?"

"You're safe with me," he answered. "I'll not let anyone harm you. You have my word."

She searched his eyes a long moment. There was ferocity in him but she sensed he posed no danger, at least to her. What she felt in that gaze and in his tone was honor, and that she trusted.

She finally agreed and showed him the way to her room.

When they reached the boardinghouse, he followed her inside and up the stairs to the floor where her room was. She fumbled with the brass key, her hands shaking too violently to fit the key into the lock. The man accompanying her gave a soft sigh and removed the key from her hands, easily unlocking the door. Then he pushed her inside the room and joined her.

"Oh, but—"

"Light a lamp so I can look at you." The man's voice was almost a growl.

"Please stop *growling* at me like that," she said, her words a little sharp due to her frayed nerves. She planted her hands on her hips, then winced at the pain where she'd scraped her palms on the stone when she'd fallen.

He didn't apologize, but he did speak more gently this time as he stared pointedly at her hands. "Please light a lamp. I wish to make sure you aren't hurt."

This time she complied. She lit a lamp and set it on the small table. It was the first time she'd gotten a good look at him. He was tall, broad-shouldered, with long, dark hair and a thick beard. His eyes were deep obsidian pools in the night. He was frightening, but there was something about him that drew her in. She wanted to paint those eyes—she wanted to understand the strange look she saw in them. She saw rage, compassion, and confusion.

"Sit." He pointed at one of the two chairs at the small table.

She did so only because she no longer had the energy to argue with him. He poured clean water into the chipped porcelain basin on her washstand and dampened a clean cloth. Then he returned and gently wiped her cheek and lips.

"Ouch, bloody hell!" she cursed, rather unladylike, flinching as pain sparked against the corner of her lips.

When he drew the cloth back from her face, blood had pinkened the fabric. The man raised a dark brow in such an elegant way that for a moment he didn't appear quite so rough and frightening. It was as if he was questioning her rather colorful curse. She didn't apologize. Instead, she gave a shrug as if she didn't care. Her mother would have been mortified by her, had she still been alive.

"That was a vicious blow you took. You need to put some salve on that cut. Once it heals, rub more salve onto the area to reduce the chance of scarring. Does your head hurt?" The man brushed his long fingers across her cheek.

His hand was beautiful, despite the rough calluses on his skin. He must have worked hard for long years to earn such hands, and she couldn't help but wonder who this man was. Heat flared in the place where his hand touched her. She instinctively caught his wrist as he touched her, but she couldn't push his hand away. Either she had no strength or he was just strong . . . perhaps it was both. Given the breadth of his shoulders and the way his clothes clung to his chest, she would have wagered the man could lift a team of horses upon his shoulders. Her head throbbed with a dull pain, making it hard to think clearly. She'd let a stranger into her room in the middle of the night. She was mad, utterly mad, to trust someone like this.

"If you feel nauseated, you must seek out a doctor. Such blows can be serious." He stared at her hand, which still held his wrist. He dropped his hand away from her face and she let go.

"How . . . how do you know that?" she dared to ask.

"I've been struck a time or two, just the way you have been." There was an odd rustiness to his voice, as though he rarely had occasion to speak. Something about that dug into Suzannah's chest, causing her to flinch. He noticed the reaction but seemed to misunderstand her compassion for fear.

"I should go. Lock the door behind me," he said.

And then the stranger was gone. In mere seconds he had *vanished*, closing the door behind him as if he'd never been there at all. Surely she hadn't imagined the entire encounter? Suzannah didn't even hear the stairs creak, and they *always* creaked whenever people went up or down the steps.

She hastily locked the door, then retrieved the cloth and wiped the dirt on her hands from when she'd fallen. Her dress had a few tears and stains, her hair was a mess, and her favorite green ribbon was gone. She must have lost it in the fight with those drunkards.

Hands still trembling, she felt overcome by a rush of emotion. She could have been hurt or much worse by those men. She buried the string of panicked thoughts of what could have happened had that man not intervened. A moment later, she wilted and eased down on her bed. Suzannah curled into a ball and put a fist in her mouth, but she couldn't stop herself from crying.

What would her dear papa think of her now? She'd failed at so many things, including her promise that she would be fine when he died. She had made him a deathbed vow, and she had broken it. Her tears flowed harder as she prayed she would fall asleep and forget all this come morning.

KIT LISTENED TO THE SOUNDS OF THE LITTLE PAINTER AS SHE WEPT. If she hadn't locked the door, he might have gone back inside her room and taken her into his arms, which was very unlike him. He was not a man used to responding with mercy or kindness, not anymore. Those traits had been whipped out of him years ago, and he had the scars to prove it. Yet this woman had somehow resurrected those things within him tonight.

With a silent curse, he left the boardinghouse and walked back to his father's townhouse in the so-called Devil's Square. He was relieved his departure that night hadn't been noticed by Palmer or any of the other servants.

He closed the door to his bedchamber and stared at his bed for a long moment. Then, with a sigh, he retrieved his blankets and pillow, and made a pallet on the floor.

As he lay down, he closed his eyes and reached into the pockets of his trousers until he found the silky green hair ribbon he'd taken from the little painter.

For the first time in years, he prayed for dreams, dreams of a little blonde creature who made the world come to life with the stroke of a paintbrush and had made him come alive with a single touch of her hand.

3

"Christ, man. What on earth are you doing?"

A voice woke Kit up from a dead sleep. He tensed out of instinct, but a moment later his mind caught up with his body and he recognized Darius as the man who stood over him.

Kit lay on his haphazard nest of blankets on the floor, and his friend peered down in obvious concern.

"What time is it?" he asked, not answering his friend's question.

"Noon." Darius arched a dark brow at Kit. "So we are not going to discuss why you were sleeping on the floor?"

"No," said Kit.

Darius's eyes softened with sudden compassion, but he said nothing more on the subject, which Kit was thankful for. Kit got to his feet and headed for the washstand. He poured clean water into the basin and splashed his face with one hand. The chilly liquid woke him up a little, but he still felt weary, as if he'd been awake for a century.

He had gone to bed close to three in the morning, and for the first time in seven years, he had slept deeply. It was as though his body had sensed he was finally somewhere safe enough to rest.

Palmer or one of the footmen had come into the room with a pitcher of fresh water, and he hadn't stirred once at the sound. In the penal colonies, a deep sleep like that might have gotten him killed.

Darius stood nearby, watching curiously as Kit gazed at his reflection in the mirror.

"I thought we might visit the tailor and then go about the business of finding you a valet."

"What happened to my man, Bradford?" He hadn't thought to ask Palmer about him last night. He'd been so focused on his father and revenge, the rest of his old life was still coming back to him in bits and pieces.

"He stayed on for half a year, but without a master, he didn't wish to trouble your father for the extra unneeded expense. Your father had his own man, but he retired after your father died, and Bradford was already gone by then. I think he's working for some textiles fellow up in Yorkshire. Most of the servants are gone now. Besides Palmer, there are two footmen, a cook, and one upstairs maid who also handles the scullery duties. You'll want to hire more staff now that you're home."

"Why did any of them stay?"

"Well . . . money, of course. Palmer made sure they received their wages. Since you hadn't been declared legally dead . . . Well, Palmer never gave up hope that you'd return, even after your father . . ." Darius cleared his throat and looked away. "Right, well . . ."

Kit's head started to pound as he thought of all the things that his life required now. Clothing, shaving, a valet, dinner parties, balls. Just thinking of those things made him ill. He was not that man anymore, but he would have to return to the life of a gentleman to exact his revenge.

"Well, make yourself ready, and we shall pay a call to Schweitzer and Davidson on Lark Street. They have the best gentlemen's coats in the city."

Kit listened to Darius discuss the latest fashions, and he was soon educated on more than he ever wished to know about how to have his cravats folded. But while he nodded and pretended to listen, Kit's mind kept straying to last night's encounter with the young woman from the theater.

He slipped his hand into his pocket and pulled out the bright green hair ribbon. His lips twitched in a near smile at the memory of his little painter standing on that ladder, painting forest imagery. He'd had the urge to climb up behind her on the ladder and cage her in from behind as he watched her paint. He wanted . . . He wanted to feel close to her, to get lost in her and her talent.

"So that's where you went. To see a woman . . ." Darius plucked the ribbon from Kit's hand and studied it in the sunlight that streamed in from the bay windows. "Who is she?"

"No one." In truth, he really didn't know who she was. He didn't even know her name.

"I saw you leave your house last night," Darius said. "I was afraid you might not return, so I waited up to make sure you came back."

"I considered it . . . not coming back," Kit admitted quietly. "Then I went to the theater, to see Townsend's daughter, but was distracted when I rescued a young woman from some drunken fools who intended her harm." He wasn't sure why he told Darius any of this. He wasn't used to talking this much.

Darius handed him back the ribbon and clasped a hand on Kit's shoulder.

"There's nothing wrong with taking a fancy to a woman. It's a good sign that you may wish to stay in London."

"I haven't taken a fancy to her."

His friend smirked. "Your ribbon collecting says otherwise, old boy. Make yourself presentable and meet me downstairs for a quick lunch. Then we'll be off."

Darius left him alone in his bedchamber, and Kit tidied up his appearance as best he could. The tailors on Lark Street would be thoroughly scandalized by his shabby clothing, but Kit didn't care. His money was as good as anyone else's.

When he entered the dining room a quarter of an hour later, Darius was eating kippers and toast with poached eggs. His eyes widened as if he'd expected Kit to be wearing something more befitting an earl than what he currently wore.

"I see we have a lot of work to do. Well, we shall make some chins wag today, won't we?" Darius recovered with a chuckle.

"This is all I have," Kit said.

He faced the sideboard full of warm chafing dishes. The smells coming from the covered dishes were divine. The footman in the corner of the drawing room watched Kit with wide eyes as he loaded up a plate with enough food for three men.

"You, lad, what's your name?" Kit asked the young footman.

"Er—Nolan, sir. Timothy Nolan."

"You are hereby assigned as my valet. Inform Mr. Palmer of your new duties, and he will see to a raise. You'll have to dress in something more befitting a valet than your livery, just as I shall have to dress in something more befitting a lord."

The young man smiled hesitantly. "You mean it, my lord?" His face reddened as he seemed to realize he had just questioned Kit.

"Yes, lad. Now, off you go. Tell Palmer and send my compliments to Mrs. Swanson on the breakfast."

"Yes, your lordship." The footman bolted from the room.

"Well, I guess that solves our valet problem," Darius chuckled. "Though now you'll need a new footman to replace him."

Kit merely grunted and sat down. His stomach felt hollow from nearly a full day and a half of being without food. He reached for his meal with one hand and halted, reminding himself to pick up his silverware first. He retrieved a spoon and broke the shell of a poached egg.

"Tell me one thing, Kit," Darius said while Kit quickly ate his food. He was not used to having any time to enjoy meals. "Just one thing,"

"What do you wish to know?" Kit asked warily.

"Anything about your life from the last seven years. Just

one thing. *Please.*" Darius leaned against the table, resting his elbows on the spotless white cloth, pinning Kit to his chair with his bright blue eyes. "I know you don't wish to discuss it, but please, for the sake of the boys we used to be, tell me *one* thing."

Kit ate more slowly and considered all the things that he had endured, all the hardships and all the endless drudgery of his life as a convict. Mrs. Swanson's food turned to ash upon his tongue at the memories.

"I was an animal," he finally said. "A beast to be burdened, to be worked, to be silent, to be beaten, to be misused in every way possible. It was a life that turns a man wild."

Darius didn't look away, not the way men and women would when faced with uncomfortable truths about the poor treatment of their fellow humans.

"We'll make them pay for this, Kit."

"And what of you? Tell me one thing about *your* life since I've been gone," Kit found himself asking as he finished his plate of kippers and eggs.

"I've been working with the Bow Street Runners."

Kit blinked. "The Runners?"

"I'm not officially on the roster. Given my title, my family would prefer to keep things quiet, but I often help on cases, when a gentleman is needed to access certain places or to speak to certain people."

Kit drank the cup of tea in front of him. Real tea . . . He hadn't had that in ages. He finally stood and looked at Darius.

"Are you ready?" he asked.

Darius pushed back his chair. "No further questions regarding my clandestine activities?"

Kit gave a wry smile. "If you wish to tell me about such things, I am more than happy to listen."

Darius chuckled. "Perhaps another time I shall regale you with my legendary tales. Today we have more pressing matters, like transforming you into a polished peer of the realm."

The butler met them on the way out of the dining room.

"My lord, you might wish to pay a call to your father's solicitor and have any necessary paperwork drawn up to formalize your control of his estate. Then I would advise you to visit Lord Lennox and get a sense of your father's accounts. I have some letters about his estate and investments, but it would be best if you spoke with him directly."

"Thank you, Palmer." Kit's headache was back. He didn't want to think of accounts, investments, ledgers or anything else that a peer's life entailed. He just wanted to be left alone, but that was not to be. His path to revenge required him to resume the life taken from him, whether he wanted it or not. Soon all eyes would be on him as the new Earl of Kentwell had returned to England.

Suzannah sat on a stone bench in Hyde Park, an easel and a fresh canvas set up in front of her. Smaller easels were arranged behind her with her finished works on display for sale. Men in fine riding jackets and shiny boots trotted past on glossy-coated horses, doffing their hats to ladies who walked arm in arm with each other, their parasols protecting them from the sun.

Gossip had fluttered like butterflies from the lips of the

beau monde all morning. Someone named Darius St. John had been seen out on the town with a mysterious stranger who was more than a little frightening but also intriguing, according to the gossips. The man had set chins wagging all over London.

"I tell you, Maximilian," one woman said as she and her husband strolled past Suzannah. "It was him, the Hollingsworth boy. The one who stole all those goods from that East India ship—what was it, six or seven years ago?"

The gentleman, Maximilian, frowned, his gray mustache twitching. "You mean Lord Kentwell's son?"

Kentwell . . . The name sent a ripple of terror through Suzannah. She craned her head as casually as possible, hoping not to be noticed as the couple moved down the path past her.

"That's the one. Cecily Robertson swears she saw Kentwell's son leaving a tailor's shop on Lark Street in some of the finest clothes a man could wear."

"Cecily saw him? She's sure?"

"Yes, quite sure. He was with the Duke of Tiverton," the woman added, "Darius St. John."

"By Jove, it could be him, I suppose. Old Kentwell bought him off the noose, and the boy was sent to Australia. That would've been about seven years ago. Christ, he must be back to claim his title as the new earl."

The woman gave a faint gasp, as if the idea was scandalous. "What does that mean?"

"It means he's a free man. He'll be able to do whatever he wishes, within the bounds of the law." The older gentleman glanced about the path as if worried about being overheard. No one saw Suzannah, however. That used to bother her, but in this moment she was relieved that she counted for nothing in this gentleman's eyes. "What did she say he looked like? I mean, seven years away in such a *primitive* land . . . He must look dreadful."

The woman shook her head, eyes wide. "She said he looked . . . *large.*"

"Large?" the older man queried in confusion.

"Yes, he was built like a warrior of old, or so Cecily says. She was practically giggling as she mentioned how he looked quite magnificent in his fitted jacket. She also said he looked positively wild. Apparently, he has a beard and long hair. She said he looked quite deliciously terrifying."

The gentleman mouthed "deliciously terrifying" and other words in bafflement.

"Oh heavens, Max, we should be off or we will be late for dinner." The woman pulled her husband along, and they resumed their walk.

Suzannah gripped her paintbrush so hard that the slender wooden stick snapped clean in two. She knew that name. Hollingsworth. That was the name of the young man her father had sent to prison.

"How much?"

Suzannah blinked as she realized a young woman was speaking to her. The girl couldn't have been more than eighteen, wearing a pretty sky-blue gown. A gentleman in his late twenties sat astride a horse not too far away. He held the reins of a second horse, which must have belonged to the girl.

"How much?" Suzannah echoed in confusion.

"This painting. The one with the horses." The young

woman pointed at one of Suzannah's finished pieces that showed a pair of horses frolicking in a field of wild-flowers.

"Oh. That one is three shillings."

"Cedric, may I buy this?" the girl asked over her shoulder.

The young man slid out of the saddle and removed a few coins from his purse. He offered Suzannah a charming smile.

"Which one do you want, Horatia?"

"This one," the girl said and pointed to the one she liked. Her brother examined it carefully and seemed as impressed as the young woman.

"Three shillings, you say?" he asked.

Suzannah swallowed hard and nodded.

"Very well. Anything for my *dear* sister." The man called Cedric tugged on one of the young woman's loose curls with a chuckle. He held out the coins to Suzannah, who accepted them gratefully. Suzannah retrieved some brown wrapping paper and folded the painting up in it before giving it to the young woman.

"Thank you. You're very talented."

The compliment made Suzannah momentarily forget her worries. It wasn't until she sat back down on the bench and watched the pair leave that she remembered the conversation she'd just overheard.

Lord Kentwell's son. Seven years . . . Had it really been seven years? She shuddered.

That trial had destroyed her father. He had refused to testify until his employer, Maynard Walsh, told him that he must. Her father had refused to speak to her about anything to do with the trial, but she'd overheard him finally agree to testify when pressed by Walsh.

The matter had upset her father so much that she'd never dared to bring it up. She'd never met the young man her father had helped to bring to justice, but something about the situation, and her father's actions in it had felt wrong. She had heard him muttering when he thought he was alone that it wasn't right to send the Hollingsworth boy to prison to hang. The entire incident had haunted her father. Even on his deathbed, he'd murmured the name *Christopher* over and over.

Now Christopher Hollingsworth was back. His death sentence had been commuted to seven years' transportation, he'd survived his time in the penal colonies, and that was the end of the story. Her path and his would never cross, and even if they did, he would never recognize her. She'd been a young child when he'd last seen her. She need not worry further about it.

She painted fiercely the rest of the afternoon, then packed up her supplies and unsold paintings and carried them home. There was a rehearsal for the play tonight, and she wanted to examine the forest again to make sure everything was to her satisfaction before she began working on another set piece.

When she reached her room at the boardinghouse, she halted just beside the doorway. She caught a glimpse of a green hair ribbon tied in an elegant bow around the handle of the door. The memory of last night's unexpected rescue came back to her. Had the tall, bearded man with calloused hands and gentle eyes returned her favorite ribbon? She set her painting supplies on the floor and untied the ribbon from the door handle. She glanced about, even though there was no one else in the corridor.

"Thank you," she whispered and clutched the silk ribbon to her chest. "Whoever you are."

"Bloody hell, you look like yourself again," Darius exclaimed as Kit left his bedchamber. The barber that Palmer had brought in had trimmed his shoulder-length hair so that it was fashionable, but not too short. Kit's beard and mustache were gone, revealing his square jaw and straight nose that led down to his stern-looking mouth.

Kit had been considered a handsome lad, but now he looked fierce, commanding. But he also felt more exposed. He ran his palm over his clean-shaven chin and grimaced.

"I feel naked," he admitted.

"I imagine you do. That was quite a beard you had, my friend."

Kit paused in front of the waist-high mirror in the corridor and ran his fingers through his dark hair.

"Oh, stop preening or Warren will tease you for being a peacock."

With a heavy sigh, Kit left his hair alone and adjusted his new coat. The burgundy-colored coat had been tailored to perfection, but Kit was not used to feeling so restricted by his clothing. He moved his arms a little, frowning. It was going to take some getting used to this style of clothing again.

"Come now, we need to meet everyone at Berkley's,"

Darius urged. He retrieved his hat from the footman, who was waiting patiently by the door.

Kit followed his friend outside, and they climbed into Darius's coach. He slid his hand into his pocket instinctively, expecting to find the green silk ribbon.

"One drink, that's all. Then you can return to your green-ribbon girl," Darius teased.

"She's not my girl," Kit replied. "I do need to return to the theater, however. I mean to see the clerk's daughter tonight." He wanted to see the woman. Assess her. Once he did, he would determine how best to exact his revenge.

Darius said nothing, but the merriment in his eyes was gone. Instead he looked worried, and for some reason that angered Kit. He didn't want his friends worrying about him. He'd survived everything life could throw at him for the past seven years.

It was his enemies' turn to worry now.

4

Kit was surprised he didn't hear actual crickets chirping the moment he walked into the main cardroom at Berkley's. The boisterous room turned as quiet as a tomb; a wave of silence hushed the casual talk that had filled the room with a comfortable atmosphere. Darius stood right beside him as dozens of faces turned Kit's way, his presence behind Kit an obvious show of support, for which Kit was grateful.

One older gentleman who held a cigar between his lips gaped at Kit, his mouth open like a fish suddenly plucked from the water. His cigar tumbled to the floor. The man standing beside him crushed the still burning tip beneath his boot before it set the rug on fire. Two others were in the midst of pouring drinks, and their brandy spilled over the tops of the glasses. The rest simply stared at Kit.

"Well, I think it's safe to say everyone now knows you're back in England," Darius said.

"Yes, they do." Kit yearned to have his beard and his

tattered sailor's clothing back. He wanted to vanish into the shadows and never be seen by any of these men again. It was too late for that. He was committed to his plan. His hand twitched, and he nearly moved to touch his smoothly shaven skin. Feeling like a stranger in his own body, he stood there trying to find some sense of recognition of himself, and failing.

A tall, blond-haired man rose from his game of cards and approached them. The man's intense blue eyes swept over Kit from head to toe, and he felt the man's scrutiny like a physical touch.

"Kentwell, may I introduce you to Lord Lennox?" Darius said.

The man bowed. "Glad to see that you are back, Lord Kentwell. We should speak about your father's investments at your earliest convenience."

Kit shook Lennox's hand. So this was the man his friends had mentioned. The powerful and wealthy baron whom they had trusted to help his father. And by all accounts, the man had done admirably.

"I understand I have you to thank for assisting my father these last few years." Kit spoke softly, not wishing anyone but Lennox and Darius to hear him.

"I require no thanks, as it was good business," Lennox replied in complete seriousness. "He was a good man, your father, and any decent gentleman should stand by a good man in his hour of need."

Kit managed a nod, but no words would come. Thinking of his father elicited an ache that left it hard for him to breathe, let alone speak.

"Do pay a call on me when you're ready," Lennox said.

With a bow, he returned to his table. The men seated with him gave Kit supportive nods of acknowledgment. He recognized one among their number as a man who'd been one year ahead of him at Eton, Charles Humphrey, the Earl of Lonsdale.

"Glad to have you back, Kentwell," his former classmate declared in a voice loud enough to cause a new ruffle of feathers amongst the older men in the room. Not that Charles cared, and that made Kit return the man's smile.

Then Kit resumed his gaze around the room, staring down each man until he looked away. If he was to feel like a damned caged animal, he could at least turn away their stares with his own. He kept his spine straight, his muscles tight, one move away from throwing a punch at any who dared utter a word against him.

"Come on," Darius murmured as he moved ahead of Kit deeper into the cardroom. "You can't go starting a fight today. The others are waiting for us."

With a grunt, Kit followed Darius through the maze of connected rooms until they reached the Bombay Room. It was a private room painted in a rich gold. The gold walls were contrasted by striking black palm fronds that were painted as if growing from the base of the floorboards to decorate the walls. The lamps were lit, enhancing the room's glow even more golden.

Christ, he'd forgotten this place. The Bombay Room. He'd come here often as a young buck with his friends during that year between age eighteen and nineteen. It hadn't changed in all the time he'd been away. He took in every detail, from the curtains hanging against the windows to the perfectly polished furniture and the fully stocked bottles on the sideboard table.

But this time, his mind was also thinking about the dozens of servants who kept the entire club, not just this room, spotless and running efficiently. He had developed a healthy respect for the working classes, more than his friends would ever understand, and it left him feeling even more detached from the so-called high society that he belonged to once more.

Felix and Warren sat at the main card table in the room, tossing a few hands of cards while they spoke softly. Felix said something with a wry grin and Warren laughed, the sound so familiar even after so many years that it wrenched his heart.

How many nights had he lain on a dirt floor listening to the snores of men around him, his muscles sore and every bone aching as though he were a thousand years old. He'd imagined himself right here, listening to his friends' laughter accompanied by the shuffle of cards and the clink of brandy glasses as they reveled in their innocent youth? The small pleasures he'd taken for granted over and over . . . they were his once again, but it didn't feel the same. Would it ever feel the way it once had? Or was he cut off from the past forever?

"Is it only you two?" Darius asked.

Felix and Warren both turned, and Felix's jaw visibly dropped while Warren let out a low whistle.

"By God, it really *is* you, Kit." Warren chuckled. "I admit, I half expected someone else beneath that hair and beard, but here you are."

Unused to his friends and their gentle teasing, Kit

grimaced and touched his face, wishing his beard to still be there. The nakedness of his face felt more vulnerable than he liked.

"Lionel had a family dinner," Warren explained. "Octavia is debuting this year, and she's practicing her skills at a few dinner parties before she's presented at court."

Lionel, Viscount Basildon, would one day inherit his father's title and become the Duke of Somerstone. Kit ran through all he remembered and all that Darius had told him of the latest news of his old friends. Octavia was Lionel's little sister; he couldn't recall much about her beyond that she had recently turned eighteen.

Warren tossed his cards down on the table in defeat. "Dinner parties are the bane of a gentleman's existence."

"The bane of *your* existence, Warren, because you cannot enjoy the subtle adventure of a good dinner party," said Felix.

"Subtle adventure of a good dinner party?" Warren snorted. "*What* adventure, pray tell?"

Felix grinned. "There's the language of the fans, of course. Do you know how many things women say when using them? I once watched an old duchess and her social rival, a wealthy countess, fight during the soup course and neither of them said a word. But the fluttering of the fans was enough to create a decent breeze in the room, and more than one footman tripped in their attempts to avoid their trays being hit by the waving of said fans."

Warren rolled his eyes. "I prefer the language of the fists. Give me a boxing match at Fives Court over that any day." He raised his fists and mock punched at an invisible opponent.

Warren and Vincent held no titles, but both came from families that were wealthy and powerful. That gave them the freedom to get into far more trouble than the others could. Warren had always been the most reckless and Felix the most adventurous. Vincent, on the other hand, was quiet but also charming. According to Darius, there hadn't been a woman yet who could turn down Vincent when he smiled.

It seemed not much had changed in the last seven years, Kit reflected. Perhaps *he* was the only one who had.

"Vincent should be here soon," Felix said. "His ballet dancer is probably keeping him late this evening," he added with a grin.

Felix, the Marquess of Grey, had had his title bestowed on one of his ancestors more than two centuries ago in honor of his startling gray eyes, a trait that ran deep in the current Hawkins bloodlines.

"Ballet dancer?" Darius asked as he handed Kit a drink.

Kit accepted it and finished his own mental list of things remembered and learned. In some ways, coming home had been like landing in a new world. He was having to relearn things that now felt foreign to him. Darius St. John was now the Duke of Tiverton. His father had passed the year before Kit's. Kit felt that tied an invisible thread between him and Darius, but at least his friend had been able to spend time with his father before he'd died.

"He started seeing her a few weeks ago," Felix explained, his lips turning up into a smile. "When will he learn? I love adventures, but not *those* sorts of adventures.

Give me a merry widow any day. Dancers are too much trouble. They expect too much. Widows, on the other hand, expect nothing but amusement."

"You know how Vin is. Every new woman gives him that feeling of 'what could be.' The man loves the idea of falling in love." Warren frowned as he defended their absent friend. "Besides, I think he likes the drama dancers provide. He's so bloody quiet all the time. I think he likes how much they chatter when he's around them."

Darius smiled fondly and glanced at Kit, as if hoping to see he too was amused by their discussion. But Kit did not feel bold enough to dive into the playful banter. His friends' lives had changed so much, and he had only been privy to the biographical details up to this point. He wanted to know about Vincent and his ballet dancers, and what Lionel thought of his sister's future suitors. He wanted to ask a thousand questions, but asking would only make him feel more on the outside than he already did.

His thoughts turned to the green-ribbon girl from the theater. What would his friends think if he shared the story of her rescue? Would they tease or congratulate him? Would he feel like he fit in once more with his old set?

Perhaps it didn't matter what he felt . . . Well, how he felt about the little painter *did* matter. Greatly. Heaven only knew why, but he couldn't get her out of his mind. She'd been slipping in and out of his thoughts all day, like a hazy, wonderful summer dream that lay just out of reach.

He raised the glass to his lips and drank his brandy, tasting it when instead he wished he could taste the painter's soft lips. She looked like a woman born for kissing. Still, the brandy had its charms. He hadn't tasted proper brandy in seven years. He'd spent the last several months during his sailor's journey drinking grog that was strong enough to strip the paint off most boats.

"Darius, we may not see the others for a few more hours. Perhaps it would be best to discuss our potential plan to deal with Walsh and Balfour." Felix looked to Darius for confirmation.

Darius turned to him. "What say you, Kit?"

Kit had spent years thinking of how he would go about getting his revenge, but all the plans he had made then seemed like terrible ideas now. What still mattered, however, was the objective.

"I want to take away from them what they love most. Tell me what they crave, what they hoard."

"Balfour craves power. Walsh yearns for money," Darius said.

"And Townsend's daughter?" Kit asked. "What of her?"

"Are we really discussing revenge against a woman who had nothing to do with your imprisonment?" Warren asked quietly.

"If she has profited these last seven years from his misdeeds, then she is as guilty as he."

"She gave no testimony against you, Kit. You're far too much of a gentleman to take revenge upon someone who was a mere child at the time."

Kit laughed harshly. "Am I?" he challenged in a low voice. "Because I rather feel like a wild beast ready to *rip* my enemies apart with my bare hands, even if they think themselves safe in the grave." He paced the room, his hands clenching as he sought to rein in the flood of rage that filled his body. It vibrated within him down to his very bones. He knew his threats went a step too far, but something in him in that moment needed to throw salt into his own wound, to feel the pain and lash out and see . . . and see if his friends would still stand beside him in his madness and rage.

A long moment of painful silence filled the room, and Kit feared he'd lost the loyalty of these men. And if he had, he alone was to blame for it. He'd lived seven years without them, but now, the thought of losing them again was too much to bear. The thought sent him spiraling into a terror deeper than the day he'd learned he was to be sent away from England to a fate unknown. Kit forced himself to meet the concerned, troubled gazes of his friends, but he did not speak.

Darius was the first to break the agonizing silence.

"Well, as much as I understand how you feel, Kit, we can't have someone naming you the Monster of Mayfair, running about tearing people into pieces. Besides, we've only just had the most excellent wardrobe tailored for you. It would be a pity to wreck it with the blood of your enemies."

"He's right," Warren added. "Now, the rending of bodies aside, I say we go after Walsh's shipping company first. Lord Lennox has made comments to me that he is interested in owning a shipping company rather than simply hiring freelance ships. What if we bring him in on this scheme and see if he won't help us? He might even buy the shipping company."

"Walsh won't sell." Kit shook his head. "When I partnered with him, he was obsessed with his legacy, and that company is it. He wanted everyone to know that he would control London's import trade." Killing his enemies wasn't an option. He'd lost seven years of his life to these men—he wouldn't damn his soul in his pursuit of revenge. But it seemed taking the company away wasn't an option either, which left him feeling hollow with frustration.

"So we destroy his legacy," Felix suggested.

"How so?" Kit wasn't sure what his friend meant to do.

Felix leaned forward, his voice dropping as if what he was about to say was a secret. "We could buy up all his debts and call them in one by one."

"I rather like the symmetry of that," Warren agreed. "You suffered for years. This would be far quicker, of course, but we would still cut him down piece by piece through his pocketbook until he has no choice but to sell. Lennox will pay a pittance for it." They all shared dark smiles.

Kit nodded. "Walsh will become bankrupt and lose all of his business goodwill." Kit began to feel hopeful once more. "And what do you suggest for Balfour?" he asked.

Felix sobered. "As a magistrate, he's almost untouchable."

"*Almost*," Darius emphasized. "I imagine Balfour has sent more than one innocent man away for false crimes, as he did you. If we research his old cases, we might discover other innocent victims. If we find the proper evidence and proof that he was paid to have innocent people put away, we could have him stripped of his magistrate's position and possibly imprisoned himself," Darius said.

"What do you think of that, Kit?" asked Felix.

All Kit could think of in that moment were the lives Balfour had ruined simply to line his own pockets. Innocent people. People who weren't as strong or stubborn as he was to survive. People who hadn't deserved the beatings, the whippings, the illnesses that came with life in remote colonies. The fury returned to him, but this time he kept it under control. His friends' warning hadn't been forgotten. If he wasn't careful, he might find himself back in Newgate Prison.

"I think it's a good place to start." He had to admit his friends' plans made far more sense than his own. He was still too blinded by rage to think clearly about the most effective path to revenge, but that rage was slowly hardening into steel. Someday soon he would be able to wield it with cold effectiveness.

"I wish to meet Townsend's daughter tonight," Kit said with a heavy finality. She was the last piece to this plan. He had to discover what she'd known of her father's false testimony. How complicit she had been, and if she'd lived on the ill-gotten gains born of Kit's conviction.

Suzannah hung back in the wings offstage, watching the rehearsal and admiring her sets. She was proud of her paintings. They looked magnificent in the lamplight with the actors moving about in front. The creative tableau of the theater spoke to her whenever she watched a rehearsal or a performance. It meant even more to her when she could see her art behind the actors. The reviews of each play always mentioned the fine quality of the backgrounds, and she rode that wonderful wave of accomplishment for weeks.

Her father had told her long ago that she had a gift, but it was easy to forget that when the expense of living alone as a single woman became too much. She would have given almost anything to paint portraits, to tell the stories of people's lives through her canvases and brushes. But no one would hire a woman for their portraits, and those who would hire her would never pay the same price they would a male artist. It seemed her fate was to paint sets at the theater and scrape by with her earnings as best she could.

The rehearsal ended, and the actors and actresses left the stage, passing by Suzannah.

"Excellent rehearsal," she said to them in congratulations. Each of them beamed back at her, their faces shining with the joy of a job well done. There was nothing quite like the excitement of a good rehearsal where you knew everything was going to work, except for the wild rush of a perfect performance in front of an actual crowd.

"Ah, there you are." Flory came up behind her. "Suzannah, there's a gentleman asking after you." The stage manager's face was a ruddy color for some reason. He licked his lips nervously.

"A gentleman to see *me*?"

"Yes, he says he wishes to pay his compliments to Suzannah Townsend. He said your performance was superb."

"My performance? I'm not an actress."

Perhaps one of the gentlemen who had paid to see the rehearsal tonight had mistaken her for an actress?

"He asked for you by name," Flory added.

"What sort of man is he?" she asked, more than a little concerned. She imagined some gentleman who wanted to pinch her bottom and offer her a ride home in his carriage.

Flory cleared his throat. "He's a good-looking one. Tall,

dark-haired, not like the usual young bucks haunting the lobby in hopes of bedding an actress. He's finely dressed too, but not a dandy. I've never seen such a finely cut coat on a man before."

Despite never having taken a lover, Suzannah was not unaware of the practice of actresses becoming the mistresses of wealthy gentlemen. Some even married them.

"Perhaps he mistook my name on the program?" she wondered out loud, still confused as to where her name, usually near the set design on the playbills, could have caught this mysterious man's attention.

"Well, he's waiting for you a few rows back in the theater," Flory told her.

"He must be confused. I will correct the mistake and point him in the direction of whomever he is interested in." She left the backstage area and pressed the curtains aside to view the darkened theater where the audience usually sat.

She glimpsed a man just outside the glow of the lamps that illuminated the now empty stage. Her heart sped up, and she had a strange sort of feeling, like when she went down the stairs in the dark and didn't realize there was one more step to go. That sensation of dropping and landing lower than she'd expected always made her stomach pinch. She had that sort of feeling now, falling in the darkness and for a moment not knowing when or where she would land.

The man held a top hat in his hands and straightened his shoulders as she approached. The small action made him look even taller. The wild, half-tamed waves of his dark hair danced about his temples, making him even more attractive. He had a hint of a tortured Lord Byron about him.

His features were painfully beautiful, as though a vengeful Venus had carved a man too perfect for mortal eyes to bear. Despite his aloof, masculine beauty, there was something intimate in his form. She felt as though if she were to touch him, it would make her come alive in a way she never had before.

Perhaps it was the breadth of his shoulders, the trim waist, and strong, powerful legs barely hidden by snug-fitting trousers that made this man in the shadows seem so sensually appealing. Her hand itched to draw him, to capture his face and form upon her sketch pad. The desire was so strong that it awoke the secretive muse within her that led her to create art that could bring tears to her eyes.

"I informed the manager I wished to speak with Miss Townsend, the actress," he said with some surprise.

Suzannah's eyes traced up the length of his form, from his elegant shoes to his crisp white cravat folded at his throat. Her breath caught. His eyes were somehow familiar. Could she swear she'd seen them before somewhere? If she had, she was sure she would have remembered his face.

"I'm afraid to disappoint you, sir. I am Suzannah Townsend, but I am not an actress, nor have I ever been an actress. I am merely a set painter." She waved a hand toward her work on the stage.

"You aren't an actress," the man said slowly, as if he was not quite sure he believed her.

"No, sir, I am not. If you can tell me which part you were thinking of, I could fetch the actresses who played—"

"No!" he said quickly and stepped toward her. That single movement was an invasion between them, and it made her nervous.

"No, it is *you* I wish to see. I was simply confused. I thought perhaps you acted in addition to painting. I blame the brandy I had at my club this evening." The gentleman suddenly smiled, and the effect was like being hit behind the knees. She steadied herself on the nearest seat at the end of the aisle closest to them.

"Do I know you, sir?" She tried to be polite, but she swore she knew this man somehow.

"Not yet, but I am hoping that perhaps you will wish to know me." He glanced down at the hat he held in his hands. "I am in need of a portrait, and after seeing your work, I would very much like to hire you."

Hire her for a portrait? Suzannah was stunned and excited, but the rational part of her feared it was a trap. Gentlemen simply did not come along and fulfill her dreams without a steep price.

"I do not have amorous relationships with my clients."

"That was not my intention, I assure you," the man said bluntly.

She scrambled to think of what he might also want of her, aside from a painting. "And I would expect a fair wage based on what other artists charge for their portraits. The *male* artists," she clarified.

"You believe I would offer you less money because you're a woman?" He lifted his eyes and pinned her to the floor with a stare.

"Most men would."

"I am not, nor have I ever been, most men. In fact, you will find me unlike any other man you've ever met." He tapped his hat with long, elegant fingers, hinting at a slight frustration, and again she felt a tug on her memory before he said, "I'll pay you double the going rate."

She gasped. "Double?"

"Double," he echoed. "If you start tonight."

"Tonight? But—"

"I have matters during my days that occupy my time. If the evenings are an issue—"

She glanced back at the stage. "Well, I must be here in the evenings for the plays."

"You have finished painting sets for this particular play, haven't you?"

"Well, yes, but—"

"Then I will be happy to speak with your manager and convince him to give you the week off, at least from late-night rehearsals. I would like to start at eight o'clock each evening. I have an excellent cook who rarely has the excuse to cook for anyone other than myself. You will dine with me, and then you may work on the portrait."

Suzannah stared at him. The man was mad. She couldn't go to some stranger's home, dine with him, and then paint him late into the night. Scandal aside, it was not safe.

"Sir, as much as I appreciate your offer, I cannot accept. I may be poor, but I am a lady. It would be highly improper. And not to be rude, but safety is a concern. You must under-stand that women cannot undertake such spontaneous requests the way a man so easily can." She had the strangest sense that he wouldn't let the matter go, and she wasn't sure she could deny this man for long. Something about him got under her skin, making her blood hum and her knees quite weak, something she'd never had the occasion to feel before. It worried her more that she couldn't think clearly around him.

"I will triple your current rates, and I guarantee that you will have a number of new clients when we are through." He didn't sound desperate. If anything, he sounded casual, like this was a fun lark and she should relax. But she saw some hint of urgency in his eyes as well. What could be so important about a portrait?

"You couldn't possibly promise that," she argued. "You cannot guarantee future clients. You haven't even seen my work."

"The Duke of Tiverton is a close friend of mine. He will wish to have his portrait done after me. As well as Viscount Basildon and the Marquess of Grey. These are simply my titled friends. I have others who will gladly commission portraits. And as for your talent, I see the sets behind you. They are exquisite. I can only imagine how you would bring life to human subjects."

"Even if I did agree to your proposal . . . I would need much more than your word that I will not suffer an assault on my person. You seem to have a great many titled friends, sir, but I do not know you or them. What assurances could you give me, aside from the word of an unknown gentleman, that I would be safe with you? I would have to have a chaperone present."

The gentleman frowned. His mouth, rather too sensual to be safe for a woman's virtue, had somehow become even more attractive. She'd never been drawn to a man when he was cross, but there was something wicked in the expression, as though he'd kiss her senseless rather than hurt her. Not that she had any personal experience with such things, but as a woman she knew on some instinctive level what this man could give her.

"What about that lad, the one who is watching us from the wings. Do you know him?"

She turned around and caught a glimpse of a boy who quickly ducked behind the curtains on the stage. It was Henry Lovelace, a fifteen-year-old boy she had convinced Flory to take in last year as a stagehand. He'd had no family and no place to sleep until she and Flory had set aside a small room at the back of the theater for him. Suzannah considered Henry not only trustworthy but a friend, and in some ways like a little brother.

A sudden heat behind her made her tremble as she realized the gentleman had come up right behind her. He leaned down, whispering in her ear.

"Have him accompany you each night. Would that be acceptable?"

She had to crane her neck to look up at him, and her stomach flipped as he shot her a bittersweet smile.

"You will see that I am no brute, Miss Townsend."

Suzannah still should have said no, but if he was honest about his offer—triple the current rate with more commissions from some of London's elite—she would be able to make a name for herself. She could afford new clothes and perhaps a better place to live that would attract more clients. She could even take Henry with her if she could afford two rooms. While he was older than most lads on their own, she worried about him being led astray or hurt by the dangers of the world.

"Must we start tonight?" she asked.

"Yes. I've been away from society for some time, and it

has been pointed out to me that unveiling a new portrait is a good excuse to invite people to one's home, so the sooner we begin, the better." He held out one hand. "Do we have a deal, Miss Townsend?"

After a moment's hesitation, she reached out to shake his hand.

"We have a deal, Mr. . . . I'm afraid I don't even know your name."

"Kit . . . Mr. Kit," he said.

"Mr. Kit," she echoed.

"I have my coach waiting outside. Collect whatever you require and bring your lad along. I shall be waiting for you."

He placed his hat back on his head and turned away. As he exited the theater, Suzannah could strangely feel his absence in a way she'd never felt anyone else's before. She stood in the shadows, a heaviness of something settling in the air as his words lingered in the silence.

I shall be waiting for you . . .

5

This was impossible.

The pretty little artist he had rescued, the one whose touch had made him feel human for the first time in seven years, was the daughter of the man who'd helped destroy his life.

Perhaps he was still in Australia, still waiting to wake up and begin another grueling day of backbreaking labor, and this was yet another dream that had devolved into a nightmare.

He stepped out of the theater and onto the moonlit street. He closed his eyes and held himself very still, focused on his breathing. It was a technique he'd used to survive in the penal colony. When things became too much, he stopped and focused inward on the sound of the air pushing in and out of his lungs. If he did that long enough, the ringing in his ears would stop and the tightness in his chest would ease.

Thoughts of that green ribbon threaded through Suzannah's hair, then wrapped around his fingers, kept intruding on his calming routine.

Christ . . . He'd told her his name was Kit. Would she figure out who he really was? What the devil would he do when Palmer opened the door and called him Lord Kentwell? The girl would likely turn and run, fearing for her life. It would be hard to blame her, given the dark places his mind had gone in recent days.

Feeling not at all well, he closed his eyes and forced himself to breathe in and out again.

"You all right, sir?"

Kit opened his eyes and saw a young boy staring at him in concern, no older than twelve or thirteen. He wore decent clothes for a lad wandering the streets. Likely, the boy ran messages around town.

"Er . . . yes. I am." Kit's words couldn't have been farther from the truth. He had to think quickly to cover his mistake. The boy was still staring at him in mild concern, and that gave him an idea.

"Lad, I will pay you handsomely to deliver a message to a house for me. You may tell the man there to pay you another shilling for your trouble once you've given it to him. But you must be quick about it."

He gave the boy instructions and then paid for a hackney to take the lad to his home. He should arrive before he and Suzannah did. He could only hope that the instructions were understood and followed correctly.

So much for rational plans, he thought with a grim sigh. He was leaping headlong into folly with this contrived plan for a portrait. He should be focusing on Walsh and Balfour.

Once the boy was safely on his way, Kit remained by his

own hired coach, counting the minutes to steady himself. His heart beat a staccato rhythm. His spur-of-the-moment plan to have Suzannah paint him was mad, but it would give him time to study her and to learn how much she knew about him, his trial, as well as her father's role in it.

Time would tell if she was as innocent as she seemed to be. If she wasn't, then his original plan of seduction and heartbreak would be his goal. If she was innocent, he would let her go, with payment as promised. That would be the gentlemanly thing to do. He'd thought that part of himself long dead, but it seemed not all of him had died when crossing the sea seven years ago.

He tensed when he saw Suzannah and the young man exit the theater. She had a canvas bag slung over her shoulder. Kit nearly reached for it on instinct, but stopped himself.

"Mr. Kit, this is Henry Lovelace, my friend."

Kit held out a hand to the lad. "It's a pleasure to meet you, Mr. Lovelace."

Henry squared his shoulders and did his best to pretend to be older, like most boys his age would when given a task. "Same to you, Mr. Kit." Something pricked at Kit's heart. He had been only a handful of years older than Henry when he had been forced onto that transportation ship.

Kit opened the coach door and held out a hand to Suzannah to help her up. Instead, she slung the canvas bag off her shoulder and let it down onto his outstretched arm. He'd intended to help her into the coach, but he'd take her bag if she trusted him with it. Then she lifted her skirts, revealing scuffed leather boots as she climbed into the coach without assistance.

Henry stifled a chuckle as he claimed the bag from Kit and climbed into the coach after her. Kit then joined them, sitting opposite them both, and pounded a fist on the roof of the coach to signal to the driver that they were ready to leave.

"Is it true Suzannah's going to paint you, sir?" Henry asked after a few minutes of silence in their ride.

"Yes," Kit said. "I've been away from London for a long time, and I need a new portrait."

The lad's head tilted slightly in puzzlement. "Is that one of those silly things rich men do?"

"Henry!" Suzannah warned in an affronted gasp.

"No, he's quite right," Kit said. "It is *absolutely* one of those silly things rich men do."

Henry leaned back against the coach cushions, satisfied with Kit's answer. No one else spoke for a long moment. Then Suzannah cleared her throat.

"What . . . er . . . what sort of portrait did you have in mind?"

"Something that will stir gossip," Kit admitted freely. "I want you to paint me in a way that shows London who I truly am."

He half expected her to demand that he explain what he meant by that, but she remained quiet, simply staring at him as though he were an intricate puzzle box she was attempting to solve. The thought of her hands, small and feminine, stroking over his body, seeking places to caress, to find ways to open him up and reveal the inner secrets of his soul, set his blood ablaze. It should have terrified him, angered him. But, surprisingly, it didn't.

When the coach stopped in front of his father's house...

now his house he had to remind himself, Kit exited first and once again held out a hand. Suzannah started to hand him the canvas bag, but he nodded to Henry behind her.

"Give your bag to the lad."

For a moment, her gaze locked with his as she came to realize what he wanted. An excuse as a gentleman to touch her, even so innocent a thing as her hand. He could tell she was trying to figure out the smartest response to his challenge. Accept his hand and see it as weakness, or meet him directly by daring to refuse?

Finally, she surrendered, whether she realized she had or not, but he hid his desire to smile in victory.

Suzannah reluctantly passed the bag to Henry and placed one hand in Kit's so he could help her down. She wore no gloves, and he felt her warm fingertips touch his. They were soft but bore slight calluses in places where she used her brushes and pencils. Kit wasn't sure what he expected to feel now that he knew she was the daughter of a man who'd sent him off to die. But what he did feel, a quickening of his blood and a flutter in his chest that wasn't rooted in plans for revenge, was unexpected. Suzannah's fingers squeezed his as she balanced on the carriage step.

She attempted to pull away once her booted feet were on the ground, but he didn't allow it. She lifted her face up, her flushed cheeks and flashing eyes only making her more damnably attractive. He liked ruffling her pretty feathers. How would she react if he stole a kiss? If he pinned her against the wall and showed her the talents *his hands* were capable of?

Instead, he slid her arm around his in a courtly gesture that he was surprised he could even remember after all these years. So many habits of his old life had been drummed out of him.

The front door of the townhouse opened, and Palmer was waiting for them.

"Ah, welcome home, Mr. Kit," Palmer said smoothly, as if he had addressed him that way his entire life. Then again, it was rather close to *Master Kit*, which was what Palmer had always called him in his youth.

"Palmer, this is Suzannah Townsend and Henry Lovelace. We require dinner, and then Miss Townsend will begin the process of painting my portrait."

Palmer's response was an instant too slow as he realized who Suzannah must be, but thankfully she didn't seem to notice the butler's reaction. Her gaze swept over the entryway, taking in the marble statues and the fine, but slightly faded, tapestries with something akin to wonder.

"Will the drawing room suffice for your preliminary sketches?" Kit asked.

She startled slightly, lost in admiration of his home. She cleared her throat and lifted her chin as she answered.

"I would have to see it first, but I believe so." She reminded him of one of the wild mares in Australia. Proud, spirited, and unbreakable. He admired her all the more for it.

"The dining room is through here." Palmer led the way, and a footman opened a door for them.

Once they were seated with Kit at the head of the table and his guests on either side, Kit noticed that Henry had been watching Suzannah's every move. She delicately touched her silverware as the first course of soup was served, and Henry mimicked her choice of cutlery from the three different spoons laid out. It was clear from the clothes the boy wore that he was either in borrowed clothes or in clothes he'd outgrown. Kit shouldn't have cared about the lad one way or the other, but he knew what it meant to struggle in a world set against him.

Suzannah finally spoke, calling his attention back to her. "You said you've been away from London?" She wore no ribbon in her golden hair tonight, and he found he missed the sight.

He cleared his throat. "Yes, I've been gone for a few years. I had business in Scotland that kept me away, and I'm just now returning home." The lies came easily, and something about that bothered him. "And you? How long have you worked at the theater?"

The second course of roast duck was brought in. "For the last year. After my father died, I began selling paintings to tourists. A man named Flory Holland found me in the park one day and thought I was quite gifted. He offered me a job painting the sets at the theater."

Kit wanted to ask her about her father, but he couldn't give his motives away just yet.

"I'm sorry to hear about your father. Do you still paint for tourists?" He was genuinely curious about that. If she painted pictures for tourists, he imagined she must make a number of good sales, with her talent.

"During the day, yes. I go to Hyde Park and paint scenes and sell them. Then in the evenings I paint the sets at Drury Lane."

"And you make a living doing this?" It was perhaps crass to ask such a thing, but Kit was determined to find out if Suzannah was living off money her father had left her, money that might have been a payout for betraying him.

Suzannah audibly swallowed, her face coloring. "I make enough."

Barely, it would seem. He remembered visiting her tiny living quarters after he'd saved her from those drunken brutes, which was no more than a broom cupboard. He only realized he was staring at her when she glanced pointedly away. In Australia he'd been largely ignored except by other convicts, and he'd learned that direct eye contact was one way to establish a power dynamic. He hadn't meant to stare her down like that—he really had just been thinking. But it was a reminder that he was no longer having to face deadly challenges from every angle. He was back in England. He was safe. Well, safer than he *had* been, at any rate.

Kit turned his attention to Henry. "And you, lad? What do you do at Drury Lane?"

"I work the ropes. I pull the sets into place and collect costumes when the actors change," Henry said with no small amount of pride. "I sleep there too, in the back behind the stage." He suddenly seemed to realize that perhaps he ought not to have said that.

"That sounds like a good position to have," Kit said to the boy.

Henry smiled shyly, pleased at Kit's approval. Kit remembered what it felt like to be a young man at that age. He would have done anything to earn the approval of older boys and men he had looked up to when he was Henry's age.

Henry, apparently emboldened by Kit's approval, now began to share stories of his life behind the curtains of

Drury Lane. They passed the remainder of the dinner entertained by Henry's tales. Suzannah seemed to relax as Henry talked, and by the end, her hesitant smile was a broad grin as she fought off laughter. She had become that pretty little painter again, the one who had bewitched him.

For the first time in seven years, the pain he'd suffered felt like it was a thing truly far out of reach, and he was glad for it. He wanted one minute of peace from the endless rage inside him.

That surprised him, though, that sudden need for peace, when he'd rarely given it a thought during his time away. He'd spent too much of his time focused on revenge because it gave him the fire to continue fighting for survival. But now he was feeling contentment as well as desire, and the mix of that was . . . unsettling. He'd taken his pleasure where he could in Australia. Quick, desperate, rough, and with a willing woman. But now *true* desire was back. He had the urge to seduce a woman and enjoy simply being around a beautiful woman. And if it also happened to further his plans for revenge, then that was a happy coincidence.

When the footman collected the dishes, Kit was slowly dragged back into himself again. The small smile hovering on his lips faded into a grim line.

"Henry, you may have a glass of sherry, if you wish. A small one, mind you. I will take Miss Townsend into the drawing room down the hall, and you may come visit her if you wish to see her progress."

Kit hoped that a glass of sherry would keep the boy occupied. He had no intentions of harming Suzannah, but he wanted to be alone with her. It was the only way he could get her to speak to him and open up about her father.

Kit rose and helped Suzannah up from her seat. She allowed it, stiffly at first, but then relaxed when he made no moves to take further advantage. He offered her his arm, and she followed him to the door.

She leaned in to whisper to him, and the nearness of her, the faint aroma of flowers coming from her hair, caused his body to tighten with desire. "I am well aware that you hope Henry will stay away from us. I warn you that I will scream very loudly and am not nearly so helpless as you may think."

Kit gave her hand a light touch, his fingers caressing hers. He wanted to kiss her senseless, but he also wanted her trust, and he wanted answers about her father. He wasn't about to risk all that for a kiss. Not yet, anyway.

She lifted her chin and said nothing more. Kit collected her canvas bag of supplies from the corridor and carried it for her to the drawing room.

"Please be careful, Mr. Kit. My life is in that bag," she urged as he slung it over his arm. It struck him that when he'd returned to London, he had carried his own life in a similar bag. He did not miss the protectiveness she held for what lay in that bag. It was full of her hopes and dreams, and she feared he would treat them carelessly. An undeniable feeling of kinship burrowed a small seed into the dark, rich, but untouched soil of his heart.

He cleared his throat and spoke honestly, his words slightly gravelly. "Your dreams are safe with me, Miss Townsend."

She gave him the smallest of nods, an acknowledgment

of that promise. He felt strangely shy, not physically, but emotionally. Lord knew he'd never felt that way before in his life.

The drawing room was cozily lit with firelight and oil lamps. Kit placed her canvas bag on the nearest chair, then looked at her expectantly.

"Tell me what you require to do your work."

She opened her bag and buried her hands deep into it, finding what she needed. "Do you wish to be seated in your portrait? If so, we could pull that settee over to face the firelight."

With a nod, he moved the furniture as she had directed.

While her back was turned as she prepared, he removed his coat so that he was wearing only his waistcoat and shirt. He'd had a chance to think about this since meeting her. As soon as the idea had sprung to his mind to have her paint him, he'd only seen one choice: to show the *real* him. The wounded, beaten, starved, scarred creature that had been molded into a strong, stubborn beast of many burdens. He wanted London to see what had been done to him. An innocent man. Suzannah would paint London's sins upon her canvas.

He unbuttoned his waistcoat and removed it. It wasn't until he'd pulled his shirt over his head that he heard her gasp.

Yes, now you see what your father's betrayal has done to me . . .

With his back to her, he smiled darkly. The rage that she seemed to rob him of when he was near her was back now. He focused on what this painting would say to his enemies. That he was back, and coming for them.

6

Suzannah gaped at Mr. Kit's bare back. It was not the nakedness of his upper body that drew her reaction, but the *scars*. Dozens of them crisscrossed his back in pale pink and white patterns across his sun-kissed flesh.

She'd seen marks like that only once before. Jude, an escaped American slave who now lived free in England, worked as a stagehand at Drury Lane along with Henry. He too bore marks like this. These markings came from a cruelty that no creature, man or beast, should ever know. She covered her mouth with a trembling hand. Only evil caused such pain in this world.

Horror, the likes of which she'd never felt before, was numbing her from the inside out. It was as though she'd fallen through the top of a frozen lake and was trapped beneath the ice, screaming, and no one could hear her. All she could think of was the pain he must have felt, the fear, the terrible knowledge that he could do nothing to prevent it. Some of these scars were new, others old, some thin and straight, others jagged. They crossed paths like highways over his skin, layering years of pain on top of each other. She was so stunned, so frozen, that it took her a moment to realize he'd started speaking again.

"I wish for you to paint me, Miss Townsend, just as I am. Scars and all. London must see this, the *truth*." He was staring at her over his shoulder, his back still to her so she could see the full effect of his trauma.

"The truth?" she asked. "What truth?"

"The truth of innocence destroyed, Suzannah." He turned toward her, the scars fading into the shadows as his eyes pinned her in place. "I was once much like Henry, innocent and young. Too naive to recognize evil when it came for me."

Suzannah was nearly speechless, and her heart battered against her ribs. She hated to see anyone hurting and seeing this man's pain hurt her far more deeply than she expected it to. "What happened?"

"I was convicted of a crime I did not commit." His calm voice could not hide the vicious edge it had to it. "I was sent to live and die as a convict, far from here—far from *everyone* I ever loved—by men filled with greed who took advantage of my innocence. Seven long years . . . that's how long I've been gone from England."

Tears blurred her vision as a terrifying truth settled within her. It couldn't be him. Could it?

"This"—he turned again to show her his back, the ugly scars, the history of his quiet rage—"was my reward for such innocence."

A man condemned, sent away as a prisoner . . . seven years ago . . .

She clutched her paintbrushes in one hand, her fingers tight enough that the wood threatened to crack. "Who . . . *who* are you?" She knew the answer, knew it deep in her bones, but she had to hear the words.

Kit let the shirt fall to the floor as he turned to her, an avenging angel with a demon beneath his skin. A man so consumed with his past, the wrongs done to him, that all she could see was a wealth of muscles, hard angles, and *danger*.

"I am a man looking for justice, and *you* will give it to me." He flexed his arms, and she saw more scars upon his beautiful skin.

Her skin prickled at being so close to someone so determinedly angry, but she couldn't look away. The way his eyes pierced her where she stood, stripped her bare and demanded that she face his truth . . . It all called to her, and her body was suddenly hotter under his gaze because of it.

"Why me?" she whispered.

"You know why, don't you, Suzannah *Townsend?*" He spoke her name softly, with an intense intimacy that sent shivers through her.

She stared hard at his face, seeking the answers there as all the pieces of his puzzle fell into place.

"You *can't* be . . ." She stepped back, then gasped and stumbled as she tripped over her bag on the floor. He moved fast, and in two long strides he caught her by the upper arms. He held her close, not allowing her to flee.

"Who am I?" he demanded in a low, dangerous tone. Their faces were inches apart now, his warm breath fanning her face. His lips were parted, as were hers, both breathing hard as if they'd run up a hill together, and now she was tumbling down the other side as she was sucked into the burning rage of his gaze.

"You are . . ." She swallowed as his hands tightened on her arms, and she trembled, her mind reeling.

"Say my name."

"Chris . . . Christopher Hollingsworth."

His hands released her, and she felt like the connection between them somehow sharpened her awareness of him even more by the absence of his touch. *Christopher Hollingsworth.* She never thought she would hear that name again once her father had died.

He'd said his name was Kit, and she knew that was a nickname for Christopher, but she'd had no idea this was him. She should have known better. A part of her had always known that he would find his way to her, to take his revenge on her because her father was gone. She didn't want to think what else he might desire, but the nebulous thought rooted itself in her mind anyway.

She sucked in a much-needed breath and was finally able to speak. "What do you want with me?"

He raised his hands again, as if he wanted to take hold of her, but then he lowered his arms to his sides as he gazed at her with an intensity that obliterated everything around her until it was just the two of them in this quiet, charged universe.

"I've already told you. I want you to paint me, Suzannah. Expose London's hypocrisy. Reveal the betrayal of innocence." He straightened his shoulders, his posture stiffening as he continued. "That will be your penance to me, for the sins your father committed by lying in a court of law and sending me to my doom. You will paint the *truth*, Suzannah."

"But my father didn't—"

"Don't lie to yourself." He took hold of her again as he spoke. "Your father testified that he saw me arrange for the theft of cargo from my own ship. He *lied*, and I paid in blood for that lie for seven years."

"Are you going to hurt me?" she asked.

He was dangerously silent for a long moment, and then a wave of regret washed over his features as he released her and stepped back.

"Set up your easel," he ordered, his tone softer. "Let us begin."

He hadn't answered her question, but she didn't dare repeat it. For an instant, she considered running for the front door of the house, screaming for help. Would he chase her down? Would he drag her back here? She didn't know.

She closed her eyes, feeling his dark, enraged presence behind her. He hadn't hurt her. She was bound to his pain by her father's blood, yes, but this wasn't about *her*. She'd seen regret in his face just now, and he'd only asked her to paint him. She could do that. She could capture what he asked. Perhaps then he would see she had done right by him. But if he dared to try to harm her, she would flee however she could.

With trembling hands, she put her wooden easel together, unrolled a few sheets of paper, and clipped them to the easel. Then she retrieved her charcoal sticks from a small case. She stood at the easel and watched him take a seat on the settee. His chest was still bare, and his body, all muscle and power, glowed in the lamplight. He said not one word, only stared at her with those fathomless eyes. It was hard to focus at first, but soon she relaxed and found her pace.

Art had always been her refuge from the harsh realities of the world. Even now, facing someone who hated her, she focused on the shapes that made his body and face rather than the angry man. The sloping shoulders, contours of muscles, the way his hair formed waves with silky strands. She drew it all, repeating the lines, learning the shape of him with the intimacy of a lover as though she were tracing him with her fingertips instead of charcoal.

At one point she was aware of Henry entering the room and seating himself nearby, but soon he was softly snoring. She kept going, her hand moving again and again until she was bone-weary. Her subject hadn't moved an inch in two hours. He seemed to possess a strength of will she did not.

"I am finished for tonight," she said quietly. Only then did he stand up. He pulled his shirt back on, then his waist-coat, dressing slowly while she packed up her supplies.

He pointed to an empty card table. "You may leave the sketches on the table."

She did as he bid and then tucked her easel and char-coal back into her bag. She glanced at the still-sleeping Henry at the same moment he did.

"You fear me," he said softly. He'd come up behind her once more but didn't touch her.

She raised her face bravely up to his as he towered above her. "How could I not?"

"*Don't*," was all he said, and then, before she knew what was happening, he leaned down and their lips met in a soft ghost of a kiss. "Paint the truth, *my truth*, and you will have nothing to fear from me." He moved away from her and gave Henry a gentle shake of the arm. "Time to take Miss Townsend home, lad."

The boy stood up and grinned sheepishly at them. "What? Oh . . ."

"Yes, it's time to leave," Suzannah told Henry.

She had to get out of this house, had to breathe in the night air, had to forget that whispering kiss. It had been a promise, but a promise of what? She was afraid of the answer . . . and even more afraid of how it made her feel. A kiss like that was as dangerous as a fire upon dry grass in a year without rain. A kiss like that held the promise to burn the world and her with it.

KIT WATCHED SUZANNAH AND HENRY GET INTO THE HIRED COACH, and then he returned to the drawing room. He replayed the evening in his mind, how she'd looked when he'd told her who he was and what he wanted from her. How she'd looked at the scars on his body. He hadn't seen pity—he'd seen *compassion*. She'd understood what he'd gone through, and rather than be repulsed, she'd looked as though his pain had become her own.

He hadn't expected that, to hurt her by showing her what he'd suffered, yet knowing she'd seen him this way and hadn't run from him gave him hope. Hope for *what* he didn't know, yet he clung to that fragile emotion none-theless.

He approached the reading table that bore her sketches with a sense of dread. What would he see? What was he *afraid* to see? She was a truly gifted artist, and he wasn't sure he could handle seeing his own truth laid bare by her hand. Was he ready to face the monster depicted on these pieces of paper?

His hands shook as he picked up of the topmost paper. He saw hard lines of charcoal and other shapes before he let his gaze take in the entirety of her work. The sketches, however brief, were like hastily stolen glances into the deepest part of his soul. Fair hands had traced the lines that carved his soul from the hard rock of his rage.

She'd created a vision of truth—half beauty, half despair—with her skilled fingers. The images seemed to whisper to him. He saw hints of what he'd once been, a handsome lad, a lighthearted young man, now torn asunder by the darkness. His eyes, so deeply drawn in shades of gray, demanded that the viewer see what time and suffering had wrought upon him. He had asked her to draw the truth, and these images could not be more true unless she cut his chest open and drew his still-beating heart.

The house around him was still, yet the memories of his past savaged his mind like an unrelenting storm. He stood alone, gazing at the face she had drawn. Memory held such power to harm or heal. Suzannah and her art had chosen to heal, to save, but why? Why had she drawn him as a man and not the monster that so clearly lurked beneath his skin?

His lips still burned sweetly from that kiss. Why had he done that? What had possessed him to kiss her, the daughter of a man who'd caused him so much pain? One word from her father, one denial, and Kit could have been set free. Fresh fury struck him, and he strode toward the fireplace, intending to cast the sketches into the flames, but he halted an instant before he would have tossed the papers into the fire.

Her kiss, the one he'd stolen, however softly, was still there imprinted upon his lips, burning him like the fires of perdition. He didn't regret that kiss, no matter how confused it made him feel.

Outside, a nightingale began to sing, its lonely song filled with mournful memories. The fire within Kit died as sorrow overcame it. He sank to his knees and let the sketches fall to the floor, far from the reach of the greedy flames. That night, with the quiet solitude cloaking him, he dared to cry for the first time in seven years.

7

Maynard Walsh leaned back in a comfortable lounge chair at White's, his gentlemen's club. A glass of warmed brandy swirled in his hand and the *Morning Post* sat folded on his lap as he savored the late-afternoon quiet. He had been away in Boston for the last seven months, expanding his business, and he was glad to be back in England. He had signed several new contracts that would prove lucrative once he paid off the capital investments used to secure those contracts.

He took a sip of his brandy and unfolded his paper, scanning the articles. He paid most attention to the business articles and less to the society gossip, but as he turned the next page, a name stuck out, a name that sent a knife of terror through him.

Maynard sputtered and dropped his brandy glass. It landed with a soft thump on the carpet, splashing the amber liquid all over his shoes. Forgetting his drink, he placed the paper on the table in front of him and read the article again.

The latest on-dits . . . rumor has it that Christopher Hollingsworth, the new Earl of Kentwell, has returned to London. Seven years ago, he was convicted of grand larceny and sent to the penal colonies of Australia as a convict. He was recently spotted on Bond Street, accompanied by the Duke of Tiverton. If these rumors prove to be true, it seems Devil's Square has added a new devil to its ranks.

Maynard's hands shook as he folded up the paper and got to his feet. "Christ!" With a furtive glance around him, he dashed from the room.

He had to find Thomas Balfour at once.

LIONEL THISTLEWAITE LOWERED HIS NEWSPAPER AND STARED AT the empty seat where moments ago Maynard Walsh had been sitting. A slow grin spread across his face.

"So it begins." He tossed his paper onto the table and stood. He straightened his coat and followed his quarry out of White's. Walsh frantically badgered a club servant, demanding his hat and cane. Lionel kept himself at a discreet distance as he collected his hat and gloves, then stepped out onto the street to see where his target was headed.

Walsh flagged down a passing coach, so Lionel did the same. He instructed his driver to follow Walsh at a careful distance until they arrived at their destination.

The plan he and the others had come up with was working. Vincent had fed a story about Kit being seen with

Darius to the papers, and it had run that morning as planned. They'd struck the underbrush and now had only to wait and see what would be flushed out. If they had successfully startled Walsh, he might panic and do or say something that would help Kit bring both him and Balfour down.

The two coaches traveled for some minutes before stopping on a street with a row of lavish townhouses. Lionel stepped out of the coach and tossed his driver a few extra coins, asking him to wait. Then he walked discreetly thirty yards behind Walsh. The man dashed up the steps of one of the houses and rapped the knocker frantically. Lionel paused two doors down, lingering to check the small pocket watch that hung from his waistcoat as any gentleman on the street might do.

When Walsh was admitted inside, Lionel came closer to the townhouse, then slipped down the small alley between the home Walsh entered and the one next to it.

The late-afternoon shadows enveloped him as he waited, considering his options. He noticed a pile of wooden crates in the corner by the garden wall. He stacked them on top of one another and then scaled the wall, dropping down the other side and landing in a crouch.

He held his breath, listening for the sounds of servants alerted to his presence, but there were none. The garden behind the house was empty, but the windows were open, and a rush of angry voices carried out on the breeze to Lionel in his hiding spot by the wall.

"What the bloody hell are *you* doing here?" someone shouted. "This is not the place we agreed to meet." The voice belonged to Thomas Balfour. Lionel scowled in the shadows. But this wasn't Balfour's home.

"I know, but this couldn't wait," Maynard shot back. "Look at this."

There was a moment of silence, and then Balfour hissed, "Blast. I paid that captain to kill him. The man swore he threw Hollingsworth overboard once they were out to sea."

Lionel's hands curled into fists as he fought his rage. Balfour had paid to have Kit killed before he even reached the colonies. Why? He'd already been convicted.

Then it struck him. Kit was a fighter. Even at nineteen he had been strong and resilient. If anyone could survive the crossing and seven years of dangerous life in the colonies, it would be Kit. And Kit would come home. Balfour must have realized that if Kit ever came back, he would be out for revenge.

You aren't wrong, Balfour, Lionel thought grimly.

"Well, he lied to you. Hollingsworth is here in London. Now. We must do something," Maynard said. "I've only just returned from Boston. We've expanded—"

"What? I told you not to sign any contracts without my approval. Your business troubles are what got you into this bloody mess in the first place. If we hadn't talked that boy into being your partner, you never would've been able to collect the insurance on the stolen goods and send him away for the theft. And if I hadn't helped you, you would be in debtors' prison," Balfour growled, and something crashed in the room.

"My sister won't like that you've broken her favorite vase," Maynard chided smugly.

Lionel's eyes widened. Maynard's sister was married to the Duke of Stoneleigh, a grizzled beast of a man who wielded great power in the House of Lords at the moment. What the devil was Balfour doing at Stoneleigh's house? Balfour was meeting Maynard's sister at her home . . . while her husband was not there.

A grin returned to Lionel's face. It was all beginning to make sense, how these two men had been connected all those years ago and why they continued to help each other now. Now that he knew the truth, he would wield it like a sword.

"What your sister likes and doesn't like is *my* concern," Balfour said coldly. "Now, have you seen Kentwell with your own eyes, or is this merely gossip?"

"I haven't seen him," Maynard admitted. "But there's mention that he'll be attending most of the events this season, including a ball at Lord Lennox's home."

"Then I want *you* and I to attend Lennox's ball and verify this rumor," Balfour ordered. "If it is true, then we shall meet at the docks, the usual place. We'll discuss our options then."

"Fine," Maynard said.

A door slammed, and Lionel guessed that Maynard had left. Lionel scaled the wall again. When he landed on the other side, a pretty housemaid was staring at him, a dustpan and a broom held in her hands. Her lips parted in shock, and fearing she would scream, Lionel put a finger to his lips and winked roguishly at her and tossed her a coin for her silence. She giggled softly as she caught the coin. He tipped his hat at her and then exited the mews to get back onto the street. He would trail Walsh and send Darius and Kit a message.

❧

A DEEP VOICE PULLED SUZANNAH FROM HER THOUGHTS. "WHO IS that?"

She was sketching again while she listened in the wings to another round of rehearsals. She'd been idly doodling while echoing the lines of the play underneath her breath. She knew them all by heart now. Suzannah glanced up to see Jude smiling down at her. He was a tall, muscular, rather beautiful man, but what she loved most about him was his kindness. Ever since he'd arrived from America, his natural joy had been infectious. Whenever he smiled, she smiled back.

She glanced back down at her sketch, frowning a little.

"You seem quite focused on this man," Jude observed. "Is he a friend?"

A blush crept across Suzannah's cheeks. The face she drew was the face that had haunted her as she tossed and turned in bed. The face of Kit Hollingsworth.

"I suppose I am quite focused. I have been commissioned to paint his portrait."

Jude pulled up a chair and sat down beside her, studying the sketches. "Is that right? You must be pleased, then. You always told me you wished to paint portraits."

"I . . . yes. I suppose. Jude, may I ask you something that may sound rather insensitive? If you don't wish to answer once I ask, I completely understand."

Jude's warm brown eyes were full of compassion. "Of course. What do you wish to know?"

"Before you escaped from America, how long were you a slave?"

Jude's gaze turned distant, and Suzannah immediately regretted her question.

"I'm sorry, I shouldn't have—"

"No, it's all right. I can talk about it. I was born into slavery. I had three masters in twenty years, each worse than the last. Just after I turned twenty, I managed to escape and sailed here." Despite his smile, she saw the pain still in his eyes. "I've been free for four years now."

She couldn't begin to imagine how hard that must have been to escape and fight his way toward a life he deserved, knowing that so many others were left behind.

"How have you survived such horrors with compassion?" she asked. "Doesn't that . . . I mean, you were treated terribly, no better than an animal. How are you not blind with rage?" The memory of Kit's eyes flashed across her mind, the rage and pain that seemed so strong it would drown him.

Jude was quiet a long moment. "I decided some years ago that I measure my own worth. I let no other person tell me what my value is. I may have scars and memories darkened with despair, but they are only memories now. They have only the power I give them, or in my case, the power I refuse to give them. Each day I choose to be the person I have the right to be, and with that power of choice, I find joy and peace."

It took her a moment to find the words to speak. She held her breath, thinking of all the moments of sorrow that had so often weighed her down. But the other questions she had would not let her stay silent for long.

"Did you . . . ever meet any convicts during your time in America? I know England stopped sending them to the Americas after the war, but . . ."

"I have met some. Why?"

Jude had trusted her with his past. Now she needed to trust him and confide in him about Kit. She took a moment to think about what she should say.

"I met a man yesterday who spent seven years in the penal colonies of Australia. He seems so broken by what he endured. Full of so much anger. So much that I don't know how he doesn't tear the world apart with his bare hands."

Jude reached out and covered one of her hands with his, giving it a squeeze.

"Some men feel helpless, but rage gives them power for a time. Anger gives them something to hold on to, like a lifeboat in a storm. A man ties himself to the oars and rows and rows. Every wave threatens to drown him. That lifeboat of rage is all he knows, but a man cannot survive forever with that rage."

Suzannah's throat tightened at the thought of someone feeling so helpless.

"How do you help them find the shore?" she asked.

"You show him the one thing that is stronger than hate and rage."

"What is that?"

"*Love*, Suzannah. Love in our fellow man, our brothers and sisters, or that one person we let in to our hearts. Love is the wind in every sail that carries a man's boat to shore. Show him love and do not back down. A man's rage can bluster and wail like the violent storms that swell the seas of a man's heart. But love calms all waters in the end."

Suzannah turned her hand over underneath Jude's and gave it a squeeze in return.

"You are a rather wonderful man, you know?" She smiled and wiped away tears from her eyes.

Jude's smile sparked with mischief. "Yes, I am," he said with a cheeky wink, and then he got up to meet his cue from the lines being said on stage so he could adjust the sets. Suzannah looked back down at her sketch and cursed as she realized she'd smeared the lines around Kit's jaw all over the sleeve of her day dress.

"Oh blast!" She frantically rubbed the charcoal off her gown, but then her gaze fell to the sketch again. Her lips parted as she saw the change the smudges had made on Kit's face. She pulled her pencil out and added longer hair and a beard more distinctly where the new smudges were along his chin and jaw.

The wild beast of a man who'd saved her life two nights ago stared back at her from the pages of the sketchbook.

His eyes . . . She knew she'd seen Kit's eyes before. He had rescued her. He could have easily killed her that night, but instead he'd escorted her home and returned her hair ribbon the next day. Why had he not harmed her then? Why had he come back the next night as himself? He had seemed genuinely staggered to learn she wasn't an actress, and that she was Suzannah Townsend. Her appearance clearly surprised him, yet he said he'd been looking for her.

Perhaps he hadn't known what she looked like until that night? If so, her rescue must have been a kindness to a stranger. If he'd known who she was before, he might never have saved her from those men. The thought made her shudder.

She stared at the sketch a long moment, wondering if it was safe to return to Kit's home.

"He's back," Flory murmured as he passed Suzannah, his arms full of costumes for the seamstress. The play's rehearsal had finally ended.

"Who is?"

"Your gentleman caller."

She leapt up, her sketches falling to the ground in a flutter of charcoal-smudged papers. "Oh heavens . . ." As she bent to collect the sketches, a shadow blocked out the theater lamp lights above her head. When she looked up, she expected to see Flory again, but a darkly intimidating face, bestowed with masculine beauty, gazed down at her.

"I thought it was wise to escort you to my home again this evening, in case you tried to change your mind," Lord Kentwell said. His lips twisted in a dark smile. "You *were* planning to keep our bargain, *weren't* you?" he challenged softly.

She blew out a breath, which sent a loose lock of hair out of her eyes and then she swept a hand over the sketches in her arms before she scowled back at him.

"I was going to keep my promise." Her tone was sharper than she would have liked.

He bent down and retrieved one last piece of paper from the floor and studied it.

"This looks like a rather dangerous fellow. It's good that you will be accepting my escort to and from the theater each evening while we work together." He turned the page around, and she saw a sketch of him with long hair and a beard. A hint of dark amusement glowed in his eyes. "I would hate for you to run into *him* again."

"That was you, wasn't it?" she asked softly. "The one who saved me from the men in the street."

"No, I don't believe it was," he said smoothly, but she had been around theater people long enough to recognize when someone was acting.

She swiped at the loose lock of hair again. For a brief instant, Kit's eyes softened, and he looked like he might smile in a pleasant way rather than grin at her like a wolf among sheep.

"Collect your things and your young protector and we shall be on our way." Kit turned and vanished into the darkness outside the theater.

A moment later, Jude came over to stand by Suzannah. He must have been watching their exchange from somewhere nearby. Perhaps he'd been concerned for her safety. "That man. He's the one you drew, the one who suffers."

Suzannah sighed heavily, trying to shuffle the pages in her arms into some semblance of order. "Yes, that's him."

Jude stared into darkened theater. "He seems to suffer less when he looks at you," Jude said.

Suzannah gaped at him. "What?"

"I saw that man enter the theater a minute ago. He watched you, thinking he was unobserved, but I saw him. That man *desires* you. You'd best take care. You may save him . . . or he may destroy you. Rage gives a man power for a time, but if he holds on to it for too long, it can destroy him as well."

Suzannah swallowed hard and then called for Henry.

"Are we to dine with Kit again?" the boy asked in excitement.

"Yes, but you must address him as *Mr.* Kit." She didn't dare tell Henry who Kit really was. This battle of wills was between her and Kit alone. She wouldn't drag anyone else into the path of his storm.

AFTER DINNER, KIT ONCE AGAIN REMOVED HIS WAISTCOAT FOR Suzannah. Henry was enjoying his glass of sherry in the library with Palmer, who was to distract the boy by teaching him to play chess. That would buy Kit some time alone with Suzannah again. He had to earn her trust and coax out what she knew of her father's involvement in his trial. That would take time and patience. She still looked ready to protest at Henry being in a different room, but she didn't speak her protests aloud. Being alone with her had nothing to do with how much he liked to watch her fall into her artistic space and give herself over to her talent. Nor did it have to do at all with stealing kisses again. Kisses and the activities that followed were the farthest things from his mind. Or so he told himself.

"Shall I sit on the settee again?" he asked, nodding toward the piece of furniture.

"Please." She had set up her easel and was fretfully moving oil lamps about on tables nearby, trying to deter-mine the best light for her to draw him. She then stood in front of him and bit her bottom lip before reaching out one hand to brush her fingers along his forehead. His hair had fallen into his eyes, and she had to adjust its placement. Her face flamed red as he gazed up at her.

"Still uncomfortable with my bare skin?" he asked.

"I'm uncomfortable simply being *close* to you, clothed or not." She toyed with his hair a bit more before nodding to herself in satisfaction.

He reached out, curling his fingers into the soft muslin of her dark purple gown before she could pull away. The gown had small flower buds embroidered on the fabric, and a sheer silk layer underneath whispered beneath his fingers. She tried to move away and was forced to halt when she realized he'd captured her with his hand clutching her skirts.

"I fear I lost my modesty in Australia," he said. "Convicts spend most of their time bare-chested, working in the blazing heat."

He watched her face, taking in her delicate features. She drew in a deep breath and then let it out. Only then did she turn to face him.

"What caused the scars?" She reached out, daring to touch him again.

Her hands were soft, but he saw strength and dexterity in them in the way she wielded her artistic instruments.

Kit glanced down at a series of claw marks along his left biceps.

"That was from a wild dog called a dingo. One night I was assigned to protect a herd of cattle. It attacked when I put myself between it and its intended meal."

She touched a light slash across his chest that bisected his right pectoral. "And this?"

"Oh, that one . . ." He chuckled softly. "A farmer's

daughter was not happy that I wouldn't share her bed. She had the unfortunate combination of being good with a knife and having a bad temper."

"Oh . . ." Suzannah tried to pull her hand away, but he caught her wrist. He had to remind himself to be gentle with her. She was so very tiny.

"Some women want to bed an English lord, even one who's a convicted criminal," he replied. "They like the idea of it."

"Oh, I thought she—" Suzannah halted, swallowing whatever she had been about to say.

"That she what?" Kit slowly pulled her hand toward his lips. He uncurled her fingers and kissed the pad of each one. Her delicate hand fascinated him beyond imagining. Her breath hitched, and he smiled at her.

"That she what?" he asked again.

"That she wanted you because you're so . . . *beautiful.*" The last word was whispered.

Her words stunned him. She thought he was beautiful? He'd been so convinced he was still a monster, a wild beast . . .

"Am I? Beautiful to you?" He mused this aloud, as if the very idea intrigued him. He then drew the tip of her index finger into his mouth, flicking the pad of her finger with his tongue. Then he playfully bit it before he let her pull her hand away with a startled gasp.

"What are you doing?" she demanded, but her voice was breathless.

"Behaving badly," he chuckled. "I'm not used to compliments, and you made me feel rather nice," he said with a wry grin. "But I'm not sure you should call a man beautiful."

"But you *are* beautiful," she insisted, then added, "However, beauty can be dangerous. A tiger is beautiful, but still deadly." She spun away and uncurled the fingers of his other hand from her gown. He let her retreat to her place behind her easel.

"If you are to apply such standards, then you must also be quite deadly, little tigress."

She tried to hide her face behind the easel as she began to sketch, but he could see she was blushing. Kit should be scowling, but somehow teasing her with suggestive talk amused him. He never thought he would miss the quaint little English roses and their modesty, but he was enjoying this immensely.

He gazed at her, watching her work. Every now and then, she would peer around the edge of the easel and gaze at him intently. He did not tease her now, not when she was working. He had no desire to interrupt a gifted artist at work.

After two hours, Henry poked his head through the doorway and glanced at Suzannah, then at Kit, before creeping in and sitting on the chair behind Suzannah to watch her work. After another quarter hour, she set her charcoal down and addressed Kit.

"I think I've sketched what I would like to paint. I've grown comfortable with your features now," she said. "I shall need to purchase a canvas. How large do you want the portrait to be?"

"Seven feet tall," he said. "And four feet wide." It was

the same size as most of the paintings hanging in the gallery above where they were now.

"That large? You're sure?" She nibbled her lip. "I will have to purchase a bigger easel."

"Write a list of everything that you need, and Palmer will see them purchased. The supplies will be here when you are ready."

She hesitated only a moment before writing out a list, then handed it to Kit. He took it and set it on a table before he hastily dressed. After Suzannah packed up her supplies, she waved at Henry, who was lounging in a chair.

"It's time to go, Henry," Suzannah said to the boy.

"Are we going to return tomorrow?" he asked Kit hopefully.

"You are," Kit assured him before Suzannah could say anything. She might try to delay her next visit.

Kit escorted them to the door, where a coach was waiting for them. He caught Suzannah's arm and slid his hand down to grasp her wrist. She turned to face him, and he placed a small purse of coins in her palm.

"This is a partial payment, along with a little more."

Her dark-golden brows drew together. "More?"

"For the lad. Buy him some clothes that fit," Kit whispered so Henry wouldn't hear.

"Oh . . . yes. I will." She looked down to their entwined hands. "Thank you."

"I was once like him. There's nothing worse than feeling like a child because you don't fit in your shirt and trousers. Henry is a young man and should feel like one."

She seemed to understand what he wanted to say, but

couldn't find the right words to respond. Instead, she simply said, "Thank you . . . I will do that."

"Good night, Suzannah."

Her lashes fluttered before she dared to meet his gaze. "Good night . . . Kit."

He watched the coach carry her away into the night and then saw a now familiar light moving in the window across the street, signaling him. Darius. He'd caught on quickly to his friends' silent method of communicating. It was close to the lamp signals sailors used to signal other ships in the fog or the dark.

"Meet . . . tomorrow . . ."

Darius must have news on Balfour or Walsh. Kit curled his fists, relishing the thought that he was one step closer to his revenge. After a moment, he returned to the drawing room and lifted his own lamp, acknowledging the signal.

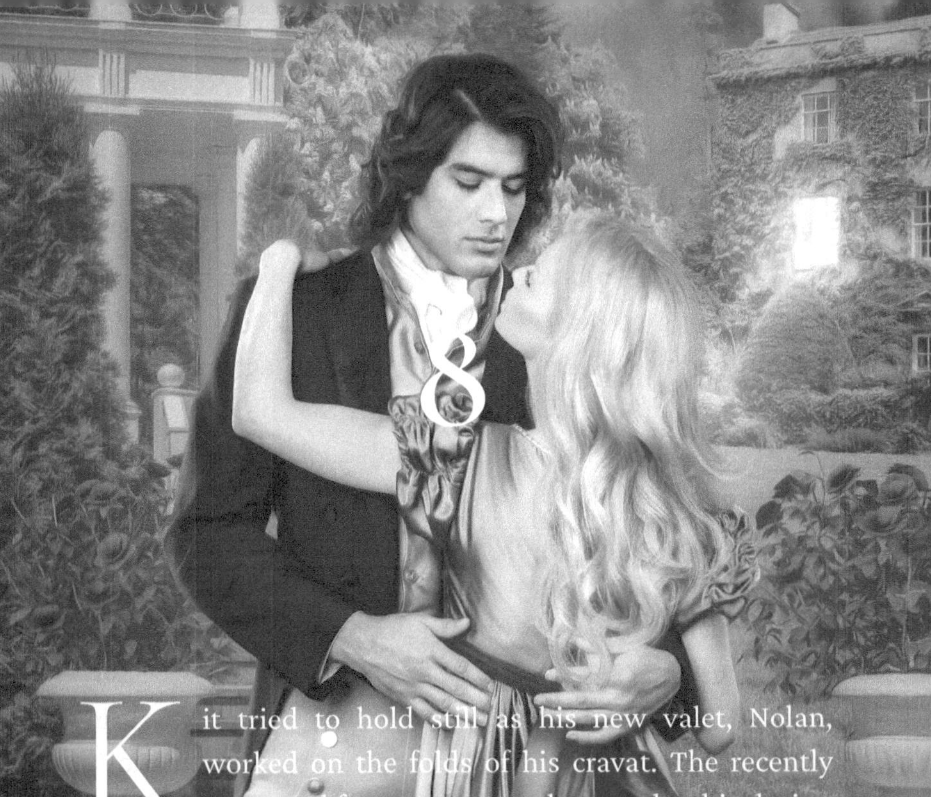

8

Kit tried to hold still as his new valet, Nolan, worked on the folds of his cravat. The recently promoted footman was rather good at his duties, but Kit was no longer used to letting anyone dress him. He also wasn't used to that annoying feeling of his clothes being so tight against his skin or wearing so many layers.

"Are you well, my lord?" Nolan asked, aware of Kit's discomfort.

"Yes, I'm fine," he lied, and then, after a moment, he decided to be honest. "I am not used to so many layers of clothing. The climate here is cold, too. I am adjusting, just not quickly enough." He slipped a finger under his cravat and tugged on it, feeling for a brief moment that he could breathe easier. "Don't fret. You're doing well, Nolan. Very well," he assured the young man.

The valet flashed a relieved smile before he retrieved Kit's evening coat from a nearby chair and helped him into it. Kit glanced briefly at himself in the tall mirror in the corner of his bedchamber and couldn't help but notice his own thunderous expression. Is this how he appeared to everyone?

Part of his ill mood likely had to do with the fact that he wasn't going to see Suzannah tonight. He'd planned on having her and Henry back at his home again, but then Darius and Lionel had informed him that he was required to attend a ball. Based on what Lionel had learned, Kit would need to make a *very* public appearance tonight so that Walsh and Balfour would see him with their own eyes. That would force the two men to act, hopefully in a reckless way, which would give him the opportunity to break the men apart and crush them.

The knowledge that he wouldn't be able to bring Suzannah to his home to work on her painting made Kit quite surly. He'd have no chance to steal another kiss or say things that got under her skin causing her to blush with beautiful fury. Instead, he had to dress up like a fool and go to a bloody ball.

Kit tugged absently on his coat with a scowl while Nolan ran a brown brush over the shoulders and back, removing any dust before he surveyed his work.

"I believe you're ready, my lord."

"Thank you, Nolan. Oh, by the by, I may be late this evening. Do not wait up for me if I do not return by midnight."

"Yes, my lord."

Kit collected his hat from Nolan and left his bedchamber. Darius and Lionel were waiting for him in the entryway, both in their best evening clothes. Kit still balked at the thought of stepping into a crowded ballroom, but at least his friends would be with him.

Once the three men were inside Darius's coach, Kit felt it safe to speak. "Does Lennox know to expect us this evening?"

"Yes," Darius assured him. "When I received the invitation, I was given a second message. He will hear our proposal this evening. Given that Lennox is throwing the ball, I imagine he has a room where we can have a discussion without fear of being overheard."

The coach stopped at a fashionable grand house on Half Moon Street. Kit, Darius, and Lionel soon joined the throng of people waiting to be allowed inside. Lamplight from the windows facing the street glowed warmly over the finely dressed ladies and gentlemen.

"Lennox never struck me as a ball-throwing man," Lionel said. "I wonder if he stands there imperiously, glowering at everyone, or if he actually likes to dance."

Darius chuckled. "From what I understand, he only hosts balls for the business connections. This is the easiest way to bring people to him where he can manage introductions and business alliances smoothly. Social engagements take away the crude talk of business between strangers. It's rather clever."

Lionel sniggered. "I'm sure a few glasses of arrack punch help loosen tongues a bit as well."

The three of them followed the crowd inside the house. People began to notice Kit, and the murmuring soon spread like wildfire. Between the whispered gossip and the sudden change from the cool outdoor air to the hot crush of perfumed bodies, Kit was suffocating. He dug a finger into his cravat and pulled, feeling like he couldn't breathe.

"Steady on, old boy," Darius said in a low voice.

Kit tried to ignore the tension building between his shoulders as his name rippled through whispers across the ballroom.

Several young debutantes scattered in a mix of squeals and giggles as he, Darius, and Lionel made their way to the center of the ballroom.

I have to be visible, I have to be seen, Kit reminded himself. But in truth, he wanted nothing more in that moment than to disappear.

There was one person he wanted to *see* him, and she was not here. He thought of Suzannah sitting in the back rooms of the Drury Lane theater, painting her sets. Was she disappointed or relieved that he'd had to cancel her session with him this evening? She was probably relieved, given how forward and intimidating he'd been with her. *He* was the one who was disappointed. Mad as it was, he felt like she was the only person who had seen the real him. Not even his friends had seen his scars yet. He had given Suzannah the truth of himself to do with as she wished, and it remained to be seen if that was a mistake or not.

Kit's gaze roved over the crowded ballroom, seeking his prey. His heart stopped for a beat as he recognized two familiar faces. *There.* There they were.

Time had not been kind to the justice of the peace who'd helped seal his fate. Balfour's face had puffed out, no doubt from the excesses of his lavish lifestyle. Kit had learned that the magistrate had taken to dining out often and had been seen visiting the more expensive brothels in

London, sometimes twice a day. The man still had a robust figure that exuded power, but he was beginning a gradual slide out of his prime.

Walsh, on the other hand, looked more nervous and wiry than he remembered. Time had put worry lines in the man's face and a twitchiness to his eyes and nose that made him look rather like a rabbit ready to bolt at any moment. That was something Kit could work with. Fear made someone easier to manipulate.

Kit's spine stiffened. Now that he had seen the enemy, he set about ignoring the two men who had ruined his life. Instead, he flashed rakish smiles at the women he passed and gave acknowledging nods to the gentlemen. He considered putting his name down on a few girls' dance cards, but the heaving bosoms of clearly distraught mothers who hovered above their precious chicks changed his mind. He wished to cause a stir, not a *catastrophe*. If he asked even one of these young chits to dance, their overprotective mothers would faint dead away. He could do without that.

Lionel came to Kit's side and handed him a glass of punch. "Lennox just gave us the signal. Follow me."

Kit and Darius trailed after Lionel. The music started and couples began lining up to dance just as Kit and his friends left the ballroom.

Lennox was waiting for them on the threshold of the doorway to a drawing room and motioned for them to step inside.

"I take it the men you wished to see have had a good look at you?" Lennox asked.

"Yes, they have."

"Good." Lennox waved to some chairs near a card table,

and the four of them sat. "Tiverton mentioned you needed my help?"

Kit glanced at Darius, who nodded at him encouragingly. "Tell him everything, Kit."

Kit drew in a breath and started his tale, beginning from the moment Walsh came to him proposing they become business partners. He was careful to leave out any mention of Suzannah. When he finished, Lionel had news to add to the story.

"I trailed Walsh to a residence yesterday," Lionel added. "It turned out it was a house belonging to Walsh's sister, the Duchess of Stoneleigh. It seems that she has been having an affair with Balfour for some years. I suspect that Walsh will use that information to blackmail, or at least coerce, Balfour into helping him."

Lennox folded his arms over his chest and leaned back in his chair.

"So it is revenge you seek?"

"Yes."

"I would warn you against this course of action," said Lennox carefully. "I've seen firsthand how a desire for revenge causes only more suffering."

"I do not care. They stole my life from me, and I will see to it that they learn what that feels like." Kit didn't care if he sounded like a callous bastard.

Lennox looked into Kit's eyes, judging how much this meant to him, what it was worth. "Very well. As our interests regarding Walsh are aligned, I will argue the point no further. How can I help?"

"Everything Walsh cares about is tied up in his shipping company. We will buy up his debts using third parties," Kit said. "And when those debts are called in, we wish for you to purchase the company for the lowest price."

Kit waited, half afraid that Lennox wouldn't agree.

Finally, the blond baron nodded. "I have been meaning to purchase my own shipping company and I do not like that Walsh has been monopolizing the ports. Send me a message when it's time to make an offer to him."

"We will." Kit stood and shook Lennox's hand. "Thank you."

As his two friends stood up, Lennox caught Kit's arm. The man's bright blue eyes were like stones beneath the surface of a frozen lake.

"Watch yourself, Kentwell. I know men like Walsh—he will be looking for any opportunity to put you back in Newgate. Or, if he fears for his safety, he may avoid using the law to deal with you and simply have you killed."

"I consider myself warned." Kit nodded at Lennox, but the man still held his arm.

"If you must have your revenge, understand this. You may find that once you have it, whatever you feel has been missing will still be gone. The greatest mistake you can make is to believe that vengeance alone is what you need."

Lennox let go and gave him a nod, but Kit left the room feeling puzzled by Lennox's words.

When he and his friends returned to the ballroom, he spotted Felix, Warren, and Vincent spread out among the crowd, socializing. Their gazes turned to him discreetly, but he gave no indication that he saw them except for the briefest meeting of eyes. He checked his pocket watch. If he knew Suzannah's schedule, she would be headed back to her small room at that wretched little boardinghouse.

For a brief moment, his mind wasn't filled with revenge. Thoughts of Suzannah dominated instead, and he had the strong urge to go to her despite having canceled their session that evening. What would she do if he turned up at her door? Could he coax her into letting him inside her small home again?

"You want to see your green-ribbon girl, don't you?" Darius asked. The three of them stood a little way apart from the rest of the guests at the edge of the ballroom.

"Who's the green-ribbon girl?" Lionel asked.

"Indeed, *who* is she?" Darius teased Kit.

Kit, with no expression at all, replied, "She is Townsend's daughter. I've blackmailed her into painting my portrait."

Lionel pinched a glass of punch from a nearby tray when a servant passed by. "Painting your portrait? Is that a euphemism for—"

"No, she's an *actual* painter. Vincent was wrong. She's not an actress. She's a set painter and lives as poorly as a bloody church mouse. I'm beginning to suspect she wasn't left any money when Townsend died. So he must have spent whatever Balfour and Walsh paid him before then."

"You said she's painting a portrait of you?" Darius asked.

"Yes. A scandalous one that will have all of London beating down my door to see it, or burn it. When she's done, you will all hire her for portraits of yourselves as well."

Lionel spewed punch everywhere. "Wh—what?"

"You will hire Suzannah to paint you, and you will pay

her three times the normal price that you would pay any male artist for the same work."

For a moment, his two friends stared at him, and he wondered if they would agree to his request.

Darius shared a glance with Lionel as he handed his friend a handkerchief to wipe the punch off his sleeve. "I'm not objecting, as such, but *why*?"

"Because I am asking you to. I can give no other reason." He wasn't about to admit how he had recklessly thrown out that offer to Suzannah in the hope that she would agree to paint him. Guaranteeing business for her had been a large part of her agreeing to his offer.

"Fair enough," Darius said without hesitation. Kit's heart was filled with a warmth of friendship he'd long forgotten. "I haven't had any portraits painted since we were at Eton. Is she any good?"

"She's gifted. Truly gifted," Kit admitted. "She paints the sets at Drury Lane in the evenings and sells her regular paintings in Hyde Park during the day."

"Interesting. Vincent never mentioned seeing her at Hyde Park. He must have trailed her to the theater and assumed she was an actress," Lionel observed with a sigh and gave his empty punch glass to a passing footman. "Well, I'm off. I promised my little sister a dance this evening, and my mother is already giving me a critical eye for failing to stand by her."

"I'm not staying either," Kit said, his gaze turning briefly to Balfour and Walsh. "Best to leave now before those two try something."

"Agreed. I'll go with you," Darius said and followed Kit to the door.

Kit decided to visit the boardinghouse and make sure that Suzannah had gotten safely home. He was uneasy at the idea of her making that walk at night, especially after her encounter with those drunken louts that first night he had met her. Checking on her would be the gentlemanly thing to do, wouldn't it?

SUZANNAH WAS PAINTING A PORTRAIT OF JUDE ON A CANVAS SHE'D stretched herself. The colors were coming along nicely, but oil was quite a bit of work. She liked to practice when she could afford the cost of oil paint. Since Kit had given her quite a large advance on his portrait, she'd been able to take Henry shopping for clothes better suited to his height and build and had enough left over to buy fresh oils. This was a good chance for her to practice in preparation for Kit's project, which would be quite large given the dimensions he'd requested.

She layered on the initial shadows of the stagehand's face and soft light browns against the white canvas. She would layer in other colors one by one. It was a technique she had learned from the previous Drury Lane set painter. He was an older man who'd retired to the country last year, but he'd been happy to give Suzannah some finer points of instruction. She'd been approaching oil painting completely wrong for years, she'd discovered. No matter the subject, man or animal or landscape, she learned that the best thing to do was to lay in the initial outlines with a light brown layer to provide a base. Then she built layer upon layer of new colors one by one. Once she'd tried that method, she'd been stunned to see how much deeper and far more real her paintings seemed to look.

She had chosen Jude as a subject because she wanted to capture the emotion in his eyes. The gentleness, the strength, the compassion and keen intelligence. It would be good practice for conveying emotion when it came to Kit. Of course, Kit's emotions were far different from Jude's. They were like two ships caught in the same storm, but one had made it safely to port while the other was still lost in the tempestuous gales.

Someone knocked at the door, and she nearly spilled the paint she was using to refresh her palette. It was close to midnight, and everyone she knew would be home by now. Perhaps she had left something behind and Flory was bringing it to her. She set the palette on the small table by her easel and went to the door.

"Who is it?" she called out.

"It's me," a deep voice said.

She repeated the comment softly to herself, wondering who on earth "*me*" was. Then she realized she recognized the voice, as well as the arrogant assumption that she should know whoever this man was.

She opened the door, and there stood Kit. Wearing fine evening clothes, his dark hair falling into his dark eyes, he painted quite the picture of a handsome gentleman of leisure. Yet there was a danger that still hung about him, warning anyone sensible to keep their distance. Her sensibility seemed to have vanished long ago when it came to this man. Every time she saw him, she was astounded at his height and the breadth of his shoulders and how he made her tremble, but not from fear. The man was as large as an old forest God from the tales her mother used to read to her as a child.

"What are you doing here, Lord Kentwell?" she whispered. "You told me not to expect your hired coach this evening because you had a prior engagement..."

"Invite me in, Suzannah." His tone was less gruff than she would have expected at issuing such a command.

"No. If you're here to ... to ..."

"Do you mean to suggest I'm here to seduce you with reckless abandon until you want no other man's touch but mine?" His lips curved in a crooked grin.

"Yes, that is something I most certainly do not want," she said as she frowned at him. How did he always know exactly what to say to befuddle her? She was supposed to be afraid of him, of what he might want, and yet he teased her about it in such a way that she now felt as if she wanted him to do just that.

Seduce me with reckless abandon until I want no other man's touch but yours...

"Then you are in luck. I wish only to see that you made it home safely since I could not escort you this evening."

She appreciated his concern but was tempted to remind him that she'd lived alone for more than a year and had looked after herself well enough. She knew, however, that he could simply bring up the night that he had rescued her as evidence to the contrary.

"As you can see, I'm quite well, my lord."

"Kit," he corrected, and with one large hand pressed on her door, he pushed it open. She stepped back as he came inside her small dwelling.

"Is it just as you remembered?" she asked.

"Yes, still as small as a broom cupboard."

"So you *admit* you were the man who saved me that night," she said with no small amount of triumph.

He snorted softly, as if this was all a game. "You *knew* that I knew that you knew that."

"I just wanted to hear you admit the truth."

Her choice of words put a slight frown on his face, a hardness. Yet if there was any kindness and compassion left in him, it lay in his decision to rescue her that night. It reminded him that he still could choose a path other than vengeance.

Kit prowled around her small room, his eyes drifting from the bed to the little table where she had her meals, then to the small wardrobe that held her few dresses and a cloak. He lingered longest on the handful of colorful hair ribbons that were draped over the back of one chair. He reached out and stroked the green ribbon, the one he had thoughtfully returned to her.

Kit noticed the easel and approached it with a curious look on his face. He folded his arms over his chest, studying the rough outline.

"Who is your subject?"

"A friend of mine, a man named Jude. He works as a stagehand alongside Henry."

He seemed rather interested. "Ah, so this is how I shall look?"

"Well, I've only just started this one. I begin with a base color of a neutral tone, like light brown, and layer in many colors in succession. Then I finish it with three layers of glaze to make it shine and feel as though one could reach out and touch the subject."

As she was explaining all this, Kit watched her, those intense eyes on *her* rather than the painting of Jude. She soon stopped talking when she could no longer ignore his intense focus.

"Would *you* want to touch me?" he asked. His voice was low, soft, almost husky, but she heard a hint of a plea in his question that was impossible to ignore.

"Would I *want* to?" she echoed, her own voice slightly breathless. She wanted to, yes, but she was also afraid of what touching him would do to both of them.

That memory of him kissing her, so faint yet intense, and the way he'd kissed her fingers, so innocent and sinful at the same time . . . She had done her best to pretend it had never happened. But she'd dreamt of it last night. She was unable to forget the feel of his mouth gently sucking on her finger and how his eyes had burned with raw passion.

"I promise to hold very still and behave . . . if you wish to touch me," Kit said. There was no coldness to his words, and she saw none of the callous wild rogue in his gaze now. There was only a plea shining from those dark brown eyes.

Jude's words about love and compassion being the way to quell a man's tempestuous rage at a world that had so wronged him echoed in her mind. How long had it been since someone touched him with love?

"Yes . . . I want to touch you." The words slipped out before she could stop herself. She wanted to touch him with love, love from one person to another who was hurting. She desired him as a woman could desire a man, but her need to touch him now . . . it came only from a desire to share compassionate love. One soul to another with the hope to heal.

He pulled out one of her chairs at the table and sat down to face her. His hands lay on his thighs as he waited for her to come near. Drawn by the temptation of touching him without fear of consequence, Suzannah stood between his knees as he parted his legs.

With a trembling hand, she brushed the hair out of his eyes. A breath of excitement rippled through her like a meadow filled with butterflies suddenly taking flight all at once. It filled her with a swirl of color and the faintest whisper of destiny on their gossamer wings.

Suzannah trailed her fingers along his cheekbones, traced his proud nose with the pad of a finger, and dared to shape the lines of his mouth. Only then did he react to her touch. His dark lashes closed as she stroked his lips, and he let out a soft sigh.

It was the sound of someone finding their way home after having been lost a very long time. The relief, the gratitude and pleasure of seeing one's front door after such a long time away. She knew that sound because it was the sound she had made when she'd first seen her sets on display at Drury Lane. As the theater had darkened and the crowd hushed when the music began, the scenes she had made rolled on stage and she'd felt like she'd found home again.

Kit had suffered seven years without the comfort of feeling like he was home. And it was her touch that had made him feel it once more. She knew this to be true, but she didn't understand how she could make him feel that way, only that she felt the sense of it mirrored in her own heart.

"Please don't stop," Kit whispered, and his eyes opened.

She saw the ghost of tears in their depths. She was never quite sure who moved first, but she was soon sitting upon his lap and had brought his head to hers. She kissed his forehead, his cheeks, his closed eyelids, and the tip of his nose and his straight chin before at last placing her lips to his.

Somewhere in the dark, secret part of her that had fallen into shadows of grief over her father's loss, a light blossomed to life. It was as though lightning had struck the dry ground of her soul, and a fire was born again, burning defiantly against the darkness.

Longing and loneliness blended with the pleasure of that single kiss. She wrapped her arms around his neck, pressing closer to him, holding on and plunging deeper into the feel of him *surrounding* her. Kit's mouth grew bolder, as if he too felt that spark between them.

The earth beneath her and the distant stars above were gone, and the brightness of the very sun vanished from her eyes. She and Kit existed somewhere within themselves, and that single kiss continued for endlessly. Until that moment, Suzannah had not believed in souls having a mate, or that two hearts could become as one. But as she felt Kit's mouth against hers, his body shuddering with the force of emotions that she too felt, she knew soulmates had to be real. They were so alike, their hearts filled with the same flame. All she could think was love called upon love in moments such as these.

Kit tightened his arms around her, holding her close as their lips finally parted. He was breathing hard, as was she, as though they had fought in battle together and now must find peace within each other's arms. He rested his forehead against hers and closed his eyes.

"I know not what magic you wield nor why it casts such a spell upon me," he breathed. "I should hate you because of your father. I shouldn't hunger for your touch, your lips . . ." He trembled again, and she nuzzled her nose against his. "But I do *hunger* . . . so much that it hurts."

"*You* are the one who casts spells," she said in the same breathless voice he had. "I should be terrified of you, and yet I cannot seem to stay away."

At last, he opened his eyes and held her tight a moment longer.

"I must go. I will have you picked up outside the theater tomorrow evening."

Before she could collect herself, she was gently set down on the chair, and then he vanished out the door before she could speak.

It was only after he left that the remnants of whatever magic had come to life between them seemed to fade. She looked about her room and noticed with delightful dizziness that her green hair ribbon was gone from the back of her chair.

She smiled, and the buzz of lazy, wonderful magic from Kit's kiss that felt like an endless summer burned strong within her again.

9

K it lay on the pallet of blankets that covered the floor beside his bed, watching the green ribbon glow in the clear morning light. He had this silly, boyish expectation that by holding the ribbon, he'd summon its owner to him.

He had slept halfway to noon, and his body was loose and warm in the sunlight. Warm, gentle sunlight—what a wonderful thing, he reflected. Bright, warm, healing. Like Suzannah. Perhaps that was what drew him to her, the sense of knowing that the more he basked in her glow, the stronger he felt. He couldn't remember the last time he'd felt so comfortable and relaxed. He had nowhere to be, nothing to do—he could just lie here and bathe in the sun, thinking of a woman whose kiss was pure magic.

With a soft smile, he smoothed his thumb over the hair ribbon and replayed the kiss from last night. He wasn't sure what had possessed him to ask her to touch him, but he didn't regret it. Suzannah's touch had filled him with a bittersweet ache for all the things he had lost in the last seven years.

What if…?

The words tiptoed across his mind, whispering tempting fantasies of what might have been. What if he had never been arrested? What if he had met Suzannah at a ball? What if they had danced together and shared a kiss on a moonlit veranda? What if he had been hopelessly in love with her and proposed marriage? What if he'd had a chance at happiness with her?

But those what-ifs would never come to pass. He was a *broken* man. Such a normal life was impossible for him, a sweet dream he could hold briefly in his hands before it vanished once again.

Vincent strode into the bedchamber and found Kit on the floor, holding Suzannah's ribbon like a lovestruck fool. "Kit…what the devil are you doing?"

"Vin, I believe it's still customary to knock before barging into someone's bedchamber, isn't it?" Kit growled as he shoved away his blankets and stood. He'd slept in his trousers as he'd often done in Australia, which his poor valet, Nolan, seemed to find frustrating.

"You slept close to noon, and poor Palmer came down the street to fetch me. He was afraid to have anyone else wake you up. What's this nonsense about sleeping on the floor?" He waved a hand at the pile of blankets. "Have a care, man. The servants are worried sick over you."

Vincent dragged a hand through his hair and scowled at Kit as if it was all his fault. It was clear that beneath his friend's frustration there was a softer emotion at play:

concern. He still wasn't used to being around his friends and feeling the depth of their brotherly love for him.

"You need not worry about me, Vin. I'm all right," Kit said, forcing his tone to be more gentle.

"*Are you?* Lionel said you went to see the Townsend girl last evening. He said you're . . . fixated on her." Vincent's gaze fell to the green ribbon Kit was idly twisting about his fingers. His dark eyes narrowed. "Tell me you didn't hurt her. We haven't proved yet if she had any knowledge of her father's false testimony."

"Of course I didn't." Kit's own temper returned a little.

"Then why—?"

"Because . . . somehow . . . I've gone mad and I've come to care for her." He wouldn't have admitted that to anyone except a friend.

"You *care* about her?" Vincent's shoulders relaxed, and he now smiled wickedly. "Well, that's an entirely different matter, isn't it?" He slapped Kit's shoulder. "Get dressed. We have much to do today."

He wasn't sure he liked the sound of that. He was tired of doing things. He wanted to rest.

"Yes. You need to buy a decent horse to ride, and you need a carriage and a team of four horses to pull it. You can't always be hiring out a hackney. It's time to think of your place in polite society now."

"That reminds me . . . When I left, my father had a nice coach and a team of four. I hadn't even given it a thought until now. What happened to the coach?"

"I believe he sold it and the horses, not because he needed the money, but because he'd stopped going out that last year before he passed."

"Ahh . . ." Kit's throat tightened as it always did when the subject of his father came up.

"So." Vincent cleared his throat. "I shall be escorting you to Tattersall's today."

Kit's shoulders drooped, and he let out a heavy sigh. "I am capable of going places on my own."

"Of course, but Darius believes, and the rest of us agree with him, that you may be targeted by Walsh and Balfour. It's just a matter of when and where. We have no idea if they will choose to come at you with legal nonsense or if they might attempt something more . . . *underhanded.* Either way, we shall be witnesses to your good character or bodyguards against any unforeseen attacks."

Kit knew his enemies were capable of either course of action. Perhaps Darius was right to be concerned. "Very well, you may play nursemaid to me today."

An hour later, Kit was dressed in his top boots, with leather riding breeches and a sloping double tailcoat made of kerseymere. He had chosen a green striped waistcoat to accent his blue tailcoat. It was the most effort he'd made to look more like the other young bucks his age since returning home. Soon, he and Vincent were in the yard of a coach maker, eyeing the available styles and colors.

"We ought to purchase a decent drag for you. Now that you're back in town, everyone will expect you to have one." Vincent crossed his arms and studied the gentleman's four-wheeled coach before them.

The coach seller shifted restlessly nearby, waiting anxiously for Kit to make a decision. The coach was a glossy dark blue and would look rather fetching with the Kentwell crest painted in gold and green upon the sides.

"I'll take this one," he informed the seller.

"Excellent choice, my lord. I will have a bill of sale prepared."

When they were alone, Vincent smiled. "Perhaps you ought to consider adding a landau for drives in the park with Miss Townsend."

Kit pictured himself in an open carriage on a fine spring day as he escorted Suzannah beneath the blooming trees in Hyde Park. Just the thought of seeing her smile shyly at him beneath the dappled sunlight made him feel . . . dizzy. The last time he'd felt like that, he'd been left half-dead outside of the settlement, working on the construction of a road. Three men had perished that day from the heat of the sun and the lack of water. He gave his head a little shake.

"I have a bit more on my mind than a drive through the park with a woman."

Vincent rolled his eyes. "Your thirst for revenge is admirable, but remember that living a good life can be a revenge all its own. If you truly like Miss Townsend and she likes you, there's nothing to say you cannot enjoy spending time with her."

The frustration that now sparked in Kit was entirely because he knew his friend was right, but letting his anger go, even for a moment, was too terrifying to consider. Anger was what had kept him alive, the spark that drove him to survive, to return home. What was he without it?

He changed the subject. "Let's go to Tattersall's."

Vincent's dark eyes ran over Kit in concern, but he said nothing more.

Tattersall's auctioneering yard, created expressly for the sale of horses at Hyde Park Corner. Good horses—or prime bits of blood, as they were called by those who frequented the yards—were sold to the highest bidder. Kit had loved coming here with his father. They used to stroll through the auctioneering yard which consisted of dozens of stables, loose boxes, and an enclosure for watching the thoroughbreds be put through their paces. They'd come here the week before he'd been arrested. Christ, it felt like a lifetime had passed since then. Yet even after seven years, Tattersall's was much the same, and somehow that pricked Kit's heart.

A black stallion was in the yard, bucking madly as several grooms desperately tried to calm the beast.

"Bleedin' bo-kickers," an older groom bellowed as he barely missed a kick from the stallion's back hooves. Several mares in an enclosure nearby shifted restlessly as the black horse railed against the control of the men who held his halter ropes.

"Beautiful beast, isn't he?" Vincent asked, clearly in awe of the raging animal.

"Yes, but they will never sell him unless they can calm him down," Kit said, falling easily back into the familiar patterns of his time laboring on the ranches in Australia. He had learned more about horses there than he had in his entire life in England.

"Ho there!" He ran forward to the enclosure gates and shouted at the grooms. "You need to calm him."

"You think we dinna ken that?" the old groom snapped. "The mad beast has lost his head."

Kit turned his attention to the group of mares. He vaulted over the railing to reach the group, where two fresh-faced lads held their leading ropes.

"Let me see this one." He took the reins of a dappled gray mare that was standing much more calmly than the others. The young man let Kit take the leading rope.

"Come on, sweetheart. Time to tame that beast." He walked the mare toward the panicky stallion, then he shouted for the grooms to let the stallion go. The grooms dropped the leads and fled the enclosure with relief. The stallion reared up menacingly as he saw the mare and Kit approaching him. The mare's withers quivered, but Kit spoke reassuringly to her.

"He's frightened. Show him how to settle down," Kit urged the mare. She nickered softly and allowed Kit to lead her toward the stallion.

The stallion tossed his head and weaved his body about as he danced uncomfortably while trying to assess the mare. When the mare drew close to him, he tried to bite her neck, but she dodged the bite and butted his flank with her head and then tossed her mane as if trying to show that she wasn't afraid but wasn't challenging him either.

"Clever girl." Kit stepped back, letting the mare move freely. She trotted along the stallion's side as they moved about the enclosure. She did not let the stallion misbehave again. Each time he tried to nip her, she herded him against the railing, and he was forced to focus on where he was moving lest he run into the wooden walls of the enclosure. Eventually he settled down, and the pair trotted side by side in long, sweeping circles. The mare was almost as tall as the stallion but slightly daintier in appearance.

"Well done," Vincent said. "How did you know that mare would calm him?"

"We had a lot of wild horses in Australia we had to

tame. They sometimes needed a companion to show them that everything was all right rather than break the horse of its spirit."

The grooms watching from the rails of the enclosure stared at Kit in wonder.

"Who owns that horse? The stallion?" Kit asked the oldest groom.

The wizened Scotsman whistled through his teeth as he admired the now settled stallion. The man removed his cap respectfully.

"Lord Burleigh. He's over there. He brought the stallion in to sell, along with some mares and geldings." He pointed to a huddled pack of older aristocratic gentlemen about forty feet around the other side of the enclosure.

"Would you mind telling him that I'm interested in that stallion, and the mare if she belongs to him as well."

"Who shall I say is interested?"

"Tell him the Earl of Kentwell."

The groom's eyes widened at Kit's title, and he hurried off to speak to Lord Burleigh. He spoke to the group of men, and soon all of their heads turned to look his way. One of the men broke away from the group and waved a hand at Kit to meet him.

"I suppose that is Lord Burleigh?" he asked Vincent. He didn't know most of the lords ruling England. He'd only gone to see his father in the House of Lords a few times before he'd been arrested. Before that, he'd spent most of his time with young men his own age.

Vincent shrugged. "Your guess is as good as mine."

They met Lord Burleigh halfway across the yard. He was

a tall man with strong features, but his face lacked the harshness that Kit would have expected when meeting a man of his appearance.

"Are you Lord Kentwell?" Burleigh asked.

Kit held out a hand. "Yes."

Burleigh shook his hand. "It's a pleasure to meet you. My groom said you wish to buy the stallion?"

"And that dappled mare, if she's yours," Kit added. "She'd be most helpful to keep him calm."

Burleigh studied him critically. "You're that boy who was shipped off to the penal colonies, though no longer a boy. I knew your father. Decent chap. He took my side in the House of Lords on difficult matters."

Burleigh was quiet a moment, and Kit glanced toward the horses, feeling strangely lonely as he watched the fretful stallion trotting smoothly now with the mare at his side.

"I don't recall what you were sent away for, but a man who understands horses is a man I'm willing to trust. You seem to know how to tame Galileo. Offer me a fair price and I'll let you have the mare as well."

"Nine hundred guineas for each. The mare has as much value, if not more, for her ability to calm the stallion." Kit didn't believe in paying below value for such a fine horse. She was like a kindred spirit to Suzannah. Both were brave and didn't cower in the face of a male's temper. He realized now as he watched the stallion and the mare moving in perfect rhythm that he was looking at himself and Suzannah, or at least the possibility of what they might be. He smiled, his chest filled with a warmth and light he hadn't felt in years.

"Well, I certainly won't turn down that price. You have a deal, Kentwell." Burleigh offered his hand again and they shook. "I'll have them sent to you in a few hours."

"Excellent." Kit had a sudden idea and turned to Vincent. "I think I need to purchase a sidesaddle for that mare."

"Oh? What for? You have a devil's grin on your face, and that means we'll either have fun or end up in a spot of trouble." Vincent wasn't complaining—he was grinning back at Kit as though either scenario would entertain him greatly.

"I'm thinking we take the horses for a ride in Hyde Park this afternoon, and if I'm lucky, I shall persuade a certain young lady to take a ride with me."

"No doubt a certain painter? Well, it sounds quite scandalous. I'm all for it, of course," Vincent chuckled.

Kit laughed. The knot of anger lodged in his chest shifted around his heart, and he could feel a fracture in it, one that might yet break apart.

The thought was not unwelcome, but it did trouble him. He'd grown accustomed to that darkness inside him, fed upon the strength it gave him, but he couldn't hold on to his anger and Suzannah at the same time. What if he lost her before he could have his vengeance upon his enemies?

Suzannah stared at her little reticule of coins with pride. She'd had quite a few visitors come by her small stand in the park today. It had proved to be a welcome distraction from thoughts of Kit's unexpected visit last night—and the kiss that had changed her life.

Stop thinking about it, she inwardly chided herself. She thanked the last customer and reorganized the paintings still for sale on the display easels. Most of her customers today had been young ladies, and many had requested horses. One young woman she'd met a few days ago had come back with her older brother and another young woman. By the looks of her, she had to be the younger sister of the young lady and her brother. The two women slid out of their saddles, and the youngest girl rushed straight to Suzannah.

"Do you paint portraits of pets?" the younger girl asked, her bright brown eyes large and beautiful and full of mischief. The older sister rolled her eyes.

"Audrey, she has far too much to do. She cannot paint your cats," the older sister said.

"So you don't paint pets?" The joy in the girl's face faded.

"Oh, but I can," Suzannah assured her. "But if they are cats, I must come to your home to see them better. I wouldn't want you to try to take them anywhere, lest they escape or get lost."

"Would you? That would be simply wonderful! We could have tea, and then you could paint Mittens and Muff."

"Mittens and Muff? Those are—"

"My cats." Audrey beamed proudly. "My dear brother, Cedric, bought them for me." She nodded at the man who still sat on his horse, holding the reins of the other two horses with a patience only doting older brothers could manage.

"I would be happy to paint them for you," Suzannah assured Audrey.

"Wonderful! Here is my card." Audrey produced a lovely calling card with her address on the back. "Please send a note to me. We shall plan a time for you to come by."

Audrey studied the paintings displayed around Suzannah and chose one of the watercolors she'd done, depicting a gentleman riding through an autumn landscape of fallen leaves.

"Oh, I simply must have this one. It reminds me of Cedric. Don't you agree, Horatia?"

The older sister nodded. "It certainly does."

Suzannah packed up the piece and was just seeing them off when she spied two men riding down the path in her direction. A third horse without a rider trailed behind them. Even at this distance, she recognized the man on the jet-black horse as Kit.

Lord, what was he doing here? Perhaps it was just a coincidence . . . Did he know she was here, or had he forgotten that she'd told him that she sold paintings in the park? She wanted to flee, but there were too many things to pack up, and he would have spotted her by then. So she stood there, feeling rather foolish as she waited for the men to reach her.

Kit slid down out of his saddle and handed over the reins to his companion, so that the other gentleman had charge of all three horses.

"Lord Kentwell, what are you doing here?" she asked in a low voice as he came toward her display. He doffed his hat to her, playing the part of a respectable gentleman. It was such a contrast to the brooding man who had removed the top half of his clothing for his portrait each night while he bared his scarred soul to her. The memory of that made her mouth run dry and her face heat up in a mortified blush.

Kit clasped his hands behind his back and pretended to admire the paintings she had out for sale. His dark eyes seemed warmer beneath the bright light of the afternoon sun. With some surprise, she realized she'd never seen him in the daylight before. He'd always been a dark, seductive presence in the shadows of the night or a darkened theater. She was not prepared for Kit by daylight. He was even more beautiful now with the afternoon light illuminating him.

"I purchased a new stallion this morning, and it seemed he required a companion to steady him, the mare you see there. It seems a shame that she should go without a rider this afternoon. I thought perhaps you would take her on a turn about the park with me? I have her saddled and ready for you."

She looked over Kit's tall shoulder at the dappled gray horse standing patiently alongside the black stallion. For a moment, she was tempted to accept. But it had been years since she'd ridden, and she couldn't just leave her things unattended.

"Oh . . . I'm honored, Lord Kentwell, but I cannot leave my paintings and supplies unattended."

"My friend Vincent shall watch over them for you. Won't you, Vin?" he called out over her shoulder, and the other man nodded. "That is Vincent Wyndam, a man of most upstanding character. Vincent, this is Miss Townsend, a talented artist whose name is on the rise."

Vincent dismounted from his horse and tossed a charming smile at Suzannah. "'Tis a pleasure to meet you, Miss Townsend."

She had the strange sense she might've seen him before, perhaps at the theater? Many men often stood in the lobby after the performance, hoping to woo actresses to their beds. Perhaps he'd been there one evening as she'd passed by the waiting crowds.

"What do you say, Suzannah? Come for a ride with me?" Kit asked.

Her face reddened further at his use of her given name in a public setting. To call her Suzannah in the dark, in the shadows, when he was baring his soul to her for his portrait—when he was kissing her—that was one thing. But now, like this in the light of day, she didn't know how to react.

"I really don't think I should."

"*Please*," Kit said. It was so hard to deny him. She had the sense that after what he'd been through in the last seven years, he did not beg for anything lightly.

"But won't it cause a stir?"

"Undoubtedly. You would be seen riding with me with no chaperone, and you aren't dressed for riding. I'm sure the society pages will be buzzing with news of my wild and scandalous behavior tomorrow. But does it matter?"

Suzannah hadn't considered it from such an innocent angle. Her thoughts had taken a far darker turn.

"I . . . er . . . was thinking more about the fact that I am the daughter of the man who once gave witness against you. In the eyes of society, we are enemies . . . aren't we?" She hadn't wanted to bring that up, but she didn't want him to lay the blame at her feet later for not having been warned.

Kit studied her, his dark eyes unreadable. "Is that the *only* reason you're protesting?"

"I'm *not* protesting," she argued.

"Good." With that, he grabbed her by the waist and lifted her up, easily tossing her over his shoulder and carrying her toward the horses.

She gasped, blood rushing to her head as she fought to free herself. She hung like a sack of grain over his shoulder, her bottom high up in the air. Anyone passing by would see her being manhandled and think he was kidnapping her. "What are you doing? Think of the scandal!"

"I *am*," Kit chuckled. "Rather than fight it, I think I might as well *enjoy* myself."

She snapped and balled a fist and pummeled his backside. "You're enjoying this?"

"*Immensely.*" His sensual laugh made the deepest, most feminine part of her shiver with excitement—until he smacked her bottom with one hand.

He lifted her high on his shoulder, and then suddenly she was turned right side up as he placed her firmly on the sidesaddle of the dappled mare.

"Oh!" She scrambled to catch the reins and steady herself on top of the horse. The moment Kit felt certain she could sit upright without falling, he returned to his fierce black stallion and mounted him.

"But my art—"

"As I said, Vincent will watch over your paintings."

She glanced at the other man, who smiled with teasing gentleness.

"Your masterpieces will be safe with me, Miss Townsend," Vincent assured her.

"You do know how to ride, don't you?" Kit asked, pulling Suzannah's focus away from her paintings.

"What? Oh yes. Not spectacularly well, but yes. I grew up riding as a child, but I don't have much practice with a sidesaddle, I'm afraid."

She squirmed a little, trying to get comfortable in the saddle and with the thought of riding in Hyde Park with someone who, until recently, had entertained vengeful thoughts against her. Had that kiss between them last night changed something in him so profoundly? It seemed unlikely . . . yet she saw less rage in him today than she had before.

"It seems you and I have something to discuss," he said, and after a moment of silence, he continued. "I have a matter to propose to you. An idea that only recently occurred to me. It's quite a mad idea, but I cannot seem to banish it from my head now."

She was almost too afraid to know what he was thinking. "What matter?"

"The matter of *marriage*," Kit said.

"Marriage? You're getting married? To whom?"

Suzannah's chest prickled as though invisible little claws were digging into her. It was silly to feel jealous and upset, but some part of her cared all too much. Had the kiss they'd shared meant so little to him that he was thinking of another woman? Perhaps she was the only one who had truly been changed by that kiss . . .

"I . . ." She swallowed down the sharp pang of disappointment. "I wish you my congratulations, Lord

Kentwell . . . to you and the lady you're to marry, whoever she is." She didn't dare call him Kit any longer—it was too intimate for a man who was to marry another woman. "Who . . . who is the woman?" she asked.

Kit flashed her that darkly dazzling smile that made her forget to breathe.

"Well, I was rather hoping that the lady would be *you*."

10

"I was rather hoping that the lady would be you."

Kit's words still echoed in Suzannah's mind later that evening as she finished sketching the newest set designs for the next play scheduled to be performed at Drury Lane. She stared into the distance, replaying the ride in the park with Kit over and over. It had been so different to see him bathed in sunlight and smiling at her when she'd only ever known him brooding in candlelight and wreathed in shadows. She had enjoyed that sunny ride, despite the shock of Kit's marriage proposal. He had raised a thousand questions with that single proposition.

Did she want to marry? Did she want to marry *him*? What would marrying him even mean? She didn't think he hated her any longer, but she wasn't certain he liked her either, let alone love her. She had no standing in society, no money, so what did he expect to gain through such a union?

There was one thing that mattered to her and that was marrying for love. Still, there was *something* between them.

Something that came alive as she sketched him upon the paper or when he gazed back at her. There were no secrets between them when he bared his soul to her like that. Touching him had been one thing, a spark of desire, but to draw him, that was to see all of him in a manner more intimate than touch. But was that enough to tie their lives together by marriage?

After he'd proposed, she and Kit had ridden in silence. He'd required no immediate answer, and for that she was grateful. Surprisingly, the silence had been enjoyable, and the breeze and the rustle of leaves in the trees and the rhythmic pace of the horses had been soothing. The complicated nature of their relationship had been, for the moment, forgotten. She'd felt no different from any of the other women riding with a gentleman, having no other care in the world than to enjoy herself.

Everyone they had passed in the park had stared at them, but Kit was unconcerned. After all he had been through, he no longer cared about such trivial matters as gossip. Suzannah had no real place in society and therefore was unaffected by the scandal as well, but she did feel a little ill just thinking of everyone wondering who the Earl of Kentwell was spending time with.

Henry sat down beside her in the front row of the theater. She liked to sit there to see how her sketches would look when she drew the overall outline of each complete scene. "Suze, are we going to Mr. Kit's tonight?"

"Yes, I shall resume my portrait work this evening. If they don't need you, perhaps you could go outside and watch for the coach?"

Henry dashed off, and she smiled and shook her head,

wishing she had a fraction of the boy's energy. Jude then came over and took the seat Henry had just vacated.

"Our man Henry looks good in his new clothes," Jude said. "How did you acquire them?"

If anyone else had asked her, it would have felt like an accusation, but with Jude it came from a place of concern.

"The man who hired me to paint his portrait gave me an advance on my payment, plus a bonus to be spent on Henry."

Jude's concern seemed only to deepen. "This man, he hasn't put you in any position you don't wish to be in, has he?"

"No," she answered quickly. "But . . . he did propose marriage today."

Jude's eyebrows rose. "This is the one who was sent to the penal colonies?"

She nodded.

"The *dangerous* one," he added.

Again, she nodded.

"You had better be careful, Suzannah."

Jude's warning brought back flashes of Kit's furious eyes and the strength of his hands as he'd caught her in his arms. He'd never hurt her, but his desire for revenge against Mr. Walsh and Mr. Balfour was frightening. He was capable of great and terrible things, and yet he was also capable of infinite tenderness. He'd saved her from those drunken men. There were a thousand facets to his personality, and she never knew what he would be from day to day. She only knew he wouldn't hurt her or Henry, and that alone made her feel safe enough to be around him.

"I am trying to be. But I swear the man has the most unbelievable way of befuddling me."

Jude's lips twitched. "The man befuddles you?"

Henry came back down the stairs along the side of the theater. "Suzannah! Mr. Kit's coach is here!"

"I had better go," she said as she leaned over and kissed Jude's cheek. "Thank you for always worrying about me."

Jude's eyes were overbright. "You remind me of one of my sisters. They sold her when she was fifteen, and I never saw her again. Esther was a woman of courage, a woman with a kind heart and a gentle soul like yours. I couldn't protect her then, but I can protect you." He caught her hand and held it. "You know you may call upon me whenever you need help."

Suzannah's heart clenched as a wave of emotions washed over her. She leaned over and hugged him tight, her eyes burning. "I know, Jude . . . I'm so sorry about your sister." There weren't enough words to say all that lay in her heart in that moment, but judging by the way his eyes glowed with brotherly tenderness, he knew what she felt. She collected her bag of painting supplies and went out to meet the temporary driver and coach Kit had been hiring out to escort them. Henry was there waiting to help her inside, and they settled in for the ride to Kit's home.

A light misting rain had begun when she'd first arrived at the theater two hours ago, but now the rain was torrential. It created a roar as it pounded the cobblestone streets. The guttering streetlamps were barely able to illuminate the street.

"Look at it coming down," Henry said as he peered out

the coach window. The rain whipped in waves down the street.

A violent rumbling shook the ground beneath them, and suddenly the horses pulling their coach screamed. The coach driver shouted, and the world around Suzannah seemed to explode. She was flung against the roof, then the sides of the coach.

Pain exploded through her skull, and everything went black. When she came back to her senses, a dull ringing filled her ears. Cold, icy raindrops coated her cheeks. She blinked, and tiny droplets clung stubbornly to her lashes. It took a long moment for her to understand what had happened. The coach had rolled over onto its side.

"Hen—Henry . . ." She tried to move, but everything hurt. "Henry," she croaked again. A crumpled form opposite her in the coach stirred and cried out in pain. *Henry*.

"My leg," Henry moaned. "It *hurts*." The boy sounded so weak. She had to find help right away, even though every movement was agonizing.

"Don't move, Henry. I'll . . . I'll get help." She tried to right herself, but her head spun. She moaned and braced herself against the coach before trying again. "Oh Lord . . ." The door was now above her and hung open at an odd angle, leaving the heavy rain to pour down on her and Henry.

Someone called her name when she started to climb out of the coach. "Miss Suzannah!" She blinked, peering through the rain at the cloaked figure coming toward her. It was Mr. Samuels, the man Kit had been hiring each night to bring her to Kit's home.

"Mr. Samuels." She reached for him when he held out his hands to her. "What happened?"

"Another coach struck us, miss. It was racing through the rain. I couldn't stop in time. My horses . . . they're dead." The poor man looked ready to weep, but he helped her out. She didn't dare look at the driver's beautiful horses—it would have broken her heart. She couldn't help but think of the two horses Kit had bought, one for himself and one for her, and how she'd feel if they had been the ones who had died. Right now, she had to be strong for Henry. He *needed* her.

"How far are we from Lord Kentwell's home?" she asked the driver.

"It's that house just up ahead." He pointed a shaky hand through the rain toward the street known locally as Devil's Square, at a stately townhouse with ivy crawling up its walls.

"Please help me down. I will go for help."

"I should be the one to go, miss," Mr. Samuels insisted.

"Please stay with Henry and make sure he can't hurt himself. I think his leg is broken very badly."

Mr. Samuels lifted her down onto the ground, and her boots sank into standing rainwater.

"I'll be back as fast as I can." She ran, pausing only once to prevent herself from being run over by another carriage that crossed her path. Then, panting hard and more dizzy than she had been before, she reached Kit's home and pounded on the door. Mr. Palmer opened it, smiling expectantly since she and Henry were due to arrive, but his smile faded at the sight of her disheveled state.

"Miss Townsend, what on earth—?"

"Kit!" She screamed his name. "*Kit!*"

Kit appeared at the top of the stairs ahead of her. He wore no coat and looked like an angel, albeit a frightening and imposing one. He came down the stairs, and before she could react, he had pulled her inside the townhouse.

"Where's your coach?" he demanded. "What the devil happened to you? Where's Henry?" His barrage of questions only made her headache worse.

"Accident . . . ," she gasped. "We had an accident. Henry's hurt. *Please*, you must help."

She was in shock, she knew it. She couldn't seem to pull herself together.

"Where?" Kit asked, his dark eyes flashing.

"Up the street."

Before she was even done pointing, he was past her and had disappeared into the storm.

Palmer tried to usher her away from the door, offering her tea and warmth, but she jerked free and chased after Kit into the misty gloom.

By the time she reached the overturned coach, Kit and Mr. Samuels were lifting Henry out of the broken conveyance. The odd angle of the boy's leg had Suzannah fighting off nausea.

"We'll take the boy to my home, Samuels. When I return, you and I will deal with the horses and the deceased man."

Her gaze drifted to the other vehicle. It was a curricle designed for racing. A body lay on the cobblestones, and by the cut of his clothes he seemed to be a gentleman. His horse was still alive but whinnying in pain and favoring one foreleg. It was a miracle the horse had survived.

Kit slung Henry over his back—the boy seemed to have slipped into unconsciousness.

"Suzannah, come with me now. I shall need your help." He moved quickly, despite the burden of Henry's body. She kept pace with him, but by the time they reached the house, her dress was soaked through and she was shaking hard from the cold.

"What—what do you need me to do?" she asked. Her teeth were chattering, but she tried to push away her own discomfort.

He pointed across the street. "You see that house?"

"Y—yes."

"That is the Duke of Tiverton's residence. Darius is a dear friend of mine. Go there and tell him I need a doctor urgently. Then return here and Palmer will find you something to change into while you sit by the fire and warm up."

Palmer ushered them inside and immediately ordered a bed prepared for Henry.

She followed Kit into the room. "What about you?" she asked as he set Henry gently down on the bed.

"That coachman needs help, and the authorities must be informed of the situation. The man from the other carriage died tonight, and that must be dealt with." Kit cupped her face in his hands. "Be strong just a little bit longer for me, darling," he said, then he kissed her hard and desperate, as though that kiss alone would have to be enough to last him a lifetime. It was over before she could even kiss him back or realize that he had called her darling. It took her another painful beat to collect herself after that. Then she headed for the townhouse across the street to fetch the Duke of Tiverton.

A middle-aged man answered her frantic knocking and stared down at her in shock.

"Please, I must speak to Lord Tiverton. I have an urgent message from Lord Kentwell."

At the mention of that name, the butler seemed to snap to attention and went to fetch his master. A moment later, a tall dark-haired man with the clearest blue eyes Suzannah had ever seen stood before her.

"I am Lord Tiverton."

"Please, Your Grace, there's been an accident. We need a doctor. It's urgent."

The duke stared past her into the stormy night. "Is Kit hurt?"

"He's fine. It's my friend Henry who's broken his leg. We need a doctor. Kit said to tell you."

The man nodded and yelled back into the house, "Chelsea, have my horse brought round immediately!" The butler hastened away to have his horse saddled. He grabbed his cloak from a footman. "Tell Kit I'm fetching the doctor."

She let out the breath she'd been holding. "Thank you, Your Grace."

She sprinted back through the rain to Kit's home. Palmer met her at the door. The old butler escorted her to a bedroom down the hall from Henry's.

"His lordship's valet brought these for you to wear. I'm afraid it will have to do until we have a chance to dry your clothes. We only have one maid, and she's too large for you to wear anything of hers." He left her alone to change.

She'd been given a man's shirt and a heavy banyan robe. Both looked as though they were brand new and barely worn. She stripped out of her wet clothes and draped them over the fire grate to dry. She donned the shirt, feeling naked beneath it, but the strange thing was that she didn't truly mind. She then put on the robe and tied the belt tight by her waist.

She was wearing Kit's clothing. They even smelled faintly like him. She closed her eyes and hugged herself, embracing the idea of him holding her, making her feel safe and warm. Did wives who loved their husbands wear their shirts and robes sometimes and feel comforted? If Kit was hers, she would relish this.

Then reality intruded. Henry needed someone to be at his bedside, and she couldn't stay here living in a fantasy that would never be.

Suzannah hastily padded to Henry's room on bare feet and pulled up a chair to sit by his side. She touched the boy's forehead and grimaced at how cold and sweaty his skin was. She took his hand and wrapped it in her own, squeezing it. She tried not to let her own worries show, lest he sense them.

"You'll be all right, Henry." She hoped that hearing his name would make him feel better, let him know he was safe.

She wasn't sure how long it was before the doctor arrived, accompanied by Lord Tiverton. After one look at Henry's leg, the doctor insisted that Suzannah leave the room while he set the broken bone.

"I should stay with him," she said. "He needs me—"

The duke placed a hand upon her shoulder, his blue eyes soft and gentle. "Please, Miss Townsend. This will be terrible to witness, and I do not want that image in your thoughts as you care for him. We will bring you back in the moment we can."

Lord Tiverton ushered her into the hall. A few minutes later, an agonized scream tore through the air. The sound dug into Suzannah's skull, reminding her of the horses' screams when they died. The boy quieted, and an awful silence smothered the house. She clenched her hands tight until the pain provided her some clarity as she considered what she was going to need to take care of Henry. Once he was well enough to move, she'd take him home and use the extra money from painting Kit to provide for Henry until his leg was mended and he could return to the theater.

The door opened, and Lord Tiverton came to see her, his face somber. "You may come in again, Miss Townsend."

She stepped back into the room and saw that Henry was once again unconscious. She sank into the chair, her legs suddenly weak. The doctor put a gentle hand on her shoulder.

"Are you well, my dear?" the doctor asked.

"Yes, I'm just . . . not used to seeing someone in such pain," she admitted.

"Ah, yes, it is why we asked you to wait outside. The sight of a nasty break can leave even a person with the strongest constitution weak." The doctor packed up his black bag and told Tiverton he would speak with Mr. Palmer before leaving.

Tiverton crouched down beside her. "Where is Kit?"

"He is just down the road. The coach was hit by a curricle. The man from the curricle died, and Mr. Samuels's horses died too." Flashes of the crash tore across her eyes. "*Oh . . .*" She covered her face in her hands, trying to quell the harsh shaking that followed. She felt as though she would fall to pieces on the floor.

Tiverton placed a hand on her shoulder, and the shuddering eased a little.

"Please, Your Grace, could you make sure that Kit is all right? It's so terribly dark, and with the storm . . ."

"I'll make sure he's all right," the duke promised and left her alone.

She sat for a long moment, holding Henry's hand by his bed. The warmth of Kit's robe and the fire blazing in the hearth slowly sank into her, erasing the cold from the storm, if not the memory of it.

"Everything will be all right, Henry. . ." She thought of how relieved she was to be here with him, under the safety of Kit's roof rather than her little cupboard at that boarding house. She stroked Henry's hair back from his face and tried to relax.

It was only later that she remembered something that had bothered her at the back of her mind. Lord Tiverton had called her Miss Townsend, but she had never once mentioned her name to him or his butler tonight. How had he known who she was?

KIT CROUCHED BY MR. SAMUELS, WHO WAS STROKING THE NECK of one of his beloved horses, weeping softly. The powerful storm had softened into a thick, misting rain. Kit was freezing and soaked clear through to the bone, but he wouldn't leave the driver or the dead man on the street. Nor could he leave behind the rush of fear that he'd felt when he'd seen Suzannah's bedraggled form as she'd stumbled into his home, crying for help. His mind had leapt to the worst conclusion, that his enemies had struck out at her to get to him. Yet the truth made him feel no better.

His skin felt tight and his bones vibrated with the echoes of his fear and panic, but he'd done all he could for the moment, and the sooner he handled this situation with the driver and the other man's body, the sooner he could get back home. And when he did, he would take his green-ribbon girl into his arms and not let go for hours until his panic and fear receded.

A wagon rolled up and a constable hopped down, his boots splashing in the muddy water that was still thick upon the streets. Kit explained what he had learned from Suzannah and the driver about the incident.

The constable, a middle-aged man named John Rivers, called for a group of men sitting in the back of the wagon to help load the deceased man's body into the back. The constable promised another wagon would be sent to collect the dead horses. The third horse, the one belonging to the dead man, swayed a little, still making sounds of distress. Its front foreleg was lifted a little off the ground, but it didn't appear to be broken.

"Poor beast," Rivers sighed. "Best put him out of his misery." He pulled out a pistol and started toward the horse.

Kit stood there, the rain drowning out all other thoughts as he stared at Mr. Samuels mourning his horses, then gazed at the third horse, who in mere seconds would also be dead. Suzannah's face filled his mind in a blinding flash.

"Rivers! Hold on a minute." He rushed toward the constable and caught the man by the shoulder. "Wait," he said. "*Please*." Then he nodded back to Mr. Samuels. "Just a minute," he said again.

The constable lowered his pistol, and Kit approached the grieving driver.

"Mr. Samuels."

The man turned to Kit, his brown eyes wide with pain. "They're gone. I raised them since they were foals, and now they're just gone."

Kit swallowed, trying not to lose his composure. "I know, but *that* horse . . ." He nodded at the one still alive. "That one might yet survive if a man who knows his horses took him under his care."

Mr. Samuels wiped rain and tears from his eyes. "I can't afford it, my lord. My coach is broken, and my horses are . . . I have no way to feed my family now, let alone take care of that one."

Kit was quiet for a moment before inspiration struck him. "I am in need of a permanent driver, and I only recently purchased a new coach that you could drive for me." Kit met his gaze solemnly. "I'll pay you well above the going rate and for the care and expenses of that horse if you will care for him along with helping take care of two horses I've recently purchased myself. You may also move your wife and children into the servants' quarters of my townhouse, if you wish. I am currently understaffed, and we have plenty of space."

Mr. Samuels blinked, his lips wide in shock. "I don't know what to say, my lord."

Kit held out a hand to him. "Say yes. Tell me you'll be my driver."

"But why me, my lord?" Mr. Samuels asked. "I've only worked for you for less than a week."

"Because I trust men who care for animals the way you do. It says much about the type of person you are." He'd never seen a good man hurt an animal.

The driver looked between Kit and the injured horse before nodding.

"I accept."

"Good." Kit now turned back to Rivers. "We'll be taking the horse with us."

"What?" The constable stared at him. "But the beast is injured. Surely you wouldn't want to waste your time on him. Besides, he's not even yours."

"I'm aware of that," Kit assured him. "If the deceased man has any family, I will pay them double the horse's value before he was injured." He provided the constable with his name and address.

Rivers raised an eyebrow. "So, you are one of them gents that live in Devil's Square, then?"

Kit would have smiled, had he not felt so bone weary. "I am. Will that be a problem?" he asked.

The constable tucked his pistol back into his belt. "Not to me. Right, then. Carry on."

Kit turned to Mr. Samuels. "They assured me they will return for your horses, Mr. Samuels. But now it's time to say goodbye to them. This horse needs you now."

The driver got to his feet and removed his cap from his head. He said a soft prayer over his fallen friends and put his cap back on.

"You're a good man," Kit said to him and laid a hand on the driver's shoulder. "Now let's walk this one back to my stables and see to his care, shall we?"

They were halfway home when Darius caught up to them.

"Thank Christ, Kit. When Suzannah told me what happened . . ." His friend's gaze swept over the driver leading a lame horse, but he asked no questions.

"I assume Suzannah fetched you?" Kit asked.

"Yes. The doctor's seen to the boy. It was a clean break, but setting it wasn't pleasant. The boy will be in bed for a few weeks before he can put any weight on that leg, even with crutches."

"And Suzannah?" Kit had had only a moment to speak to her before he'd rushed to the scene of the accident. He'd taken her at her word that she was all right, but now he feared she'd been hiding some injury.

"She's terribly shaken but bearing up well. Still, it would be best to watch over her tonight. She shouldn't be alone."

Kit agreed. As of tonight, she and Henry would be his guests. He still had plenty of empty rooms, after all.

When they reached his home, Kit and Mr. Samuels put the injured horse into a stall and a messenger was sent for a veterinarian to take a look at him.

Kit and Darius returned inside and told Palmer about their new permanent driver, who would need dinner and a bed in the servants' quarters tonight. He'd inform his butler about moving the driver's family in tomorrow.

Darius took hold of Kit's arm as they stood in the entryway.

"And what about you? Will *you* be all right?"

Kit shrugged. "Warm brandy and dry clothes should do the trick."

Darius's blue eyes penetrated Kit's heart. "I meant with that girl here. She's under your roof tonight."

"Being here is a safe place for her."

"You know what I mean. What about *you*?" he persisted.

With any other man, Kit would have assumed the question was whether the girl was safe with him. But his old friend meant it another way, that it might be difficult to have someone under his roof he couldn't trust.

Kit swept his hair out of his eyes and relaxed. "I think I need her here. She calms me. I know it makes very little sense. I don't even know that much about her, but it doesn't change how I feel. I shouldn't trust her. But I do."

Something about Darius's soft smile brought back memories of their youth that Kit had feared were long forgotten. It opened up the core of his soul.

Suzannah had made him feel that same way, but instead of thinking of the past like he did with his friends, thinking of Suzannah had turned his mind to the future, a future that was no longer bleak. When he thought of her, his mind always seemed to fill with endless sunlight.

"If I didn't know any better, I'd think you might be falling in love with her," Darius teased gently.

"If I was still capable of love . . . I think I would be. She would be the one I would give everything to." It was becoming easier and easier to speak openly of his feelings with Darius, and even his other friends.

"Do you remember what your father used to say when we were young boys?" Darius asked.

Kit shook his head.

"No matter how far a man falls, he can always get back up and climb again. You are not incapable of love, old friend. I think you're capable of loving fiercely, as all great loves should be. Do not hold yourself back because of fear or doubt."

Darius smiled and left Kit alone in the entryway. Kit turned to the stairs, his shoulders sagging as the last of the tension bled out of him. He knew Suzannah was close, and after everything he'd seen and felt tonight, he wanted to hold her in his arms and see for himself that she was unharmed.

He could have lost her tonight. It could have been her cold body lying in the street. He banished the dark thought and went up the stairs to find her.

Darius's words echoed in his mind.

I think you are capable of loving fiercely, as all great loves should be.

11

S uzannah woke to the sensation of being carried. She struggled to open her eyes, the cry of shock dying in her throat when she recognized Kit's face above her. Kit was carrying her . . .

She was cradled in his arms, leveled against his firm chest like a child. She gripped the damp material of his shirt, as if suddenly afraid she might fall.

"Kit?"

He glanced down at her, the shadows of the hallway shrouding his eyes. "You shouldn't sleep in a chair, Suzannah." His voice, gruff but low, made her shiver. "The boy will be fine tonight. I'm taking you to my bed."

"Your bed?" Her heart pounded wildly as he maneuvered through the large oak doors of a bedchamber she'd glimpsed before, but it was certainly not the spare room Palmer had made up for her.

"Yes." The flex of Kit's jaw betrayed a hesitation that didn't show in his voice.

"But why?" she persisted.

"Because I wish it. It will calm me to know you are close and safe, and that I am nearby if you need assistance in the night. Besides, I will sleep on the floor," he added as he strode deeper into the room and placed her carefully on the bed.

Suzannah scrambled to her knees, fidgeting with the clothes she wore—*his clothes*—so they would adequately cover her. "You can't sleep on the floor. Surely—"

"I am no stranger to sleeping on the floor." He turned away from her and walked over to a washbasin. His dark hair was damp, the long ends curling above his ears and the collar of his soaking shirt, which clung to his frame in places, showing hints of the muscles she was becoming more and more familiar with, every sketch she drew. She'd always been so aware of him, of his strength and might, and how easily he could hurt her if he chose to.

Just then she felt a far different awareness, one entirely of the feminine kind. A strange and wonderful heat pooled low in her belly as she thought of her hands touching those muscles, caressing the slopes and sinews in a far more intimate way than from safely sketching at a distance.

She cleared her throat. "Kit, thank you for your consideration, but I cannot take your bed while you sleep on the floor."

"It will not trouble me, Suzannah. In truth, I haven't slept in a bed in seven years."

Whatever she'd been about to say was forgotten. Her throat closed up with a sense of dread as he continued.

"Beds were not provided to convicts, as a general rule. We slept on straw mats or in empty stables. The women were luckier, if one could call it that. They were often given employment in the homes of settlers for their sentences. They had beds, but that didn't stop a man from taking advantage of them whenever he wished."

Suzannah's stomach churned at the thought of any woman being hurt like that against her will.

Kit was quiet a long moment before adding, "I can't seem to get comfortable anywhere but on the floor." He turned his face slightly, so that his dignified profile was all she could see. "It is what I am used to."

Seeing this harsh reality of his past was like cold water upon her face, much like when she'd first seen his scarred back. She was suddenly less weary than she had been moments before. She sat up in his bed, pulling his robe close around her body.

"Kit..."

He braced his hands on the washstand and met her gaze through the mirror, waiting for her to continue.

"Why did you really bring me here, Kit?" She needed to understand this man whose personality had more facets than a cut diamond. What would she see if she managed to see into the heart of him?

"I barely understand it myself," he confessed, his words soft but full of confusion. "I should want nothing to do with you, but the moment I first saw you, you became an obsession. There is no other word for it." He slowly turned to face her. "I wanted you before I knew who you were. And then when I learned who you were, I tried to believe I only wanted vengeance. But I can no longer pretend. You could have died tonight, and Christ, it's been killing me every second not to hold you." He turned to face her, and she gasped at the stark, desperate need she saw in him. A need to hold on to something after a tragedy . . . a need that she felt as well. "*That* is why you will be sleeping in my bedchamber tonight. I *need* you near me."

"Because . . . because you care about me?" The thought made her dizzy. Was that part of the reason he had proposed to her in Hyde Park? Was his affection strong enough that he wanted to truly share his life with her as a husband and wife would? She bit her lip, not daring to bring up the proposal, not yet.

From the moment he had saved her from those men, she had seen him as wild and dangerous, and yet with her he had only ever been gentle. Even with his anger, he'd treated her with tenderness. Something within her unfurled itself in the darkness like a moonflower spreading its petals in search of twilight. This mysterious, wounded man held such fire and sweetness within him, a compassion that shouldn't have existed after all that he had endured. All he wanted was to hold her, and she didn't wish to deny him that when such a thing was so easy to give, when she *wanted* to give it with all her heart, when she needed it as much as he did.

She moved over to one side of his large bed and pulled back the covers beside her, placing one palm down on the empty spot in open invitation. "If you sleep upon the floor, you cannot hold me in your arms." She held her breath, waiting to see how he would react.

Kit stared at her. His fathomless eyes widened a little before narrowing again as he reached up and pulled his neckcloth off. He let it fall to the floor before he unbuttoned his waistcoat and shed that as well. His shirt came next, and her womb clenched as he pulled it over his head and bared his upper body to her. As before, she was in awe of his beauty and ached at the echoes of pain cruel men had left on his flesh. Yet this time, he wasn't undressing for her to paint him; he was undressing so he could lie beside her. It was an intimacy she had never experienced before, and it both thrilled and terrified her.

He turned his back to her and bent and removed his boots and stockings before removing his wet trousers and small clothes. She glimpsed his hard muscled buttocks as he walked toward the dresser opposite the bed and retrieved a new pair of underclothes. Suzannah couldn't help but imagine digging her hands into his backside as he lay above her. The feverish thought flamed her cheeks, but she didn't look away from him. When he turned toward the bed again, they simply stared at each other for a long moment before she nodded at the place in bed beside her..

She waited for him to join her beneath the covers and welcomed him into her arms. He was so large that he dwarfed her when he pulled her close. He tucked up the bedclothes around them, and the heat of his skin warmed her chilled body. She'd never lain beside a man before, let alone a mostly naked one, but this felt so soothing.

"I love how warm you are," she whispered as she tucked her head under his chin.

"I was cold until I met you." His deep, rumbling response sent ripples of emotion through her. Something was changing between them, something that once it began couldn't be undone. If she gave in to this, then she would have to have all of him, not just a part. When she loved someone, she loved everything about them, even the darkest parts.

"Kit, if we continue on like this, then I must know you. The *real* you. No more mysteries. Tell me everything."

"Everything?" He let out a heavy sigh. "So much of what I am is full of darkness."

She lifted her head up to look at him. He brushed a lock of her hair out of her eyes and stroked his thumb over her lips.

"Very well, then you must tell me everything as well," he said.

She was sure she had far less to tell him than he did her, but she didn't say that. She merely nodded again.

"How much do you know about your father's involvement in my conviction?" Kit asked.

"How much?"

"Yes. Tell me everything you know. We must discuss this before anything else." He stroked her cheek, and she closed her eyes as she savored his touch.

"I honestly don't know much. He refused to talk about the matter with me, but I remember he was sad and fearful whenever he thought of it." She could recall him pacing at night, wearing paths in the already threadbare carpets as he walked.

"Fearful?"

"Yes. I always thought he was afraid of *you*. Of what might happen if you returned to London. But—" A flash of an old memory came back.

Kit propped himself up on his hand as he lay beside her. "What is it?" His other hand slid down her shoulder.

"Well, it's strange. I didn't remember until now, but

his employer paid a call to our home a few days after you were arrested. Papa kept saying you were innocent. They argued fiercely behind closed doors. I was supposed to be in bed, but I remember hearing their raised voices through the closed door. Walsh said, 'Think of your daughter . . . What if something befell her?' I always thought he meant about what would happen if you came back." Her brow furrowed, and she closed her eyes again. "But now, as I relive it in my mind, I believe his tone was threatening, not concerned."

Kit's face was illuminated by lamplight as she saw a spark of new knowledge in his eyes.

"What? What did you think just now?"

"Did your father ever say he thought I was innocent before Walsh came to see you?" He shifted to prop himself up against the headboard.

"Yes . . . once. But he never talked to me about it. I only heard him muttering to himself one evening after he read about your arrest in the *Morning Post*."

"Damnation," Kit cursed. "He wasn't paid, then, to testify against me. It sounds as though he may have been blackmailed into it."

"You thought he'd been paid?" Suzannah flinched. "Did you think that I . . . benefited somehow?"

He nodded slowly. "That was why I came to find you at the theater. I had to see if you were living lavishly after inheriting your father's money."

A bitter laugh escaped Suzannah. "I hope you realize how untrue that assumption is."

"I do . . . and it's all the more clear that they threatened your father into lying by mentioning you."

She nibbled her bottom lip. "You really think they would have hurt me?"

Kit's hard stare made her flush with embarrassment.

"Of that I have no doubt. If my father hadn't saved me, I would have hanged. A friend of mine overheard them talking after they realized I was back. Balfour said he paid the captain of the ship that took me to Australia to throw me overboard, to make sure I died before ever reaching Australia."

"What?" She bolted up in bed, the covers dropping around her. She pulled his heavy warm robe tighter around her, glad for its warmth.

"They wanted no loose ends. It's a miracle they didn't kill your father. Presumably, they left him alive because his death might have been perceived as too suspicious. Luckily for them, he didn't live long."

Suzannah flinched. Hearing her father's death so casually dismissed hurt as much as if she'd been struck. Kit didn't miss her reaction.

"I'm sorry. These last seven years have made me cold. We both lost our fathers, and I keep forgetting that."

"We did," she agreed. "And our mothers too." Even though those deaths were so long ago, it still left an emptiness inside them both.

Kit cupped her face. "We are orphans together."

She blinked away a sudden rush of tears at his words.

"Don't you dare cry. That might be the one thing you could do that would break me." Despite his playful tone, his eyes reflected the pain she herself was feeling.

"I spent so many years afraid of you, of this cruel,

frightening man returning to London and what you might do when you learned who I was."

He closed his eyes as though to hide himself from her penetrating gaze. "And now?"

"Now I am thankful to have been so wrong."

"You don't believe I am guilty of the crime I was sent away for?" Kit held her gaze, but fear of what she'd say glinted bittersweetly in his eyes.

"I don't," she replied without hesitation. She trusted him and trusted what she had learned about him. "I trust you," she said with her whole heart. She did trust this man now, after everything they'd been through.

"Then marry me." He shifted slightly toward her, the faintest angling of his body in her direction, and she felt shielded from the world as he trailed his fingertips down her neck before tracing patterns on her exposed collarbone.

She hadn't expected him to ask that question again so soon, but she'd been thinking about her answer ever since the ride in the park.

"Kit, I want to marry for love," she confessed in a soft whisper.

He smiled at her with a crooked grin. "Then love me." She'd never seen him smile like that before and wondered if this was how he'd looked at all of the young women before he'd been sent away.

"Love you? Just because you command?" she asked with a soft laugh when he arched a brow at her.

"Just because I *ask*," he replied before he leaned in toward her.

He nuzzled her nose with his, almost kissing her until she

gave a desperate sigh. Only then did he press his lips to hers. She was always startled by how soft his mouth was. So much of him was hard as stone, and his skin was a deep gold from years in the sun, but his mouth was exquisitely soft and warm. She opened her lips, letting his tongue dance with hers. How could something that felt so heavenly be considered so wicked?

She scooted up his body, needing to get closer to him, and he pulled her farther onto his lap. He leaned back against the headboard and parted her knees as she straddled his waist. The shirt she wore rose up her thighs, and she shivered as she felt his hard cock beneath her. Kit groaned, his large, beautiful hand settling on her bottom, cupping and squeezing each buttock lightly. Pleasure zinged through her as sharply and as wonderfully as the strings of a violin being played by a master.

"Be my *wife*, Suzannah," Kit whispered between kisses.

His mouth was dangerous and made it hard to think past how much she adored it when he kissed her.

"I need to be loved in return," she said, surprised at the firmness in her voice. "When I marry someone, I want both of us to love each other."

He tipped her chin up, their gazes locking. "It's been a very long time since I felt anything like love, and I don't know if I'd recognize it if I did. But what *you* make me feel . . . I cannot imagine feeling that for anyone else." He smiled wryly. "I know that's not a romantic thing to say. Lord knows I'm far from romantic. But like most creatures on this earth, I need sunlight to survive, and you . . . you are sunlight to me. Perhaps that is love—I cannot think of what else love would be other than finding sunlight in the soul of another person." He brushed his fingers through the messy waves of her hair that fell about her shoulders.

"What if you tire of me or become ashamed? I am not a gentleborn woman. Society will expect you to marry someone more worthy of your title."

"Society can hang itself, as it wanted to hang me. If my punishment has taught me anything, it is that this so-called *society* is full of injustice, and a society that would deny people from marrying who they choose is not one worth defending. As for tiring of you, I believe I could spend decades trying to find the bottom of your mysteries and still discover more. Does that reassure you?"

Having this conversation after the ordeal she'd gone through was likely not the most intelligent thing to do, but a voice whispered to her not to turn her back on this man.

"I . . ." Suzannah delved deep into her heart, thinking it over before she finally acknowledged the hope she saw burning in his eyes, wanting to give it more light. "Yes."

"Yes?" he echoed hopefully, his voice rough with emotion.

"Yes," she said with more confidence. Saying yes to marrying this man meant more than just being his wife. Infinitely more. Kit had suffered much, but he had not been broken. The man she was with now had become stronger through his ordeal, and more considerate. He might think he'd forgotten what love was, but deep down she did not believe that about him. He deserved to be happy, and she was happy with him. And Suzannah was already tumbling down that dangerous slope toward love with him.

His hands on her bottom tightened as she lowered her head down to his for another, deeper kiss. She moaned and rocked against him, seeking something she didn't quite understand. She only knew that it felt natural to rub herself against him. There was a quickening beneath her skin that excited her in all manner of ways.

"Let me touch you," said Kit. "Let me help you find your release. It will help you sleep after what you've endured tonight."

"My release?" she asked, unsure if she understood. "I don't wish for this feeling to go away." She liked feeling excited, like she was close to something wonderful, even if it was a little bit frightening.

He nibbled on her earlobe, and heat pooled low in her belly, making her squirm on his lap. "Far from it. I wish to make it more intense." He made a soft humming sound in her ear that vibrated through her body, making her feel more alive than she ever had been.

He shifted down the bed and rolled their bodies, trapping her beneath him. He grasped her wrists in one hand and pinned them above her head in the blankets. Then he kissed her with ruthless abandon while still being careful not to crush her. Rather than being frightening, however, being caged beneath him felt *safe*.

Excitement shimmered within her, and she had a sudden flash of memory. Her mother was holding her hand, and they were running toward a lake. Even as she ran on her tiny legs, she was fascinated by the light that rippled across the surface. It had been so bright it looked like diamond dust had been scattered over its surface. The sight had entranced her. When Kit kissed her like that, she felt like she was running toward that lake, ready to dive into the shimmering glory of a perfect day. She was so close she could almost feel the cool water on her feet.

She tipped her head back as he kissed his way down the column of her throat. One of his hands slid up beneath her shirt to caress her hips. Only after she was breathing hard with excitement at his intimate touch did he part her thighs.

"Open more for me, darling. Let me touch you. Let me please you."

His words stunned her. This was a titled lord, a man who could take what he wanted, yet he was begging now to please her. The heady dizziness within her only grew as she parted her thighs farther. She swallowed a startled cry when he stroked a gentle, questing finger over the folds of her sex. His tongue thrust into her mouth, slow, languid, mimicking that single finger that now teased her before it slowly penetrated her. It didn't hurt, but the feeling of foreign invasion was so strong and unexpected that she wriggled beneath him, trying to get comfortable. He began to thrust the finger in and out of her, while his mouth moved over hers more and more hungrily.

"I'll always be gentle," Kit murmured, then chuckled. "Unless you want me to be something else."

That vow of gentleness only made her crave his wildness that much more. She struggled beneath him, wanting her hands to be free so she could touch him, but he kept them trapped.

"Please, Kit. *More*. Give me more." She did not care how greedy or desperate she sounded.

He added a second finger alongside the first, stretching her entrance, but not to the point of pain. He moved his fingers faster and faster and his kiss roughened, almost becoming savage as he claimed her, capturing her soul within this moment. *Forever*.

There was no going back, not now, not as she chased that feeling of perfection in his arms. When the unexpected pleasure hit, she couldn't even scream. She could only gulp for air as her body tightened and waves of physical ecstasy rippled out like a stone upon that shimmering lake within her mind.

Kit tore his mouth from hers, gasping as he held himself tight above her. Something wet coated her belly, and he feathered breathless kisses against her temple. They shared the air around them, their eyes locked on each other as something passed between them. An acceptance of something, but Suzannah couldn't put her finger on what. Then, with a sigh of reluctance, Kit rolled off her.

She lay there as he got up from the bed and went to the washstand, returning to her with a wet cloth. She was too limp to struggle or pull away as he cleaned her body. She'd been embarrassingly wet, and yet he didn't seem bothered by it at all. He put the cloth in the basin and returned to her, turning down the lamp that still glowed on the nightstand. He then curled her up in his arms and kissed her cheek.

"You're mine," he whispered in the dark. She burrowed closer, offering her silent agreement with his words.

Yet he wasn't owning her, not like another man might. In those two little words, she heard the hope of a man who'd had nothing of his own for so long that he was overcome with joy at once more having someone to call his.

She would be his wife. Kit would be her *husband*. She too would have someone to call her own.

As she listened to his breathing, she couldn't help but wonder what her father would think had he still been alive. If he were, she knew he'd want to help Kit clear his name just as she did. She loved him, and she would do anything to help him. And perhaps someday he would feel safe enough to say that he loved her too.

She kissed his chest and smiled drowsily as she listened to the steady beat of his heart. The pulse beat deep into the earth as if to say, *I'm alive,* in defiance of those who'd tried to destroy him.

12

P almer opened the door to his master's bedchamber. It was a little after dawn, and he was used to the master coming downstairs early for breakfast. The townhouse was quiet, yet it was not an *empty* quiet. For the first time in years, they had guests, albeit under somewhat dramatic circumstances, but they were still welcome to Palmer, who adored having company in the home.

However, Palmer was concerned for their current guests, and his concern was strong enough that he felt he ought to speak to Master Kit right away. The boy Henry was resting. Palmer had given him another drop of laudanum to settle him two hours ago, but Miss Townsend was nowhere to be found. The bedchamber Palmer had prepared for her was empty, the door ajar with her clothing still hung on the fire grate, dry and ready to be worn, but the lady herself was missing.

Palmer eased the door to Kit's bedchamber open and

peered around. The master usually slept on the floor, the poor lad. It broke the man's heart to assume that Kit had lost his sense of creature comforts while serving out his sentence. But what Palmer saw now made his old, wrinkled face break into a smile.

Master Kit was asleep in his own bed for once, but he wasn't alone. Tucked in Kit's arms was Miss Townsend. Kit held on to her the way a small child might clutch his favorite toy to his chest for comfort. Palmer's brow furrowed. He would have to have a discussion with Master Kit about his responsibilities to the young lady. Miss Townsend was not from an aristocratic family, but she was an innocent woman, not Kit's mistress, and if Kit had compromised her, he should do right by the young lady.

But that discussion would have to come later. Palmer was not going to wake Master Kit, not when he looked so peaceful. Palmer quietly closed the door and let the pair sleep.

Kit woke at the sound of a door softly closing. He lifted his head and blinked as he realized he was holding a woman. For once, the soft mattress did not bother him—at least, not as much as he'd expected it to. The woman was soft and warm and smelled faintly of rain and flowers. He buried his face in the coils of her hair on the pillow, breathing in her scent and enjoying this moment with her.

Suzannah. The little painter was in his bed, in his arms, and the thought made him smile. Until the rain scent in her hair brought back memories of last night and the terrible accident. It could have been her he'd carried home, her who had suffered a shattered leg and blinding pain. It was only by luck alone that the poor lad had been hurt and not Suzannah. The thought of either of them in pain filled him with a desperate fear and rage that went beyond words, but he couldn't have borne it if Suzannah had been hurt. It might have killed him.

She slept deeply, unaware of him relishing holding her in his arms, which was just as well. He'd pushed her quite far last night with his insistence that they marry, and then he'd touched her in an intimate way, offering a taste of what he would give her once she was his. He had every intention of being a dedicated and loyal lover to his future wife.

My future wife . . . He rolled the words over in his mind and found he liked the sound of them. Yes, they would marry quickly. He needed her to live here under his roof with as little scandal as possible. He didn't care about such things himself—how could he?—but he would not let Suzannah suffer if he could help it, to be slighted by rumors of her sharing his home and bed before marriage. As soon as time would allow, he and Darius would visit the Doctors' Commons for a special marriage license. With such a license, they could be married in a day or two.

He shifted to sit up, then leaned over and kissed Suzannah's temple before he slipped out of bed. She let out a soft sigh and rolled over, seeking his warmth, her hand exploring the empty pillow before she settled back into sleep. Something fragile and warm fluttered in his chest as he watched her, knowing she missed him even in sleep. He'd never thought he'd ever want anyone to need him, but knowing that Suzannah needed him soothed him in a way he'd never imagined.

Kit rang the bell for his valet and stepped into his dressing room. Nolan met him a few minutes later with clean clothes and helped him dress.

"How is young Henry?" he asked the valet. He was careful to keep his voice down.

"His leg pains him, but the doctor seems to have done a fine job of resetting the bone, and it will heal. I broke my leg as a boy when I was not much older than Henry. The challenge will be keeping the lad in bed long enough to let the bone mend before he puts too much weight on it."

"We'll find a way, even if we must tie him down," Kit said, half joking. "Would you have Palmer inquire whether a local dressmaker might visit my home?"

"A dressmaker, sir?"

"Yes, Miss Townsend agreed to marry me last night. She shall need a new wardrobe if she's to be a proper countess."

The valet beamed. "I'll see it done, my lord, and I hope I am the first to offer you congratulations."

"Thank you, Nolan." Kit patted the valet's shoulder. "Tell Palmer I shall be down directly."

Suzannah was still asleep when he went downstairs to the dining room. He couldn't shake off the warm, contented feeling he'd had at the sight of her in his bed, and for that he was glad. When he entered the dining room, he saw Darius reading the *Morning Post* at the table while sipping a cup of tea.

Darius lowered his paper. "Good morning," he said with a bemused smile.

"Did you sleep here?" Kit asked. He couldn't begin to

imagine how the devil his friend had already arrived here, dressed and reading the paper at his dining room table. Had Darius even slept at all?

"What? No," his friend chuckled. "I returned home after you tended to the driver. The others will be along shortly, so I thought I would arrive here first."

Kit took a seat close to Darius. "Is there news?"

"Yes, looking into Balfour's old cases has borne some fruit. Felix sent me a message last evening, which I forgot to tell you in the midst of last night's excitement." He closed his paper and set it aside on the table. "Speaking of which, how did last night go?"

For the first time in seven years, Kit felt a flicker of his old self—the playful, lighthearted young buck—come to the surface.

"As to how last night went, you can congratulate me."

"Oh?" Darius's blue eyes burned with curiosity. "On what?"

"On my upcoming marriage."

Darius broke into a grin. "Congratulations. That *is* wonderful news."

A footman came and poured Kit a cup of tea, which he drank gratefully, and then he leaned back in his seat. His smile slipped a little.

Darius noticed. "You aren't happy?"

"I am . . . ," Kit admitted. "That's what confuses me. I'm content for the first time in years, yet I *am* worried." He toyed with his cup and saucer.

"Worried about what?"

"I fear what Balfour and Walsh may try to do. What if I cannot keep Suzannah safe from them? Revenge has filled me for so long that I fear I may never learn to be content without it. What if I lose her because of it—?"

"Kit, a man must fight every day to keep his happiness. After your future wife is safe, we will help show you how. I think it would be wise to have one of us with Suzannah whenever you cannot be with her."

"I agree. I have a feeling she will insist on finishing her work on the sets for the play, and I do not wish to be the sort of man who denies her the activities that give her joy, but she shouldn't be alone. Especially not there." He understood probably better than Suzannah could ever know what the bond of camaraderie felt like. The people who worked with her at the playhouse were friends, companions, confidants, and they needed her the way she needed them. He wouldn't deprive her of such an important connection. Everyone deserved to feel like they belonged somewhere.

Palmer opened the door to the dining room, allowing Vincent and Lionel into the room. Trailing closely behind were Warren and Felix.

"Excellent, everyone is here," Darius said.

"Shall we discuss our plans while we eat?" Kit offered. The others agreed.

Kit joined his friends at the sideboard, where a dozen chafing dishes lay ready for them. It was so strange to be among his old friends like this, eating fine food in a fine dining room. *His* dining room. There was still a part of him that wondered if he was dreaming and would soon wake up on the dirty floor of the stables. It was going to take a while to get accustomed to his old life again.

Felix nudged him in the ribs. At first, he thought it was

just to get him to move so he could reach the cold meats. "You all right, Kit?"

"Yes," he lied.

"Kit has some good news to share," Darius added with a cheeky smile as he sat down with a plate of food. The others joined him at the table and stared at Kit expectantly.

"I am to be married."

Lionel gaped, open-mouthed, unable to speak. Felix laughed, and Warren blinked in astonishment. Only Vincent seemed unsurprised.

"You're marrying the Townsend chit, I take it?" Vincent guessed aloud.

"You are?" Lionel echoed.

Kit nodded.

"When did all of this happen?" Lionel asked. "I've missed more than I thought. Bloody dances and dinners..."

"I know it's rather sudden, but I think she and I shall do well together," Kit said. He tried to eat, but he felt oddly nervous. Part of him needed his friends' approval of the match.

"Well, now you've sunk us," Warren said. "Damnation. Once our mothers hear of you tying the knot, the rest of us are doomed. *'Oh, Warren, even Kit, who was banished to the penal colonies, has come back and found a wife. What's your excuse?'*" He mimicked his mother's tone, and the others laughed. Just like that, the tension Kit felt evaporated like morning mist.

"Wedding talk aside," Darius cut in, "we need to catch up on what Felix has uncovered about Balfour."

Felix swallowed a bit of poached egg and cleared his

throat. "I've spoken to nearly twenty families of victims transported for crimes where Balfour presided over their cases. None have heard from the sentenced people since they were transported. No letters or anything."

"That's not uncommon. We could barely afford to eat beyond what we were provided by those we worked for. It was nearly impossible to buy paper and ink for letters," Kit added softly. "The men we worked for had only the duty to feed us and provide a place to sleep and a few bits of clothing. They had no other requirements to treat us well."

"I assumed that might be the case. As to the men and women Balfour sentenced, more than half are reported to have died on the crossing over," Felix continued. "That's also no particular surprise, except for the fact that in each of these cases Balfour had some type of benefit that was later revealed. Sometimes a business transaction or shares in a company he acquired. Sometimes there was more of a personal connection, like a maid who accused an acquaintance of Balfour's of assault would suddenly be convicted of a theft at another house."

Kit sighed heavily. It was as he'd suspected. "He's using the law as a battering ram to get what he wants."

"Yes. His cases, when taken one at a time, don't look particularly suspicious. One could easily make excuses for him," Felix said. "But when pooled together, it becomes an obvious abuse of power." Felix shot a glance at Warren. "Tell them what you learned last night at the docks."

Warren leaned forward in his chair as all eyes turned to him. "Does the name James Murray mean anything to you?"

Kit's throat ran dry as old, terrible memories of the

crossing to Australia returned to him. "Yes, he was the captain of my transport ship. He was a hard man."

"Well, I happened to come across him in a tavern. Apparently, he's recently retired from transporting prisoners. He remembered you clearly when I spoke of you. He said he's willing to testify that he was paid to kill you. He admitted to taking the money but said he had no intention of fulfilling his end of the bargain."

"And he didn't," Kit confessed. "The crossing was a terrible journey. Many men and women died, but he didn't cause their deaths. At least, not directly. Illnesses borne of close confinement did that for him." He'd seen more than twenty prisoners die of consumption in less than a month. He'd been one of the men required to help sew the bodies up in canvas bags and toss them overboard, and it was a lucky thing he hadn't caught it himself.

"How are Walsh's debts coming along?" Kit asked.

"We have purchased every business and personal debt we could," Lionel said. "All we need to do is tell our intermediaries to begin calling them in. Once that's done, Lennox can come and make the offer to buy the shipping company."

"Start calling in the debts today," Kit said.

Lionel answered with a nod.

"Once Walsh realizes we are crushing him, he will run to Balfour for help," Vincent said. "What if Balfour attempts to help him?"

"That's exactly what we want." Kit smiled grimly. "We'll take every penny from them both, and when they have nothing left, we'll bring the law down upon them." Revenge was so close now he could taste it.

~

Suzannah stretched in the bed, basking in the swath of sunshine that warmed her skin. She froze midstretch as she realized it was not *her* bed. She was at Kit's house in *his* bed.

Oh Lord . . . Had she truly agreed to marry him last night? She had . . . and he had touched her in the most intimate, exciting ways possible, giving her an exquisite pleasure she'd never imagined. She covered her face with her hands, mortified, and yet also strangely delighted.

A light rap on the door had her scrambling for the covers, but it wasn't Kit who entered. It was the elderly butler, Mr. Palmer.

"Good morning, Miss Townsend. I dried and pressed your gown as well as your . . . er . . . underthings." He blushed to the roots of his white hair as he set her garments on the foot of the bed.

"Oh, thank you so much, Mr. Palmer." She was incredibly grateful for the old man's thoughtfulness. "Do you know where Lord Kentwell is?"

"His lordship is having breakfast downstairs, should you wish to join him."

"Thank you, Mr. Palmer." She waited for the butler to leave before she retrieved her clothing and dressed. She was glad to discover that her boots had dried despite the leather having been soaked clear through the night before. She propped her foot on one of the two armchairs and began to lace up her boots. Her gaze roved around the room as she did, and she spied something sitting on the windowsill she hadn't noticed the previous night.

Unable to deny her curiosity, she finished lacing up and

went to the window to pick up the object. It was a beautifully carved elephant made entirely of ivory. The elephant's features were so perfectly etched that she half expected it to lift its trunk and trumpet proudly. She placed the elephant back on the windowsill with care, wondering where Kit had found it. It was exquisite. She glanced around the room once more, admitting to herself that she felt nervous about sharing breakfast with Kit and was looking for any kind of distraction. After what they'd done the night before, she was more than a little embarrassed. He'd pleasured her, and now she was supposed to sit there and drink tea with him in the light of day as if nothing had happened.

She smoothed her skirts in an effort to calm her racing heart and finally left the bedchamber and went down the stairs. She remembered the way to the dining room easily enough, but she paused at the sound of deep masculine voices on the other side of the closed door. Should she wait before entering? It was clear from the male voices that Kit was not alone. She didn't know who was with him, but they were likely from Kit's elite social circle. She was rarely around polite society like this and wasn't certain what the proper thing to do was.

"Go on in, miss. You won't disturb them," Palmer said with a fatherly smile as he joined her at the door with a tray of letters and calling cards resting in one hand. He opened the door and nodded for her to enter ahead of him.

The discussion ceased immediately as six men practically leapt to their feet.

Suzannah's breath caught at the sight of Kit in light tan trousers that hugged his muscular thighs. The burgundy waistcoat he wore lightened the intense dark brown of his eyes. He was gloriously masculine and yet almost painfully beautiful . . . and he was hers. There was an undeniable surge of feminine joy knowing that this man had begged to pleasure her last night. Yet remembering that encounter had her blushing wildly.

Kit came toward her and cupped her face in one palm, smiling down at her as if they were the only two people in the room. Lord, she loved that smile of his, the one that made him so relaxed, so sweet . . .

She was grateful for his height and physical presence as he turned to the other men while he stood beside her. She felt strangely safe when he was near her. The gentlemen in the room were all finely dressed in waistcoats and trousers that must have cost a small fortune. That meant they were as she suspected, high society. She gulped past a hard lump of panic.

"Good morning, Suzannah," Kit said in a soft tone, calling her attention away from the other men for a moment. The distraction calmed her, and she drew in a breath. Then Kit spoke to the others. "Gentlemen, this is Suzannah Townsend. Suzannah, these are my friends." He pointed to a man she recognized from last night. "You remember meeting Darius St. John last evening?"

"Yes, it's lovely to see you again, Lord Tiverton." She dipped into a curtsy, and he bowed to her.

"It is certainly lovely to see you again under much better circumstances." Darius's blue eyes twinkled. His hair, which had appeared as dark as a raven's wing last night, now revealed hints of dark amber-colored strands. Seeing him and Kit in the same room together, they could have passed for brothers.

Kit gestured to the other gentlemen patiently awaiting their introductions. "As for these men"—he nodded at the man on the opposite side of Darius—"this is Lionel Thistlewaite, Viscount Basildon." Lionel was also dark haired, and his hazel eyes shimmered with a keen intensity that made her feel like he could see straight through her.

"This is Felix Hawkins, the Marquess of Grey."

Felix smiled at her. The only fair-haired man in the room, his light gray eyes sparkled with life. He was much like one of the dashing heroes in the novels she loved to read, and he looked as though he would pick up a fencing foil and leap into action at any moment.

"Last but not least, these are Warren Burville and Vincent Wyndam. Vincent you've met during our ride in the park," Kit said with a glance to the remaining men. Warren was as tall as Kit and almost as broad in the shoulders. But his brown hair and jade-green eyes made him seem less frightening. Still, he exuded an air of danger and recklessness that would appeal to a great many women. He was what ladies in polite society would likely call a rogue or a scoundrel. Warren winked at her, and her face flushed.

She cleared her throat and looked toward Mr. Wyndam, taking in his chocolate-brown hair and eyes to match.

She gasped as she suddenly remembered what had seemed so familiar about him. "I've seen you . . . at the theater. You've been to a number of performances."

Vincent smiled roguishly at her. "Ah . . . yes, that you have. I was . . . keeping an eye on you and, well, the actresses, of course."

"Someone doesn't seem to understand the nature of stealth," Lionel murmured to Vincent.

Vincent shot him a baleful glance. "I wasn't trying to be stealthy."

"I think he was suggesting you should *practice* a bit more," Warren added. The room dissolved into an amusing squabble that seemed better suited to boys in the school-yard than a nobleman's dining room.

From what she could glean of the conversation, these men were Kit's friends, and they had been keeping an eye on not only her but also Mr. Walsh and Mr. Balfour. She could only assume that it had something to do with Kit's conviction seven years ago. But in all the ruckus, they seemed to have forgotten that she was even there.

Suzannah glanced around the room, and Palmer caught her eye as he let out an aggrieved sigh, which made her bite her lip to hide a smile. The butler set the tray of letters down on the table with a loud rattle. The men stopped talking all at once. Palmer cleared his throat and inclined his head to Suzannah.

Kit took his cue from his butler and departed from the table and came over to her, offering his arm. "I believe the lady requires food to break her fast," he said to his friends, then looked down at her. "I'm so sorry, Suzannah. We've been terribly rude." Kit's eyes twinkled. She was so taken aback by the fact that he seemed delighted with how this meeting with his friends was proceeding that she took his arm when he offered it without question. He walked her to an empty seat close to Darius and pulled out a chair for her.

"Please sit." Kit gently urged her into a chair, then retrieved a plate and went to the sideboard behind her to fill her plate with food.

"Forgive us for our boyish behavior just now. We wish

to offer our sincere congratulations to you and Kit," Lionel said to her.

"Oh? What f—" She stopped herself short, realizing it could only be one thing.

"I informed them this morning that you agreed to marry me," Kit said as he placed a plate of food in front of her. It was far too much, but the smells wafting up were divine. Kit's cook, Mrs. Swanson, prepared magnificent dinners, but it seemed she handled breakfast equally well. It momentarily distracted her from the thought of Kit's announcement.

"I thought we might be married tomorrow morning. Does that suit you?" Kit asked her.

She pulled her focus away from the food, even though her stomach rumbled.

"*Tomorrow?*" The single word escaped her in a squeak. She'd guessed he might want to marry soon, but not that soon. She wasn't even sure this was a good idea. She'd gotten carried away last night, swept up in the feeling of belonging that he created within her, but in the light of day, when she was thinking more clearly . . . Well, she half expected him to rethink his marriage proposal as well. She'd lived too many years with shimmering dreams being ripped away or suffering disappointments to trust anything wonderful, even marriage to Kit. She needed time to adjust to this entire idea, to see if it would even last.

Suzannah took in the expression on Kit's face. His dark brows drew together, and he brushed away an errant lock of hair from his face, which made his usually harsh brow seem softer, sweeter.

He answered her softly. "I think it's wise not to wait.

You can be moved in here today, your belongings removed from that boardinghouse and—"

"Wait," she interrupted. "My lord . . . Could we please *discuss* this for a moment somewhere privately?"

The gentlemen around them were now studiously avoiding looking at her, all except for Warren, who was paying close attention to her and Kit whispering. Vincent jabbed him sharply in the ribs with an elbow so that he turned away as well.

"Yes, that's a good idea. Come with me." Kit led her out of the dining room and into a drawing room nearby and closed the door. He leaned back against it and folded his arms over his chest, waiting for her to speak.

"Why must we rush this?" she asked. "I've only just started to like you, my lord, as well as trust you, but are we not still strangers to each other?"

Kit pushed away from the door and came toward her. "Suzannah, please, you must call me Kit. I know the decision to marry may seem hasty, but it's my wish to protect you. You've heard us speak of Walsh and Balfour, and they are dangerous men. I shudder to think what they would do to you once they learn that I've been seen with you. They'll wonder what your father told you, and they'll seek to silence you. I cannot let you be hurt . . . or worse. Not because of me. If you're my wife, I'll be able to properly protect you. If something happens to me . . . you'll be taken care of legally and financially."

"So . . . you only wish to marry me to *rescue* me?" The revelation stung far deeper than she'd expected. "I don't need to be rescued, Kit. I can leave London. I can vanish—"

"Vanish?" His brows formed dark slashes over his eyes.

"That's the very last thing I want you to do. Nor should you be expected to run when it is *they* who should be running. What I want . . ." His voice trailed off, and with a frustrated growl he seized her roughly, pulling her to him so he could silence her protests with a kiss that scorched her soul.

She melted, unable to stay clearheaded when it came to this man's kisses. He parted her lips with his tongue, and she delved and dueled with him, their mouths like a fire raging. He cupped the back of her head and fisted his hand in her hair, tugging on the strands. His possessive, *animal* need to control her only made her burn hotter. She clung to Kit's shoulders and struggled to get closer.

After a long moment they broke apart, their harsh breathing mixed as they still clung together.

"Marry me because you *want* me . . . because we *need* each other. Forget Walsh and Balfour. This . . ." He feathered his lips over hers. "*This* is why we belong together. Don't deny it." He said the words with such earnestness that she truly did feel a connection to him, one that made very little sense, but it was real nonetheless, and she would not deny it.

"All right." She trailed her fingertips over his burgundy waistcoat. "But answer me one thing."

"Ask whatever you wish."

"That ivory elephant on the windowsill in your room. Is that something you had before? After you left England?" She had so many questions, but that one came to her above all the rest.

A cloud fell over his countenance. "That was a gift from someone I met in Australia. An Englishman who let me work on his land in the last year I was serving my sentence.

He was as close to a friend as I had while I lived there. He knew that I was innocent. He trusted me and paid me fairly so I could buy my way home. That elephant was to be a reminder of who betrayed me. Elephants have long memories. They travel hundreds of miles to visit the site where their kin died. They never forget, and neither will I."

Kit lifted one of her hands up to his lips, kissing her knuckles with tenderness. "Does that answer your question?"

"Yes . . ." She bit her lip. "And what of Walsh and Balfour? Are you and your companions planning some scheme of revenge? What happens to me when that is done?" She wasn't a fool. Kit must have had a plan, she was sure of that now, she just wondered what part she was to play in it.

He bit his lip, hesitating only a moment before he spoke. "Yes. We have set certain things in motion, and when the time is right, I will take away their wealth and their freedom, just as they did to me. When that is done, when it is safe . . . you and I shall be free of them."

"Tell me I can trust you," she begged softly. "Tell me that once this is done, we can try to find love in each other."

His eyes glinted with tender humor. "I thought you already loved me?"

"Do not play with me, Kit. I need you to consider this seriously." She smacked a fist against his chest, which made him laugh and pull her closer for a kiss to her temple.

"I am serious about this and about us," he said. "More than you can imagine. I assure you that all will be well."

"You cannot promise that."

"Perhaps not, but I learned over the last seven years

that what a person believes in may be the only thing that helps them survive times of strife."

Suzannah brushed her fingers over his cheek when she saw that flash of old pain in his eyes. She had to trust him. She *wanted* to believe that a hasty marriage would not be a mistake.

"Very well, then . . . tomorrow," she agreed. Part of her still worried that this was all a dream. Was she really going to marry the Earl of Kentwell in less than a day?

She gasped in horror. "Oh heavens, that means I'll be a countess."

"You do not seem pleased by the prospect," Kit observed with a sardonic look.

"I do not know anything about being a lady of quality, having dinners, balls, or even dancing." She swayed as a wave of dread made her suddenly weak in the knees.

"Fear not, you will learn," Kit promised.

"You were born into this life. I was not," she argued. "What if I make a fool of you?"

He placed a finger to her lips. "You would *never* make a fool of me. I already bring with me enough scandal for both of us. I rather think people will wonder why *you* have chosen to marry *me*, rather than the other way around. Why not have Palmer instruct you in the things you are worried about? He's deuced good at all of that."

She nibbled her bottom lip, still fretting as she considered his suggestion. "You don't think he would mind?"

"Not at all." Kit leaned down and kissed her again, making her dizzy as he clutched her shoulders. His tongue sank between her parted lips and teased her wickedly.

"How on earth do you do that?" she demanded when they finally broke apart.

"Do what?" He tilted his head, smiling at her as if he knew exactly what she was asking but would never admit to it. *Wicked man . . .*

"That thing with your tongue," she whispered.

"A man must have *some* secrets, darling." He chuckled and gave her bottom a playful pat. "We should return to breakfast. You need to have a proper meal to start your day. Then we will discuss your lessons with Palmer. Darius and I shall procure a special marriage license and arrange for the ceremony. By tomorrow, we shall be man and wife."

"Man and wife . . ." Suzannah echoed the words with a mixture of excitement and fear.

13

Suzannah survived the breakfast with Kit and his friends. They took turns delighting her with tales of Kit's boyhood and the harmless but amusing antics he had gotten up to. At first Kit had glowered in embarrassment, but he soon relaxed and even smiled a little. That made her happy more than anything else, just seeing him smile. The stark fortress surrounding Kit's heart was crumbling. The more open his heart became, the better chance she had to make him fall in love with her.

Once the servants cleared the plates away, Kit pulled Suzannah to one side of the room to speak privately.

"While Darius and I are obtaining the special license, I've decided that you will go shopping on Bond Street for a new wardrobe. Lionel's sister, Octavia, has recently come into society. Lionel has sent word to his mother that he shall be taking you with them when he escorts them on their shopping today. You are to buy a wedding gown and anything else you may require. Do not fret about cost—money is no object, as far as I'm concerned."

"Surely I do not need so very much?" She hated to think of him spending money on her for something she'd only wear once.

Kit's expression softened as he stroked the ribbons in her hair. "Purchase a hundred gowns, if you like . . . and be sure to buy plenty of ribbons."

She blushed as she felt the stares of his friends upon them. Kit had mostly shielded her from their view, but they were tall enough that she glimpsed them over the mountain of his shoulder.

"Buy sheer underthings, kid gloves, boots and slippers, silly bonnets. Buy it all, my darling," Kit said more quietly. "Give me the joy of being kind to you. Let me gift you these things and know that they are yours because I care."

He *cared* . . . How could such a small word mean so much to her? How could this man, once such a dark, brooding, and frankly terrifying man, elicit the softest of emotions within her?

"All right." She couldn't deny him anything when he asked her like that.

With a triumphant smile, Kit kissed her forehead. "Now, wait here for Octavia and Lady Somerstone. Darius and I must leave now. I shall see you this evening for dinner."

Darius bowed and followed Kit out of the drawing room. The rest of Kit's companions politely excused themselves, except for Lionel.

"My mother and sister will be along presently. I shall make the introductions when they arrive." He smiled at her, but Suzannah was still more than ever aware of her lack of social standing compared to both Kit and his companions. She wasn't sure how to act or what to say without Kit there to guide her.

"Lord Basildon . . . your mother and sister won't mind that I am unfit as a shopping companion, will they?" She feared being stared at and judged by other fine ladies if she appeared beside a duchess and a young lady of quality.

He offered her his arm to escort her to the drawing room. She slipped her arm in his, feeling as shy as the first time Kit had done that. She was unused to men escorting her to different rooms in the house. It was silly, but also strangely charming.

"Unfit?" Lionel echoed the word as if he'd never heard it before. "How so?"

"I mean, well, I am no one of importance, and they will surely be embarrassed by associating with a disgraced dead man's daughter."

Lionel's hazel eyes focused on her sharply. "Miss Townsend, your father suffered no disgrace. And as for you, you are the farthest thing from being *no one* I could possibly imagine." He urged her to sit in a comfortable chair and then knelt unexpectedly at her feet and took her hands in his. "In fact, you are everything. Kit, the old Kit I know, is coming back to us. I know you do not know that Kit, not yet, but someday you will see him as the man he was before he was betrayed. And for that, for bringing our friend back to us, you are more valuable to me than the king himself. You have my undying loyalty and my vow of protection."

He spoke so earnestly that she could not deny the truth of his words. Unprepared for this raw show of emotion,

Suzannah wiped at her eyes as she fought off tears. How could she explain to him all that she was feeling? Just a short time ago she was merely a woman who painted sets at the theater on Drury Lane, yet now she was on the verge of becoming a countess and being thrust into the most elite circles in England with no preparation whatsoever. Everyone had been kind to her and treated her like a lady, but somehow that only made her nerves worse.

"I'm so sorry, my lord, it's all rather too much, you see . . . I cannot seem to believe that this isn't all some dream that will vanish and I shall be living once more in a tiny cupboard, as Kit calls it."

"Do not apologize. You've had the only world you've known ripped away from you, and you've been tossed into a new one. I doubt I would have handled it much better, were it me," Lionel teased gently and produced a handkerchief as he stood.

She accepted it gratefully.

"Dry your eyes, my dear. I dare not think what Kit will do to me if he hears I made you cry."

She laughed and apologized profusely as she wiped at her tears before returning the handkerchief to him.

"Lionel Richard Thistlewaite! What on earth have you done to that poor woman?" a regal voice bellowed from the doorway.

Still wiping at her eyes, Suzannah spun in her seat to see a pair of women in the doorway of the drawing room. They stared at Suzannah and Lionel in clear concern, and she understood how it must have looked, her crying and him kneeling beside her in a room with no chaperone.

"Mother." Lionel stood up and inclined his head at the

striking woman in her mid-fifties. The manila silk gown she wore was exquisite and turned an iridescent gold in the light as she moved. She wore no turban, the way many women her age might, but rather she had her hair styled up in a lovely tumble of waves. The young woman beside her was a russet-haired beauty of perhaps eighteen who watched Suzannah with keen interest.

"Might I remind you that not all tears are unhappy ones?" Lionel added when his mother continued to stare at them in concern.

"Yes, well, you can forgive my misunderstanding. I've never seen you make a woman so emotional before. You usually have them eating out of your palm and swooning, dear. Not that you'd bother to marry any of those nice young girls you're always dancing with, and I dearly *wish* you would."

"That is certainly a matter to discuss another day," Lionel replied with a wink at Suzannah.

Suzannah stood and approached the two ladies with Lionel at her side, ready to make introductions.

"Mother, Octavia, this is Miss Suzannah Townsend. Miss Townsend, this is my mother, Lady Somerstone, and my sister, Octavia."

Octavia was positively beaming at her. Lady Somerstone, on the other hand, smiled politely but remained a little reserved.

"It is lovely to meet you, my dear. My son has informed me that you are to marry Lord Kentwell?"

"I suppose I am."

"You *suppose?*" Lady Somerstone echoed. "My dear, are you or aren't you?" The woman's tone and air were so clearly of ancient English aristocracy that Suzannah rather felt like she was in the presence of a queen.

"She is," Lionel cut in. His mother ignored him and continued to stare at Suzannah, waiting for an answer.

"I am," Suzannah finally said as she lifted her chin and looked resolutely back at Lady Somerstone. She was taking a leap of faith for Kit, and she supposed she must commit to that and accept whatever came next. Time would tell if trusting her heart had been a mistake or not.

"Excellent. As I understand it, you wish to learn how to be a countess. Your first lesson is that a woman in your position must always be decisive, even if you secretly feel conflicted about something. You must show confidence in your decisions to others." Lady Somerstone seemed to relax, as if she sensed Suzannah had made the decision to throw herself on Kit's side. "Then let us hunt down a wedding gown worthy of a countess."

And just like that, she was taken under the wing of the Duchess of Somerstone. They rode in a fashionable carriage with Lionel dutifully accompanying them to Bond Street. Octavia peppered Suzannah with questions and observations. By the time the carriage made its first stop, Suzannah had heard so much of the business of "Lady this" and "Lady that" and "Lord so-and-so" that she felt certain she would mix up all their names and various scandals.

The first shop they entered was full of lavish fabrics, exquisite gloves, beautiful ladies' boots and slippers, as well as a number of other things a lady could desire. Suzannah had never imagined such a shop existed. She wandered around, clutching her hands together because she was too afraid to touch anything. She was more than aware that she was out of place in her plain gown and scuffed black boots.

A plump woman with a brightly colored turban wrapped around her head sniffed and raised her nose up as Suzannah finally dared to pick up a pair of kid leather gloves. The buttery leather was so soft that Suzannah wanted to rub it against her cheek, but she didn't dare because she could feel that woman's gaze upon her.

The duchess joined Suzannah at the display of gloves.

"Lovely choice, my dear, quite lovely." Then she turned toward the other woman. "Oh hello, Prudence, I'm glad to see you out and about. I feared that perhaps you would not have the proper credit to shop . . . given your husband's debts."

The woman gasped in outrage and threw down the bonnet she'd been holding and stalked out.

Lady Somerstone smiled smugly and then whispered softly to Suzannah, "She's a terrible gossip and has no place to judge anyone, let alone you. Now, let's find you a wedding gown to make our young Christopher swoon."

Suzannah couldn't help but blush and then smile at the way Lady Somerstone called Kit "young Christopher."

Octavia linked her arm through Suzannah's.

"See? No one will dare cross you when my mother is on your side. You have me, of course, but I'm far less imposing than my mother. Give me another twenty years, though, and I'm sure I'll be a fierce lady indeed." Octavia winked at her, and Suzannah adored the way it so reminded her of Lionel. She finally began to enjoy shopping.

By early evening when she was deposited back at Kit's home, she was certain of two things: she would never dare cross the duchess or those she loved, including Kit, and Octavia was indeed her bosom friend.

Suzannah climbed wearily out of the coach and gave her heartfelt goodbyes to Lionel's mother and sister. Lionel and one of Kit's footmen carried two stacks of boxes containing everything a countess could possibly need for a wedding and a honeymoon, and much more besides. It was more clothing than Suzannah had ever owned in her life. There were dresses for walks, riding habits, evening dresses, carriage dresses, day dresses, tea gowns, and some whose purpose she had already forgotten.

Lionel had remained with them the entire time, but during the fittings he had elected to sit on one of the couches, reading a paper and ignoring all mention of fashion. She knew his presence was not for the sake of his kin— but because Kit wished for her to be protected at all times by himself or his closest friends.

"I shall remain with you until Kit returns," Lionel said as he followed Suzannah inside Kit's townhouse, carrying the last of the boxes.

A footman helped Suzannah remove her cloak. The footman who had accompanied her on the shopping expedition began to take the boxes upstairs to her bedchamber. About half of the gowns she'd purchased still needed to be sewn and would be delivered in the next week. All that mattered for now was that she had what she needed for tomorrow.

Palmer greeted her just inside the door. "Ah, welcome home, Miss Townsend."

"Thank you, Palmer. How is Henry?" she asked.

"He's fairing much better. He and I played some chess

this afternoon before he rested. He's only just finished dinner and is sleeping."

"That is good news." Suzannah was more than relieved to know Henry was doing well when she wasn't able to watch over his recovery as much as she wished.

"Palmer, is Kit home yet?" Lionel asked.

"Yes. He arrived a few minutes before you. He's presently changing for dinner. Are you staying for supper, Lord Basildon?"

Lionel shook his head. "Afraid not, old boy. I have more chaperone duties for Octavia this evening. We have yet another ball." Lionel bowed to Suzannah and put on his hat. "I shall see you tomorrow, Miss Townsend."

"Good night, Lord Basildon." She nodded to him as he departed, then sighed and faced Palmer wearily. "What time is dinner?"

"In a few minutes, but it will only be you and Master Kit, I believe," Palmer said a little glumly. "The other gentlemen are busy this evening. You need not change if you do not wish to."

She was relieved that she and Kit would have a private dinner, but even more relieved that she didn't have to change her dress yet again.

She was debating whether to go up and see Henry now when Kit appeared at the top of the stairs. He was smartly dressed in tan trousers and a bishop's-blue waistcoat. He had forgone a tailcoat, and somehow the intimacy of that decision made her belly flutter. She liked Kit dressed more casually. It made it easier for her to feel his equal.

He greeted her as he reached the bottom of the stairs. "Suzannah. Did you have a fruitful day out?" He offered her his arm. She looped her hand through his arm and walked with him to the dining room.

"Yes, we did. But I fear you will receive a rather large bill from the modiste. Lady Somerstone kept adding items to the list, and I do not think there is a force in all of England strong enough to stop her when she has a mind to shop."

Kit chuckled, and the warm, rich sound delighted her. "The bill does not concern me. I have grown used to only purchasing necessities, and while it feels wrong to buy any excesses for myself . . . you are an entirely different matter. You are in need of a wardrobe, and I rather like the idea of spending money on you."

"I understand that some women may like to feel spoiled, but I confess, it makes me feel uncomfortable. My father . . . he used to spend almost every spare bit of money on me and often went without. It . . ." She swallowed as her throat tightened. "I know that you have far more than he did, but still, I shall never want anything in excess for myself. Otherwise, it feels as though . . ." She didn't dare continue.

He studied her for a long moment, and she sensed he was somehow peeling away the layers of her words the way she did old layers of oil on a painting when she was attempting to fix an old set at the theater.

"Does it make you feel as though I've bought you?" Kit asked.

She nodded but said nothing.

As they sat for dinner, Kit brushed his knuckles over her cheek, his dark eyes studying her seriously. "A man cannot buy a truly free creature. You are free, Suzannah. Never forget that."

Was she, though? At the moment, she felt quite caged in, and it did not matter that the bars were gilded.

Kit continued. "I was thinking . . . After we are married, we could take my coach and travel to Kentwell House . . . the family estate. It's three hours outside of the city, and I have not yet visited it since my return. It would give us time to be together without fretting about my other concerns here."

She did like the idea of getting away from the city. "I didn't know you had a country estate."

"It's closed most of the year—or it was while I was away from England, but my father was buried there, and I would like to pay my respects. I also need to see what needs to be done about the estate's restoration. It's an old home, but its bones are good. With money and love, it could be grand again."

Her heart lightened at the thought of restoring something old and broken into something beautiful. "I would like that." Perhaps Kit would allow her to redecorate it. She would certainly enjoy an artistic endeavor like that.

"So, tell me about your day. What did you think of Octavia and Lady Somerstone?"

As they ate, Suzannah shared her adventures in the realm of Bond Street. Rather than becoming bored, Kit seemed delighted by her tales.

When they finished their meal, Suzannah's heart raced as Kit escorted her upstairs to his bedchamber. They stopped just outside his door, and the quiet, lamplit hallway seemed charged with an intensity that deepened both her excitement and trepidation. She wasn't sure whether she wanted him to insist that she share his bed again or if she wanted to be taken to her own room down the corridor. Kit's face was unreadable. He wanted *her* to be the one to ask about his intentions.

"Shouldn't I sleep alone in my own room?" she finally asked. "Isn't that considered proper?"

Kit lifted her chin with gentle fingers. "It is. But is that what *you* want?" There was no challenge, no accusation, just a soft and concerned question. His eyes were gentle as he gazed down at her, and they asked her to speak the truth.

What did she want? Ever since she'd kissed him, she longed to be in his arms, to feel that wonderful blend of excitement and contentment that he'd brought out in her. Yet this need for intimacy, for this man who was in so many ways still a stranger, scared her.

"What do you want?" she dared to whisper.

Kit's eyes were intense now. "I want to hold you in my arms, but my desires should never come before yours. I believe that marriages . . . intimate relationships should be built on trust. Partnerships. Do you agree?"

She let his words sink in. "Yes." The man was too good to be true, she knew that, but shouldn't a woman trust someone she was starting to love? She cleared her throat. "Let's sleep in your chambers."

He leaned down and stroked his thumb over her bottom lip before he kissed her. She tasted his hunger, his need, and rather than simply endure it, she embraced her own need for him and let it feed her own desires in the kisses she returned. He gripped her waist roughly with one hand and fumbled to open his door with the other. His clear excitement for what was to come next stirred an excitement in her too.

"Kit . . ."

"Yes?" he breathed against the back of her neck as he urged her to step into his bedchamber.

"Are you going to take me tonight?"

He gently herded her toward the bed, his mouth still playfully landing kisses upon her neck and shoulders. She gripped the post of his bed and rested her head against the strong wood as his fingers eagerly dug into the laces of the back of her gown. He removed her clothing quickly, though not roughly.

"Kit . . . ," she said again. "Are you?" She demanded an answer this time, even as she faced the fact that she was completely naked while he was still fully clothed and standing right behind her.

Kit gripped her upper arms, nuzzling the tangle of her hair that tumbled down her shoulders and back, which made her shiver with longing. She should be frightened. Any sensible woman would worry about taking things so quickly, but Kit's manner, the way he kissed her, the way he touched her, left her dizzy and wild with need instead. He was like an animal seeking his mate, needing to join himself to her, and he had no thought past that primal need to connect. He played no games of seduction. He simply wanted her, and she wanted him back.

"Tell me I can have you, Suzannah," he demanded. "Tell me you're mine." His hands slid down her hips, slowly exploring her body.

She wanted to be his when he asked her like that. To belong to this man was a promise to surrender to his desires and demand her own be satisfied. But it was more than that, and she knew it. This man had been alone for so long, craving someone to be his in all ways of the body and heart.

She turned in his arms, her bare breasts brushing against his waistcoat, her nipples hardening into points at the gentle abrasion. She raised her gaze to his and knew what she wanted.

"I'm yours."

A fire lit within his dark eyes, and he cupped her face in his hands as he kissed her. This kiss was different than the others. It was as though before now he'd been holding himself back, and now he was unleashing all of his passion into her. She felt consumed by it, as though she was the only thing sustaining this powerful, beautiful, and wounded man.

He lifted her up and set her on the side of the bed, his mouth never leaving hers. Suzannah's head spun as she clawed at his chest, trying to find the buttons of his waistcoat before she gave up and simply tore at the silk. Buttons shot everywhere, and Kit laughed softly against her lips.

"Minx," he breathed in delight at her show of desire. "Showing your claws at last."

"Get out of your clothes . . . *now*," she growled at him. Some distant, well-behaved part of her would be scandalized by her behavior later, but at this moment she didn't care.

Kit shrugged out of his waistcoat, and then he pushed her flat on the bed. "There will be time enough for that." He grasped her legs, gently opening them as he bent toward her. He moved quickly, and before she realized what he was planning, the blasted man had his mouth between her legs. She shrieked at the unexpected sensation of his wicked tongue flicking against her in ways she hadn't even dreamed of.

"Oh . . . my . . . God . . . *Kit* . . ." His name escaped her lips as a moan. She'd never experienced anything like this, not even when he'd touched her the night before. She threw her head back and clutched the bedding in her fists as Kit continued to pleasure her with his mouth. It seemed to go on forever, this wonderful, wicked thing, before Suzannah's eyes rolled back in her head and a wave of ecstasy nearly killed her. Legs trembling, she gasped for breath, but Kit showed no mercy. All she could do was surrender to him.

When he finally lifted his head, she stared down the length of her own naked body to meet his gaze. He slowly straightened to stand up and unfastened his trousers.

He leaned over her and braced one hand by her head. "I'm sorry, Suzannah."

"For what—?" Her words turned into a gasp of pain as he entered her in a hard thrust.

"Try to relax and breathe deeply," he said soothingly. "I promise never to hurt you like this again, darling."

She did relax after a moment. When she breathed in and out slowly, the pain transformed into an awareness of him, feeling him *within* her. They were connected so deep, it was as though their bodies and souls had become a single flowing ribbon of brilliant color tumbling endlessly down a wildflower-covered hillside. She'd never imagined a feeling like this was possible.

Kit held still above her. "Does it still hurt?"

"I . . . no." She tried to move her hips upward, and the sensation of him sliding deeper felt wonderful, yet strange.

"Good," he groaned. "Because I want to make love to you, Suzannah." He pulled to sit her up and urged her to wrap her legs around his waist. He then lifted himself up upon the bed and carefully laid her down beneath him in the center of the bed before he kissed her and began to rock over her. As he thrust in and out, he captured her hands and laced his fingers with hers. There was no part of her that felt untouched by him. They were joined in every way possible, and the sensation was overwhelming.

Kit's mouth moved to settle over one of her breasts, sucking her nipple, then laving it with his tongue. Suzannah squeezed his hands hard as she felt another wave of pleasure build inside her. She whimpered, and his warm breath fanned her heated skin as he nuzzled her other breast. "Kit . . ."

He chuckled wickedly. "I never loved hearing my name more than listening to you moan it."

When he freed her hands, she buried them in his hair and pressed him closer to her breasts, urging him to do more. The delicious tug of his mouth on her breasts sent tingles deep into her very center. After a long, delicious moment, he kissed his way back up to her mouth and laced his fingers through hers once again. Then he began to really move.

Suzannah was not prepared for what it would feel like to make love, to miss the feel of him within her as he withdrew and the rush of pleasure as he surged back inside. She chanted his name like a prayer as he claimed her. Whatever she had secretly held back from him before, she now surrendered as Kit loved her with his body. The pleasure that came was pure, explosive, and filled her mind with colors that she wished she could capture upon a canvas. She was unmade as ripples of joy both of the heart and body spread out to her fingers and toes.

Kit shouted her name, hoarse and desperate as he plunged twice more before she felt a soft heat fill her while he came apart. He gazed down at her, his breathing hard as he tried to find control of his body.

"It's all right," she soothed, somehow understanding that he had been as affected as she was.

"It's . . . never been like that before," he confessed, his voice raw with emotion. "It's never . . ." His voice trailed off as fine lines crinkled at the corners of his brown eyes.

"Never?" she asked him.

He smiled. "*Never.*" He rolled them so she lay by his side, but the action pulled him out of her body, and she felt an unexpected tenderness between her thighs. Kit cursed and then apologized to her with soft kisses to her temple softly before he tucked her closer to him, their legs entwined. He was still wearing his trousers around his ankles, and the thought of that made her stifle a giggle.

"Does it hurt? I should have been more gentle for your first time." He stroked her face, and the calloused pads of his fingertips made her heart ache. Those rough fingers spoke of the struggle he'd been through, working to survive in Australia.

"It's tender," she admitted, "but I don't think I'm hurt."

"I'll have a hot bath drawn for you in the morning," he said.

She sighed like a contented kitten and burrowed closer

to him to absorb his warmth. "Hmm . . . that sounds nice. Oh, I forgot to ask. Was your errand successful, my lord?"

"Errand?" he asked with a smile.

"Hmm . . . you know . . . the license." Her voice was delightfully drowsy.

"Oh yes, Suzannah, I have obtained the license. And you found your dress, of course."

"Yes, I—I have a suitable dress for . . . tomorrow."

"And the other part of *your* errand?"

"What other part?"

Eyebrows raised, smile like the devil, he said, "The sheer underthings and ribbons?"

She blinked in surprise at him remember that request.

"Well, darling, did you buy them?"

"Yes . . . I certainly did. Oh, Kit, you *are* wicked." She playfully pushed against his shoulder.

"Yes, the wickedest," he assured her with a leonine grin and then kissed the tip of her nose before he grew serious again. "You . . . won't have any regrets tomorrow?" Kit asked her as sleep crept closer and closer to her.

She closed her eyes and yawned. "About what?"

"About marrying me."

"I could never regret that . . . not to a man like you." She pressed her cheek against his chest, feeling his pulse beat steady. After what they'd just shared, she knew now she wouldn't have any regrets.

"And what sort of man am I?"

Suzannah was exhausted and could barely think clearly as she answered. "A good man. A man deserving of love."

～

Kit swallowed hard against the lump in his throat.

"A good man . . . A man deserving of love . . ."

He held on to her for a long while, but when he was certain she was deep in slumber, he slipped out of his bed and tucked the covers around her. It wasn't easy to leave her in his bed, leaving the sweet scent of her that permeated the air with roses and springtime. The warmth of that bed and the warmth of his future wife were far too tempting, but he had a mission tonight. He stared at her sleeping form as he dressed and pulled on his boots, then quietly left the room and found a footman still awake in the downstairs entryway.

"My lord?" the man asked.

"I shall return in a short while. I hate to ask this, but will you please wait up for me?" He didn't want to bang upon the door late at night and wake everyone.

The footman straightened up and fetched Kit's hat for him. "Of course, my lord."

Once Kit was ready to leave, he chose not to wake poor Samuels at this hour of the night so he found a passing hackney on the street and rode to the docks, where his friends had reported that they had seen James Murray.

The dockside tavern that Felix had told him about was not a place a decent London man would ever find himself in, but Kit had faced far worse in the colonies. A few bare-knuckled bruisers didn't frighten him. But the foul stench of unwashed bodies, mixed with the brine of brackish waters from the nearby docks, combined with the tart scent of ale and other things in the air made Kit's body tense with disgust. Had he softened so quickly? He'd lived in conditions like this for years, yet now all he wanted was to go home to Suzannah and his warm bed.

As he moved through the tavern, a bar wench shrank back in fear and men stepped aside, all too aware of his strength and size and the menace he carried with him.

A familiar figure was seated by the wall near the fire roaring in the hearth. Kit walked over and pulled back a chair at the table across from him. The man was nursing a pint of ale from a tin mug. Kit waited for him to lift his head and look at him. The man's eyes flashed with recognition, then horror. Kit almost smiled.

"You . . ." James Murray's eyes bulged.

"Hello, Captain."

"I already told those men of yours that I would testify for you," Murray hastened to say.

"Thank you," Kit replied.

"Is that why you're here?" Murray asked. Waves of whiskey rolled off the unshaven man's breath.

Kit was quiet a long moment before he finally asked the question that had plagued him.

"Why didn't you kill me?"

Murray seemed to sober a little at the question. "Why?"

"Yes, you took the money, and you knew it would be a risk not to do what you'd been paid to."

Murray took a long gulp of his ale before he spoke.

"I could say it was because of your father. I didn't want some fancy earl raising questions and making my life unnecessarily complicated. But the truth is, I saw something in your eyes that day when you came to my cabin. You had more than vengeance in your eyes—you had righteous indignation. Divine, even. It was like Nemesis herself had blessed you and damned all those who'd wronged you. I wanted to play no part in whatever happened next. I feared that if I tossed you overboard you'd survive. Better to leave you alone and pray that on the day you came back for revenge, when you inevitably found me, you'd have no cause to kill me." Murray's gaze swept over him. "By the looks of you, the labor made you quite capable of snapping my neck, or worse."

Kit didn't disagree. He could very easily have killed Murray.

"You shouldn't be here in a place like this. If the men who paid you to kill me learn where you are . . ."

Murray paled, and Kit realized that it hadn't occurred to the old sea captain that he would be in danger.

"Surely you don't think . . ." Murray glanced at the less-than-reputable people in the tavern.

"Take a hackney to this address and tell the man there I sent you. He'll know what to do." Kit passed a slip of paper with Darius's address on it to Murray. He would have offered to escort Murray himself, but as the two had been speaking, he'd counted at least five men watching them too intently to be casually interested in them as strangers. It seemed he had been right in his concern that Murray would be discovered by Walsh and Balfour.

"You must leave this place at once," Kit whispered. "I'll hold them off."

"What? They're here already?" Murray gaped and snatched up the address from the table.

"Go. Now," Kit growled as he stood up.

Murray leapt to his feet and bolted for the door. Kit tossed some coins on the table and moved to block the exit once Murray had left. If Kit had delayed even a few seconds, the five men would have beaten him to the door and caught up with Murray outside. Instead, the men were forced to turn their wolflike focus onto Kit. Kit smiled.

"Evening, gentlemen."

The biggest brute sized him up. "We ain't got no problem with you."

His grin grew as he removed his cloak and hat and set them down on the nearest table. "I'm afraid you do. The men who hired you? I'm the one they really want."

"If that's true, I bet they'll pay double for you, then," the leader said with a dark chuckle. Two of the men behind the tallest fellow removed small daggers from their belts.

"I imagine they would . . . if you were to succeed." Kit slowly raised up his loosely balled fists. "But I'm afraid all you will find here tonight . . . is pain." It'd been far too long since he had broken some bones, and a dark part of his soul craved it now.

A quarter of an hour later, he was the only man still standing. He licked a split lip and flexed his bruised hands. Broken chairs and shattered glasses were strewn over the floor. Five bodies lay upon the ground, while many others cowered at their tables or had fled into the night.

His attackers were all still breathing. Kit knew better than to kill them, no matter how much he might wish to. He wouldn't dare give Walsh and Balfour cause to put a noose around his neck. He removed several pound notes from his coat and laid them on the nearest table, then nodded at the barkeeper. He retrieved his hat and cloak, flashed a wink at a frightened serving maid, and walked out into the night.

When he returned to his home a short time later, he found Suzannah awake, dressed in his robe and anxiously pacing the floor of his bedchamber. She'd purchased a new robe for herself today, and yet here she was wearing his. Something about that stole his breath.

You truly are mine . . . aren't you? He couldn't help but think this as he cleared his throat to catch her attention.

"Kit!" She flung herself at him the second she saw him. He wrapped his arms around her, holding her close. He buried his face in her neck, kissing her ever so softly in the tender place where her shoulder met her throat. She smelled divine, even better than what he remembered from a mere hour ago when he'd left her.

He let out a slow sigh and just held her, feeling the rightness of her in his arms and knowing this was where he belonged. Here in this bedchamber with her. A comfort like he'd never known filled him so completely that he couldn't breathe for a long moment. He simply felt it, that sense of *belonging* that he had thought he had lost forever.

"Where the devil did you go? I woke up and found you gone. One of the footmen said you left, and . . . I thought . . . I was . . . I worried that . . ." She began to ramble, still panicked, and he could feel her anxious breaths against his chest as she burrowed deeper into his embrace.

"What did you think happened?" he asked as he tilted her face up to look at him.

"I thought perhaps something bad happened to you, or that you didn't want to go through with the marriage after all. Oh—you're hurt!" she gasped as she got a better look at his bruised face. "What happened?"

"I had an old friend to visit, and someone was trying to hurt him. I put a stop to it."

"With what? Your face?" she snapped. "Your eye is blackening, and your lip is bleeding."

"I assure you, the other fellow fared far worse."

She pulled out of his arms to grab a cloth and wet it in the nearby basin. "Stop joking. Sit down. *Now.*" She pointed at one of the armchairs by the fire.

He sat obediently, amused and delighted to see her caring for him, mirroring what had happened the night he'd rescued her.

"Idiotic man," she grumbled as she cleaned his cuts and then lifted one of his bruised hands and placed a tender kiss to his aching knuckles. "Going off in the middle of the night to get into fights? Please don't ever do that again."

"It's not as if I left the house looking for a fight," he said defensively. "Besides, I am more than capable of taking care of myself."

She met his gaze and brushed his hair back from his eyes. "You *aren't* alone anymore. You have friends to help you fight your battles, but even then, you shouldn't be fighting at all because it frightens me, Kit. What if something happens to you and tonight changes everything?"

"What do you mean?" He wasn't following her.

"What if it isn't just me you leave behind? What if it's *us*?" she emphasized, placing a hand on her abdomen.

"Us . . ." He repeated the word, his mind suddenly spinning wildly. He'd been so focused on claiming her earlier and hadn't given a single thought to the possible results of their union. Even now she could be with child. *Their child . . .* He didn't know whether to shout or to just clutch her to his chest and hold on so he wouldn't cry. The unexpected joy at the thought of sharing a child with her, with his own ray of golden light . . . His future, once dark, seemed now to be illuminated.

Suzannah smiled mischievously. "It's only a small chance."

"Small chance be damned. I think we should work on increasing the odds straightaway. What do you think?" He pulled at the sash of the robe that covered her.

"Men seem to think sex renders females weak, but I rather think it's the men who become quite senseless from it."

He curled his arms around her waist, gently pulling her to stand in the space of his spread legs.

"Well, I certainly do become senseless with you," he agreed. "And I'm ready to become even more senseless." He silenced her laugh with a deep kiss, and he scooped her up and carried her to his bed. They fell back onto it with her on top of him. Neither of them said anything more for a long while as they diligently and thoroughly worked to increase their *chances*.

14

S t. George's was filled with people, far more than Kit had expected to be present at his wedding. He stared over the packed crowd, a mix of friends and curious onlookers, as he waited anxiously for Suzannah to arrive. He clenched his hands tight in front of him, but his nervous reaction didn't go unnoticed by his groomsman.

"Steady on, old boy," Darius said calmly beside him.

"The last time everyone stared at me like this, it was at my sentencing," he muttered. "I didn't wish for my wedding to be such a spectacle . . ." He tugged at the tight cravat, feeling like it was cutting off his air.

"There she is." Darius nodded at the back of the church. The doors opened and Suzannah came in. Dressed in a cream-colored gown, trimmed with lace, she presented a picture of loveliness to rival any of the highborn ladies of the beau monde. Her face was still flushed with the passion of the previous night, and Kit's heart beat faster seeing the glow on the face of his well-loved woman.

Those seated on either side of the center aisle whispered excitedly as she walked past. When she finally reached Kit at the altar, she smiled shyly up at him. Blushes suited her nicely, and he wanted to make every excuse to see her blush once they were alone. Green ribbons were threaded through her hair, reminding him of the night they'd first met. Something spinning in his chest left him feeling strangely dizzy.

"My green-ribbon girl." He reached out a gloved hand and stroked his fingertips over her own, briefly, but the contact heated between them.

The ceremony was a blur and Kit held on to her hand the entire time. That simple act grounded him in the moment and deepened his connection with her. He never could have imagined that the daughter of a man who'd helped ruin his life was now one of his truest joys. Suzannah was a gift. He could not deny that now.

The wedding ceremony ended, and they faced the crowd. His friends cheered. Warren whistled, causing an older woman seated behind him to wallop Warren on the head with her reticule.

"Come along. We have a wedding breakfast to attend." Kit gently tucked her arm in his as they began the long walk down the aisle to the carriage waiting outside. Men shook Kit's hand in congratulations, and women wiped their eyes with fancy handkerchiefs. Something prickled at him with unease, and he searched the crowd around them. All he could see were happy wedding-guests, hearing the excited voices of everyone talking at once.

Then, just as they were about to reach the door, Kit saw something out of the corner of his eye. It was like catching sight of a black shadow that fractured the light ominously on a sunny day. The shadow transformed into a man as he emerged from the crowd, a pistol in his hand. It was Walsh.

"You've ruined everything!"

Kit's life slowed to a crawl as Walsh fired the gun. Suzannah cried out, and he caught her limp body in his arms.

"No!" He collapsed to the ground, his wife in his arms. Blood stained her gown, and the bouquet she held was sprayed in red.

Suzannah's lifeless gaze stared up at the painted angels on the ceiling far above them. He let out an unholy roar of violence and pain.

The shout sent him flying upward in his bed. Kit flailed as he realized he was in the dark, his body coated with a cold sweat and the bedsheets all tangled around him.

"What's wrong?"

He turned, seeing Suzannah's form in the shadows beside him. She was here. She was *alive*. She wasn't on the floor of St. George's, her lifeless body sagging in his hold.

"Oh, thank Christ," he moaned. The pounding terror that threatened to crush his ribs faded slowly. He pulled her into his arms so he could feel her heartbeat against his chest.

"What is it?" Suzannah cupped his face in her hands, and his eyes adjusted to the darkness so he could just make out her fear and worry. "*Please* talk to me." He grasped her wrists gently, holding on to her just as she held to him and pressed his forehead to hers.

"It was a bad dream, that's all."

"It must have been a terrifying one. You almost fell out of bed." She stroked her hands on his neck, soothing him.

He had never met a more caring woman in his life. How had he been so bloody lucky to find her?

"It was," he admitted. "I dreamt that Walsh shot you mere moments after our wedding." He wasn't sure it was wise to tell her this, but he was determined to be honest with her in all things.

"Oh . . . ," she breathed and held him a little tighter. "I'm sorry." She then kissed him softly on the lips, a kiss to soothe rather than seduce.

"Why are you sorry?" he asked when she finally broke off the kiss. She was killing him with her sweetness.

"Because I don't wish for you to worry about me. It's the last thing I want."

He cupped her chin and held her gaze. "I'll never not worry about you. You're mine. I care about what's mine. I *protect* what's mine." He wanted to reassure her that he could take care of her, but having to confess his nightmare of watching her die hadn't helped make him feel like his own words were true. He hadn't felt this helpless and afraid since the day he was sentenced and sent to Newgate.

"Why don't you go rest?" Suzannah said. "Dawn is a few hours away, and we shall need energy to handle our wedding guests."

He pulled her down beside him. "Why don't we run away to Scotland and forget everyone else?"

"You know we cannot do that. Your friends want to see you married. It will make them happy. And what of Palmer, Mrs. Swanson, and Henry? They all deserve to see this. I care even less for a public wedding than you do, but we owe it those we care about to have the ceremony here." She settled against him, hand on his chest, which he covered with his own.

"Sleep," he urged her.

"Only if you do," she argued as she yawned. He could hear how sleepy she was.

"I will."

But he lay awake, watching the sun come over the horizon and light the bedchamber with its rays. He feared that if he closed his eyes that awful nightmare would be waiting for him. He left Suzannah to sleep a bit longer while he got up and dressed.

After he had put his clothes on, he told his valet to send a message to Darius that he needed to change his plans for the wedding. Unlike in his dream, he had never made his intent to wed public. He'd always intended this ceremony to be quiet and secret, for Suzannah's safety. He'd still wished to have the ceremony held in St. George's—it was something his mother had wished for when he'd been younger. But St. George's was far too public.

It was better that he and Suzannah steal away and marry in a small parish church outside of London. Walsh and Balfour wouldn't be able to find them unless they followed him, and he would make sure that would not happen.

Darius arrived just as Kit was sitting down to a quick breakfast.

"You look like you've just come from hell, old friend," Darius said in concern. "Did you sleep at all?"

Kit jumped right to the point. "I decided we can't marry in St. George's."

"Oh?" Darius didn't argue, but he took a seat facing Kit at the table.

"I fear Walsh or Balfour might try something. We avoided announcing the wedding in the papers, but I worry it's not enough. I want to take Suzannah out of the city. I want to take her somewhere *safe* for the wedding, somewhere private."

"Very well. Palmer will be disappointed, as will Mrs. Swanson, but if something is worrying you, you should heed that instinct."

Kit rubbed his eyes and sighed before he looked at his old friend. "I've come to care about her. God knows how it happened so fast, but I can't let her be hurt because of me."

"I agree," Darius said. "Now that Walsh's debts have been called in, the man will be desperate. There is nothing to tie you to the debts, he will no doubt assume you're behind it. I admit, it worried me less when it was only *you* we had to watch out for. A young innocent is another matter entirely. Suzannah is a strong woman, but also kind and trusting. She would be an easy target for retaliation."

"Exactly." Kit was glad his friend agreed.

"What about the little church near your estate? You mentioned you wish to take Suzannah home for a time as a brief honeymoon. Would that parish suffice?"

Kit nodded. "Yes. That church is out of the way. Walsh and Balfour would not immediately think of it. I suppose the clergyman there will be furious at the unexpected ceremony, but so be it."

Darius chuckled. "No man of the cloth would ever refuse á hefty sum of coin donated to his parish. I'm sure the church roof has a leak or two."

"Send word to the others of the change of plans," Kit said. "I will tell Mrs. Swanson to pack up what she's been preparing and we can take her and Palmer with us to the country house." Kit would've preferred not to worry about having to escort his cook and his old butler to the country, but he couldn't exclude them from his wedding. Palmer and Mrs. Swanson had been in his life since he was a young boy. They were, in some ways, *family*. And Henry would have to come too, despite his leg, or else Suzannah would be upset, and Kit wouldn't allow that to happen.

"I'll see it done."

"Good. Let's plan to depart in two hours," Kit said. The quicker they could leave London, the better. He only prayed his enemies would not discover his plans.

MAYNARD WALSH STARED AT THE PILE OF LETTERS HE HAD OPENED a short time ago. His heart pounded, and there was a bitter taste in his mouth as his body started to spiral into terror. He held the top letter in one trembling hand as he reread the words.

DEAR MR. WALSH,

Your line of credit at our bank has not been extended at this time. A private group of investors have purchased your debts from us and have notified us of their desire to call in your debt. You have one week to pay the following amount—

. . .

MAYNARD DROPPED THE LETTER AND SWALLOWED HARD. HAD IT just been one debt, Thomas could have assisted him, but *all* of his debts had been called in at every institution. He had no way to pay that much back for several months, and *that* was assuming he could operate his shipping company without a single expense, which was impossible. He had dockworkers, sailors, and captains to pay, and those were just the most immediate expenses.

Kentwell was behind this, he had to be. It was too orchestrated, too perfectly timed. A well-delivered death blow.

He was finished. He couldn't recover from financial ruin like this. Maynard's gaze strayed to the drawer of his desk that held his pistol. He stared at it for a long moment, thinking of how easy it would be to use.

No, he should speak to Thomas first. Thomas always had a plan. When they had learned that the captain Thomas had paid to kill Kentwell had returned to England, Thomas had sent men to help the man "disappear."

Maynard collected the letters and shoved them into a small leather case before he left his office. Thankfully, Thomas was at home for once that evening. Maynard was used to spending hours trying to track him down, either at his club or the various brothels across London. When the butler showed Maynard into the drawing room, he found Thomas sitting on a settee scowling, a snifter of brandy in his hand.

"What is it, Maynard? Your sister is on her way, and you know I don't like to be disturbed when I have my time with her."

Maynard opened the leather case over a nearby reading table, and the creditors' letters spilled out.

"What are those?" Thomas demanded.

"What do you think?" Maynard snapped, his own temper flaring. "My credit lines have been closed. My debts have been called in."

"I'm sure I can cover them—"

"No, you can't. It's all of them, Thomas. *Every last one.*" He enunciated the last three words heavily.

Thomas set his glass of brandy down and stood, his gaze distant. "It's *him.*"

"Yes."

"Then I have more bad news. The captain, James Murray, still lives. It seems Kentwell came to his rescue and spirited him away. Five of my best men ended up unconscious in a tavern."

Maynard broke out into a cold sweat. "He's too strong, Thomas. We never should have sent him away. The man is a bloody mountain." When he had glimpsed Kentwell at the Lennox ball, he'd been terrified of the sight of him. The young, innocent lordling he had lured into his scheme was gone. Kentwell was now an unstoppable force of vengeance.

"If Murray had done what I paid him to do, we wouldn't be in this mess." Thomas paced the room, hands clasped behind his back. Suddenly he stilled, and a cruel smile stretched his lips. "Are you familiar with the legend of Achilles, Maynard?"

"No, can't say that I am." Maynard had always been more of a numbers man than literature.

"According to myth, Achilles's mother dipped his infant

body into the river Styx, which made him invincible to injury, all except for his heel, which was where she held on to him when she plunged him into the water. That one small spot was his weakness. What we need to do is strike out at Kentwell's weak spot. We must find his heel."

"But you said yourself he couldn't be beaten by your best men."

"Every man has a weak spot. Even a strong man cannot turn a knife in the back or a shot in the dark. When we strike, he must not see it coming, but it will bring him down. I've been tracking his movements, and we will find a time when he is vulnerable. We must be patient, that is all."

Maynard frowned. That was easier said than done. Balfour didn't seem to understand the depth of trouble they were in.

"I . . . think we should sell the company."

Thomas whirled on him. "What?"

"We cannot operate without capital. Lord Lennox sent me an offer to buy our company."

"Don't be a fool. Do not sign anything. Once Kentwell is dead, I think you'll find those calling in your debts will become more . . . lenient."

Maynard silently brewed with anger. The man was so full of undeserved confidence he had become blinded to reality. But Maynard held the majority of the shares and could sell without Thomas's permission. As much as he wanted to keep his company, he was not about to face debtors' prison over it.

"I should get back to my office," Maynard muttered and left Thomas alone. Let him plan murder—Maynard would plan for escape instead. If he sold the company to Lennox, he might get enough to sail to America and start over. It wasn't what he wanted to do, but it was his best option. He didn't want to deal with Thomas or his schemes ever again. He was done with him.

Suzannah stared at the front door of the quaint country church. In one hand she held a bouquet of pink peonies, which set off the frost blue of her silk wedding gown. Her hand trembled a little as she faced the open doorway.

"Are you all right?" Darius asked. He had stayed by her side every second that Kit had not been able to, except when she had changed into her wedding gown at a little inn a mile back on the road.

"Y—yes . . . Oh Lord, I am nervous, though."

"That is perfectly understandable. You've only known Kit a handful of days."

"Are you trying to bolster my spirits or dampen them, Lord Tiverton?" she asked, her voice now holding a slight edge to it.

He chuckled. "Bolster most certainly, but please understand that if I didn't think this was a good idea, I would have convinced Kit not to go through with it—for your sake as much as his."

Somehow, that reassured Suzannah. Darius was a nobleman, not because of his birth and title, but because of something deep within him. He was an honorable soul, and because of that, she trusted him.

"Kit is a good man. I only wish you could've known him

before he was sent away. This angry, brooding Kit, that is not the man he used to be."

They both stared through the interior of the church's open doorway. Kit was waiting for her at the altar.

"I'm glad to know him as he is now, even with his scars and pain. I love him, as foolish as that may seem. But I love him as he is, the man who suffered and fought to survive and come home. Maybe someday I will see that other softer, sweeter man, but this one waiting for me . . ." She nodded toward Kit. "He's the man who fights for what he believes in. He didn't come home for vengeance, no matter what he says. He came home for love, and I will give him mine."

The Duke of Tiverton blinked and cleared his throat. "I could trust no one else but you with my oldest friend, Miss Townsend."

Her eyes began to burn with her own tears. "Heavens, we shall both be weeping before we get to poor Kit, and he'll wonder what has happened." She tried to give the duke a watery smile as he discreetly wiped at his eyes.

"Quite right. Today's a day of joy, but Kit won't under-stand our tears of happiness."

The pair made the walk down the aisle with only Kit's friends and servants in attendance, all clustered toward the front. The mossy scent of old wood and recent rain, combined with the muted splashes of sunlight from the stained-glass windows, made everything perfect. Even the off-key organ being played by an elderly woman with thick spectacles, who kept having to peer at the sheet music over them before playing more than a few notes at a time, added to the effect. Suzannah would have wanted no other wedding than this. Henry and Mr. Palmer were in the front row, Henry sitting in a wheeled chair that they'd brought from London. He held a cloth bag of rice at the ready for when the ceremony was over.

Suzannah was lost to a wave of gratitude and love all around her, and when as she took Kit's hand and spoke her vows to love, honor, and cherish, she was somehow *found* again.

Oh, Papa . . . I wish you were here, she thought. *But know that I am happy, truly happy.*

Kit held her hand tight, making his own vows to love and honor her. His cheeks turned slightly pink as he added that he would cherish her. Her tall, handsome husband truly was a multifaceted gemstone. She knew his value, and it had nothing to do with his title or his money. He was a man who hadn't let life keep him down, no matter how often it struck him down. He kept getting back up, fists raised, ready to do battle once more.

Since she had lost her father, she had struggled and fought, but the world didn't see women or their struggles the way they did those of men. She may not have faced enemies upon a battlefield, but she'd fought every day for food on her table and candles to light her way at night when she worked. She'd fought off the unwanted advances of men and fought every day to have the world see her value.

Kit had seen past her situation and had seen her heart and talent the moment he'd met her. How could she not love a person who saw the truest version of others?

They were pronounced man and wife, and Kit took her in his arms and kissed her. She dropped the bouquet of peonies at her feet to curl her arms around him. Someone whistled appreciatively. The shrill sound had Kit pulling away sharply, searching the small parish church for danger. It took her a moment to realize his nightmare was coming back.

"Kit," she said, cupping his face. "I'm still here." She kept speaking softly until his gaze met hers and he calmed.

"Yes, yes. It's all right," he murmured to himself and squeezed her. "We should go. Mrs. Swanson will not want us to be late for the wedding breakfast."

Kit had sent some of his new staff ahead of them to his country home, Kentwell House, where they were preparing a breakfast for the small retinue of guests.

"Congratulations, Suzannah!" Henry bellowed with all the excitement of a young man his age. Rice pelted Suzannah and Kit as they passed by the boy.

"Not *inside*, blast you!" the clergyman cursed and marched over to Henry, demanding he surrender the bag of rice. Kit let out a loud, joyous laugh as he ushered Suzannah away from the commotion.

"I'll be finding rice everywhere for the next week," Suzannah said. It was in her hair and most certainly down the inside of her dress.

Kit ruffled a hand through his dark unruly hair, and rice cascaded over them both, making her laugh.

"And I shall have a pleasant time peeling away your clothing to look for stray grains," he whispered. Just like that, her body was flooded with heat and desire.

"Hush, we haven't even had our wedding feast."

Today was so different, so full of hope and light. If they could just find a way to send Walsh and Balfour to prison, they could live like this every day, with joy rather than always looking over their shoulders.

"Come along, *wife*," Kit teased as he led her to their waiting coach.

Her first glimpse of Kentwell House was through a wooded path lined with towering rhododendrons heavy in bloom. It reminded her of an old fairy tale castle that lay forgotten deep in the woods, hidden by enchantments of an old sorceress. An ancient magic hung in the air. She'd always liked old places, like crumbling castles and ancient rambling manor houses. Her father used to take her for picnics near old ruins. She would bring her sketch pad and try to capture the beauty of these forgotten places with her pencil.

Kentwell House was an old stone manor that, judging by the structure of the architecture, she guessed was built in the late 1600s. It was not done in the Tudor style, but a more medieval stonework. Green ivy flourished along the west wing, and in the east was a delightful mess of wildflowers and English roses where the garden had been left unattended for years.

The coach stopped, and Kit leapt out to help her down. She removed her bonnet and gloves, letting her bonnet hang like a basket by its ribbons on her arm as she followed Kit up the steps. Four other coaches soon followed, but Suzannah ignored the other guests as she waited for Kit to open the large oak door. When he did, her breath caught at the sight of the home's interior. Through the dust and the gloom, she saw the old glory of this place gleaming with promise. It was a manor waiting to be lived in, to be *loved* again. She bit her lip and followed Kit inside.

We are here, she thought. *We are home.*

"What do you think?" he asked. "Is it worth saving?"

She looked from her husband to the house, fighting back tears as she knew what he was truly asking her.

"Yes, most definitely worth saving."

A smile spread across Kit's face so bright that she felt it illuminate her like a late-spring sun.

"It will require a bit of work," he added.

She smiled back. "I'm not afraid of work. But first we have guests to tend to, and then our honeymoon."

The scoundrel playfully leered at her. "I need no reminding of *that*, darling wife. I promise you shall be *well* ravished."

"I shall hold you to that promise, husband." And she would, because Kit was an exquisite lover. All she had to do was hurry this wedding breakfast along so she and Kit could run off to the nearest bedchamber.

15

There was something wonderfully wicked about watching her half-naked husband dig up dead plants in the garden while Suzannah *pretended* to sketch the flowers and the house instead of his glorious body.

Suzannah had done a few quick sketches of the plants, of course, but the pages beneath that first were only of Kit. She had done her best to capture his powerful frame and the ribbons of muscle that defined his arms, and she was fairly satisfied with her work. Late-afternoon sunshine gleamed off his sweaty skin as he toiled away. Suzannah could not imagine any other titled gentleman would do such work shirtless, shovel in hand, working the land with such fervor and passion. The years Kit had labored in Australia had made him capable of handling any task set before him.

Suzannah, however, was more than content to sit upon the stone bench, her bright pink skirts pooled around her, to sketch and embrace the cool breeze. It had been two wonderful weeks since they'd arrived at Kentwell House for their wedding breakfast. Once the guests had gone, she and Kit had the house to themselves, except for Henry. Kit had taken the boy to the pond every day to fish on the dock, just the two of them. She had observed them in deep conversation from time to time. When she asked Henry once what he and Kit talked about, the young man had squared his shoulders and shook his head.

"'Tis subjects for gentlemen," was all the boy would say.

Naturally curious, Suzannah had climbed onto Kit's lap that evening, and after a fair number of coaxing kisses, she'd gotten him to reveal the general nature of his and Henry's discussions.

"I tell him the things my father told me at his age. Things about how a man should act, how he should treat women, how to conduct his business with honor. We live in a world where titles make a man, but someday things here will be more like in Australia where a man is judged by his deeds, not his birth. Henry shall need to learn to stand on his own as a good man."

After that, Suzannah hadn't worried about their secret talks. Whatever Kit was telling her young friend, it could only be to his benefit.

Everyone in the house, even the servants, soon fell into an easy rhythm of life, as if they had all lived there for decades. Suzannah woke every morning to Kit's eager mouth upon her body and his hands gently exploring her until she was begging for him to take her. As she lay sated and drowsy in bed, he and Henry would head for the pond, before returning to have lunch with her. And while Henry rested, she and Kit would tackle some part of the house or the grounds that needed their attention.

Often she would end up sketching new concepts for renovation or ways to rearrange the furniture while Kit did most of the heavy lifting. They worked together wherever they could, cleaning up the house and making a decent list of repairs needed, as well as furniture they would like to replace. They had also created a list of staff positions that would need to be filled. Suzannah had been concerned about the cost, but Kit's financial position was far better than when he'd left, thanks to his friends convincing his father to invest his remaining funds with Ashton Lennox.

Just after he'd been sentenced, his father had used most of his fortunes to help get Kit's sentence commuted from death to transportation, but after Kit had been sent to Australia, Lennox had stepped in and helped his father recover financially. The baron had a talent for doubling or tripling investments, and the fortune spent on saving Kit's neck from the noose had not only been recovered but added to. Once assured these changes to the house would barely touch Kit's wealth, she gave in to her own excitement at the possibilities of restoration and redecoration of the estate.

Having finished his work on the garden for now, Kit abandoned his digging and wiped his face on a cloth before coming toward her. She realized too late that Kit was stalking her like a tiger in the grass, and she squealed when he scooped her up from the bench and carried her to a large blanket he had laid out on the grass nearby.

"Kit!" She dropped her sketch pad in an attempt to hold on to him. He caught the book with one hand before he settled her beneath him on the grass. He placed his knees on either side of her body, trapping her beneath him as he opened the book of her drawings. His eyes widened, then narrowed.

"These are some *interesting* sketches of flowers," he mused as he paged through another few sketches. "Although the subject of your work seems to have shifted from flora to fauna."

"Oh, Kit, *really*." She rolled her eyes and reached for the sketchbook. He raised it out of her reach and kept her pinned beneath him on the ground.

"If it is nature in the raw that interests you, perhaps you need a better look at your subject." He set the pad aside and then bent to kiss her. She clutched at his shoulders, feeling the heat of the sun emanating from his bare skin. She moaned. He always felt so real to her, so impossibly, wonderfully alive.

"We are out . . . in the garden . . . ," she breathed between kisses.

"And?" he questioned before he nibbled her bottom lip. "It's my garden."

"We cannot do . . . what you're thinking . . . *outside*. Someone could see us."

Her husband chuckled as he kissed her neck. "Let them see. I care not."

"Oh, but I care—"

He silenced her with another heated kiss that was far too sinful for her to think through clearly. He pushed her thighs apart and reached up her skirts, finding his way to the heat of her. To her embarrassment and his delight, she was already wet and aching for him.

"Now I understand," he said. "My minx likes to watch me work in the yard. Makes you wet, does it, darling?"

It was true, and she dared not deny it, not with the way his fingers stroked her between her thighs and made her wild with sensual hunger. She gasped.

Kit worked to unfasten his trousers with a sinful chuckle. "Then I shall take you here among the roses until you scream with pleasure," Kit warned with a sinful chuckle as he worked to unfasten his trousers.

She wriggled beneath him, desperate for him to do exactly that. Their gazes locked just before he surged deep into her. She groaned as their hips collided with the force of his entry. Kit braced his body above hers and began to move roughly in Suzannah just the way she liked. Her body hummed with pleasure as she raised her hips to meet his, no longer caring that they were sprawled out on the lawn in full view of the house.

He was right—once he was deep inside her, she didn't care where they were. She dragged her nails along the back of his neck, and he hissed out a breath. His hips jerked in response to her caress. Just as he had discovered all the places that could drive her wild, she had learned much about him. Her husband had quite a few sensitive places, and whenever she encountered a new one with her mouth or hands, he went mad, bucking into her until she came hard enough to see stars.

"Naughty little creature, aren't you?" he grunted, punishing her with pleasure as he drove into her again and again.

She loved it when he spoke so wickedly to her and used his powerful body to make her feel like she was soaring through the clouds. He took her right to the edge of where she thought she couldn't stand another climax and drove her headlong into a burst of pleasure all over again.

"Yes . . . oh yes . . . Kit, *harder*," she begged, reveling in his fervent lovemaking. He pounded into her unrelentingly until her body unraveled and became nothing but a wave of beautiful, endless sensations. Her lashes fluttered as she sagged limp beneath him. He pumped twice more into her before roaring out his pleasure like some wild beast. Then he collapsed on top of her, letting her briefly feel his weight before he carefully moved off her. Her skirts were still up to her thighs, and the bright sun touched her pale skin. Kit reached out, placing one palm on her leg, and stroked her inner skin with his tanned fingertips. He seemed to marvel at the contrast of their skin, just as she did.

"You're so bloody soft, and yet your legs grip me so tight when I ride you," he said, his tone soft and heavy with satisfaction.

"I do not mean to grip you so hard . . . ," she confessed, slight worry in her voice. "Is a lady not supposed to . . . er . . . do that?"

"I like it. In fact, I quite *prefer* it. The first time I took you, I was worried you could not handle my strength. I often forget how strong I am." He was not bragging, for she heard concern in his voice. "But I discovered that despite how small you are, you're quite strong. It makes you perfect for me." He slid his hand up to the juncture of her thighs where she still recovered from the wake of her climax, and she jumped as he gently teased that sensitive area. She clapped her thighs together and begged for him to stop, which only made him roll over her and kiss her while his fingertips drew out a longer, softer climax.

"No more. Have mercy, husband, I beg you . . . ," she gasped at the abundance of pleasure that threatened to kill her.

"I suppose I shall have to carry you back into the house like some ancient warrior with his war prize. I think I'd like to strip you naked and take you hard among a bed of soft furs."

The image he painted for her nearly made her pass out. She couldn't stop imagining what it would feel like to have those soft furs rubbing against her breasts and belly while the rough hardness of him took her from above. Kit had introduced her to all sorts of wonderful positions to make love, some of which she'd never thought were possible.

"You are a wicked man," she replied, her breath still coming out in soft pants.

"And you love that about me," he said with smug confidence.

She agreed without hesitation. "I most certainly do. But is there something I can do so I can torture you with pleasure like you do me?" she asked quite seriously. She stroked a hand down his chest to his open trousers, closing her fingers around his half-erect shaft. He closed his eyes and let out a sigh of pleasure at her touch. He made it so easy to be bold, to touch him in places she would never have dreamed of touching a man.

Kit's eyes burned with wicked fire and his voice deepened. "If you wish to have *those* secrets, I shall be happy to teach you, but that we'd best do out of sight. If the servants saw you take my cock in that pretty little mouth, they would perish on the spot." He stroked his fingertip over her bottom lip.

Suzannah's womb clenched sharply in response to the image. This man had turned her into a wanton creature in such a short time. Her maidenly reservations were clearly and blessedly a thing of the past.

All she needed to do was take him into her mouth and do what he did to her when he feasted on her between her legs? That seemed simple enough. She tried to push him to lie on his back, but he resisted.

"Tonight, darling. You've exhausted me enough already, minx. Let your husband rest." He sighed and kissed her before he fixed his trousers and she fixed her skirts. They lay on their backs, watching the clouds drift through the vastness of the skies above. Kit was often quiet, but she'd learned that his silence did not come from anger or disinterest. His life had changed so much. He shared his thoughts often with her, but sometimes, like this, they both quietly enjoyed each other's presence without the need for words.

When she was on the verge of falling asleep, she reached over and caught his hand in hers, holding on to him.

"Was there anything about Australia that you didn't mind?" Suzannah had been coaxing him to open up more about his life in the colonies. He had shared stories of hunger, beatings, harsh weather and even harsher masters, as well as his deep longing for home.

Kit was quiet a long while before he spoke. "When you come to a place that feels like it's on the edge of a vast wilderness, it's as though you stand on the edge of the known world and that one more step will send you careening into the dangerous *unknown*. But it's there, at the edge of the world, that you see who you truly are and what you're capable of. You can either fall to your knees and give up or you can throw back your head and cry out, *'I have earned my place between the stones of the earth and the light of the stars above.'"*

She closed her eyes and imagined Kit doing that, shouting in defiance of the heavens. "I shall never know what that is like," she sighed.

"Oh, but you do," Kit said.

She opened her eyes and saw that he had turned to face her.

"Not all battles against the unknown are done in faraway places. Some occur right here." He touched a fingertip to her chest above her heart. "The moment you began painting my portrait, when you took the risk of coming home with me, you were having that moment. *I* was your wilderness, Suzannah, and you held your own against me."

A blush rose in her cheeks at his words.

"Kit, I really do love you," she whispered. She held her breath, waiting for him to say what she needed to hear most.

He squeezed her hand in return. "What little I remember of love holds no candle to what I feel for you. I believe there is no word capable of the summation of what my heart feels for you. Except to say that you are everything to me."

This time when he kissed her in the grass beneath the brilliant blue skies, she tasted his love, felt it burn clear through her. Loving Kit was like climbing up to the top of a mountain in the middle of a tumultuous storm and being gifted the power of lightning. His love electrified her and stopped her heart all at once before sending her flying back into life, feeling more alive than she ever had before.

"Thank you for *loving* me, Suzannah," he whispered against her lips.

If only he knew that love had been so easy to give. Love was the one resource a soul never ran out of. Love was a candle that never burned low. It was a light from a thousand stars on a cloudless night. It was the breeze in the sails of a ship far from home.

She wished in that moment that they didn't have to return to London, because she feared that she would lose him forever. But she was discovering that life was forever a lesson in learning to find joy, and someday . . . someday the specter of Kit's past would be gone forever, and she would be free to love him without the fear of losing him.

THE LAST FEW WEEKS IN THE COUNTRY WITH SUZANNAH HAD BEEN nothing short of heaven for Kit. He had never imagined he could feel like a young man again, with only hope and excitement ahead of him.

For long stretches during the day, he forgot he'd ever been away. As time went on, his painful memories from the colonies seemed to exist only in the land of dreams and nightmares, rather than the other way around. It was as though he and Suzannah had always lived together among the flowers and the towering trees that dappled the ground with sunlight.

Only at night, when the shadows settled around him and the smoke from extinguished candles coiled in the air like vipers, did the reality of the past return, and he remembered why he'd come home. *Revenge.* Walsh and Balfour still had to pay for their sins. He could not let that go, no matter the time that had passed. Now he began to wonder if his need for vengeance had, in fact, been a curse.

Suzannah was still working on her portrait of him, but he found he cared less about it than when he'd originally commissioned it. How had everything changed so quickly? He had come to London with his heart burnt to ash, yet between Suzannah and his old friends, his heart had risen from its ashes like a newly born phoenix.

"My lord?" Palmer said, disturbing Kit's ruminations. The butler stood in the doorway of the study that had once belonged to his father. It had been locked, but Kit had reopened it earlier in the day, cleaning out old papers and wiping dust off the bookshelves. The maids were far busier tending to other rooms.

"Yes?" He leaned back in his chair, hearing it creak ominously beneath him. It was another piece of furniture that would have to be replaced.

"A messenger came from London. It seemed urgent."

Kit bolted upright. "What is it?" He held out a hand for the letter, expecting bad tidings from Darius.

"It's actually for her ladyship," Palmer replied. "I was seeking her out and assumed she was with you."

"No, she's painting in the drawing room."

"Ah." The butler turned on his heel and left without another word. Kit smiled. The old man still adhered to strict customs and would not hand over the countess's letters, not even to her husband.

He followed Palmer down the corridor to where Suzannah was working.

"Oh, good morning, Mr. Palmer." Suzannah set her palette and paintbrush down before rubbing her nose with the back of her hand. The action smeared paint over the tip of her nose, confirming his belief that she was as adorable as she was talented. He wanted to see her progress, but she would not allow it. She insisted on revealing the portrait only when it was ready, and he was content to agree.

"I have a letter for you, my lady. It was delivered from London. The messenger said it was urgent." Palmer walked over and passed the letter to her.

"For me?"

Suzannah's gaze turned to Kit, but he had as little idea about its contents as she. She took the letter and broke the seal, unfolding the paper to read the message.

"It's from Flory."

"Flory?" Kit vaguely remembered the name but couldn't recall from where.

"The stage manager at the theater. Someone's ruined the sets for the play! All my work . . . Oh, Kit, we must go back to London. I need to fix the sets. They don't have anyone else who can work as quickly as I can."

The hazy contentment he felt slipped away, but she was right—Suzannah would have to go back. The play and crew needed her. He would not deny her something that mattered so much to her.

"Palmer, please have Nolan pack my things and one of the maids pack Suzannah's clothing for our return to London. Have our coach made ready."

"Are we all to return with you?" Palmer inquired.

"You, Henry and Mrs. Swanson, yes. Leave half the footmen and maids here to continue cleaning. While we're back in London, we'll begin the hunt for new staff as well as new furnishings."

"Yes, my lord." Palmer left them alone.

Kit caught Suzannah by the shoulders. "Darling," he breathed. That term of endearment came so easily to him when he spoke to her. "It will be all right. We shall be back in London this very evening, and you can go to the theater straightaway. I'll go with you."

"You will?" she asked, the hope in her voice knifing through his heart.

"Of course, darling. If there is any way I can help, I shall." He cupped her face with a soft smile, then brushed the paint from her nose. He kissed her deeply. She melted into him and he felt as though he was falling, but in a wonderful, wild, uncontrolled sort of way, like when he'd been a lad and rolled down a hillside meadow, gaining speed.

"I love you," he whispered against her lips. She stilled, her mouth trembling a little, and he opened his eyes to look at her.

"You do? You're certain?"

In answer, he kissed her again, opening his heart fully to her. He felt her arms tighten around his back in response as she sensed his love and reciprocated it.

I love you, I love you, I love you . . . , he repeated over and over in the most ancient language of love that needed no words to be understood. He would let no shadows gather, not now, not when he was so full of light.

16

Flory paced nervously behind Suzannah. "Do you think you can fix it before the house opens this evening?" He nodded at the ruined scenic drops she'd worked so painstakingly on.

Suzannah glanced at Kit. "If we put our all into it. And perhaps if someone could help us with the underpainting?"

"I'll see who I can spare," Flory said. He turned to say something to a man who was with him, but a crash from behind Suzannah's scenic drop stopped him.

The play was opening tonight, and there was still much work left to do. After a frantic day of work, she had managed to repaint the damaged sets. Other props and even parts of the theater had been damaged as part of the mysterious vandalism, but Suzannah's responsibility was limited to the backdrops.

Kit put an arm around Suzannah's waist and kissed her temple. "I know we've been here most of the day, and I wish I could stay longer, but I'm afraid I have to go, darling.

Darius is here. He'll keep watch and escort you home tonight."

She could see Darius and Vincent standing side by side at the edge of the stage. She didn't want Kit to leave, but he and Vincent were meeting with a magistrate today to discuss Captain Murray's testimony, and Kit could not miss such a meeting.

Reaching up, she brushed a spot of green paint from Kit's cheek with her smock apron, making him smile in a charmingly boyish way.

"I'll see you tonight." He stole another kiss, this one far less innocent, which roused a few whistles from the stage-hands nearby. Blushing, Suzannah shoved at him.

"Go on, you mustn't be late."

He smiled at her and gave Darius a slap on the shoulder before he and Vincent left. With a sigh, she turned back to her work.

Three hours later, she'd done all that she could to repaint the countryside and the villa scenic drops, which had been crudely painted over. It wasn't her best work, but it would suffice.

Jude strolled over to her, admiring her work. "Always working miracles."

Suzannah chuckled. "I try."

"How's Henry?"

"Better. His leg is healing. We're having to remind him to rest."

Jude laughed. "That sounds like the lad. And you? Flory said you married that man who came here. Lord Kentwell?"

"Yes . . ." This time her answering smile was softer, sweeter. "Oh, Jude, you were right. He has been so wonderful. He is so close to banishing that darkness inside him."

"Because he loves you," Jude said.

"Yes, and because I love him." She couldn't hide her blush this time, but she didn't care. She was too happy to care whether she looked silly for loving him.

"And what about him?" Jude pointed to Darius. "He always has someone watching you?"

"Kit has enemies, and he worries they might come after me. He worked with me all morning but had to leave, so he had Darius take his place."

Jude watched Darius lounging near the changing screens where the actresses were. But the man's eyes were on Suzannah, not on the pretty women preening nearby.

"I never thought I would see the day where a duke played watchdog."

"You know him?" Suzannah asked Jude, quite surprised.

"Not personally. But I've seen him around the city. He assists the Bow Street Runners from time to time. That is something I would like to do, but they will not hire a man like me. Tiverton seems to be a good man. He's been in some rather dangerous situations from what I've heard. Your husband chooses his friends well."

"Yes, he does."

When they'd returned to London, Kit had learned that their plan for Ashton Lennox to buy Walsh's shipping company interest had been successful. And since Lennox hadn't pay Walsh enough to satisfy all of his debts, so Walsh disappeared shortly after to hide from the remaining creditors who were actively hunting him. Balfour was quiet too, which Suzannah knew worried Kit.

He'd been notified that his cases were under review by a chief magistrate, and Suzannah feared that the two men were planning to find a way to avenge themselves upon Kit.

"Well, I finished what I needed to do." Suzannah squeezed Jude's hand. "I should go home."

"You're missing opening night?" he asked.

"Only this one. I'm simply too tired. But I was thinking of inviting Kit and his friends to come to the next performance." She always loved opening night, but repainting everything in such a short time had exhausted her.

"I shall see you later," Jude said.

"Good night," she called after him before she collected her bag of paint supplies and carried it over her shoulder to Darius. He made polite excuses to the three actresses who were giggling and batting their lashes.

"My deepest apologies, my beautiful ladies, but I must escort Lady Kentwell home to her husband."

The actresses all swooned as if Darius had broken their hearts.

"Do you suppose Kit and Vincent will be home in time for dinner?" she asked.

He took the bag from her and slung it over his shoulder. "I believe so. They should be back by now. I can't imagine it would take more than three hours for Mr. Murray to provide his account of events to the magistrate."

Suzannah and Darius exited the theater. He helped her into the coach and hit his fist on the roof to signal they were ready to leave.

"Kit said you would be willing to come to one of the performances?" she asked hopefully.

Darius chuckled. "Yes, we are all coming. He's rather proud of your work, you know."

"Is he?" She knew she was fishing for compliments, but she couldn't help it.

"Most proud," Darius assured her. "He's thinking about asking the king to commission you for a portrait."

"What?" she gasped. "*The* king?"

"Yes." Darius grinned. "*The* king."

"Oh heavens . . . oh Lord . . ." She closed her eyes, suddenly dizzy at the thought of even being in the same room as the king.

"He's just a person," Darius replied. "*Quite* human. Don't forget, you are now a titled lady within his social circle. Lady Kentwell . . . wear the title with pride."

"Still, he is the king, and up until a short time ago, I was just a poor painter," Suzannah almost moaned. "What would I even say to the king? What does one talk about with royalty?"

He chuckled. "With royalty? You simply sit back and allow them to do the talking. In my experience, they don't need anyone to add a thing to their conversations."

Darius suddenly sat up and peered through the curtains of the coach.

"What is it?" she asked.

"We didn't take the left turn we should have—"

The coach jolted to a stop, and their driver shouted at someone. A pistol fired, someone cried out, and through the small window Suzannah saw a body fall from the top of the coach to the ground.

"Get down!" Darius gripped her arm and pulled her to the floor of the coach. "Don't do anything unless I tell you."

He pulled out a pistol that he had hidden under his coat. "Take this." He pressed it into her palm. "Do you know how to use it?"

She nodded numbly. Kit had taught her how to fire one while they were at the country estate. But shooting at bits of chopped logs was very different than shooting at a person.

Darius pulled out a thin rapier from underneath the seat of the coach. How many weapons did he have stashed nearby?

The coach door was thrown open and Darius flew out, sword ready as he stabbed the man who'd wrenched open the door. She could hear the blade sink into flesh, and she covered her mouth, swallowing down a wave of nausea.

Focus! she silently yelled at herself as she held the pistol ready and stayed crouched on the floor. The clang of steel and the grunts of men fighting echoed all around her.

"Find the woman and kill the spare!" a hard voice yelled.

Darius suddenly appeared inside the coach and grabbed Suzannah, hauling her out the other door. For a moment she stood there, frozen with terror.

"Run, *run!*" he bellowed and shoved her ahead of him.

If there was one thing she could do, it was run. She dared look back only once. Darius was silhouetted against the moonlight as he stood his ground, blocking the men from getting to her. His rapier gleamed dangerously in the moonlight. She felt like a coward for leaving him like this, but she would only endanger them both if she stayed. She had no way of defending herself against these men with only one gun.

Men converged on Darius, and the sounds of a struggle followed by a single gunshot echoed all around her, making her gasp.

"Find her!" The voices were like the howling of wolves as the men hunted her. She took a blind turn and found herself at a dead end. Trapped. She spun around, raising the pistol at the men who now advanced on her.

"Come here, pretty bird," one man crooned as they fanned out around her, closing in. "Put away the pistol—you'll only make it worse for yourself. We were told to bring you in alive, but no one said anything about not breaking a few bones." The man cracked his knuckles as he stretched his hands, as though eager to curl his fingers around her neck and squeeze.

He was right, she knew logically that one bullet would not save her, but knowing she could at least reduce their numbers by one . . . That was something, wasn't it? One less man out there to hurt other women.

Suzannah waited until the biggest man was close enough to touch her, then fired. The light in the man's eyes flickered and then died. He fell to his knees and then toppled over. She stared at him and then back at the other men.

"Little bitch!" one of the men shouted and hit her hard in the cheek with a meaty fist. She crumpled from the blow but didn't pass out. She was lifted up over a man's shoulder, who carried her down the street past a field of bodies, some writhing in pain, others unmoving. One body she recognized with terror and heartbreak.

"Darius . . . ," she wheezed through the pain in her skull. He couldn't be dead . . . He couldn't. *Oh God, please no . . .*

Jude saw the horrifying last moments of the fight in the
alley near the theater. Suzannah fell when one of the men
hit her. Jude's fists clenched, and he nearly stepped out of
the shadows to intervene. But four-to-one odds were
beyond what he could win, at least without a weapon.
Where the devil was Lord Tiverton? The man should be
here—

Jude's stomach dropped when he noticed a finely
dressed body among the carnage by the coach. Tiverton had
fallen defending Suzannah . . .

The men who carried Suzannah passed by the bodies
and climbed into another carriage, which soon vanished
into the darkness. The wounded hobbled away as Jude
rushed over to the fallen duke, turning the man's body over.
He had taken a bullet to his shoulder and a knife to the
stomach. The blade was still partially buried in him.

"Christ . . . ," Jude muttered.

Tiverton's lips parted and he gave a barely audible
whisper. "Suzannah . . ."

"*Christ!*" Jude said again with a frightened shout. The
man was still alive!

"Hold on, Your Grace." Jude examined the blade's loca-
tion and noticed the tight weave of Tiverton's silk waistcoat, which seemed to wrap around most of the blade. Silk
was strong, and even the sharpest blades could only lightly
pierce the material unless thrown with great force and
great speed. After this careful examination, Jude felt it was
safe to remove the blade. To his relief, his hopes were
confirmed. The blade had barely sunk into Tiverton's flesh.

He lifted Tiverton up onto his shoulders, carrying him toward the coach that had been abandoned. The driver was dead, but Jude knew how to handle a team of horses.

He placed the duke into the coach, made a makeshift bandage for his shoulder, and climbed into the driver's seat. He lashed the horses' flanks with the leather ribbons and clicked his teeth. The horses bolted into motion. Jude knew where to go. He only prayed the man did not die before he reached his destination.

Kit stared at the clock on the mantel in the drawing room. Suzannah and Darius should have been home by now.

"Something's wrong," he muttered to Vincent.

His friend took a sip of scotch and then stood, collecting his pistol from a nearby table. "I agree. Darius is *never* late."

"We must go to the theater. Find out when they left and whether anyone was asking after them." They moved quickly, meeting Palmer in the corridor. Kit was about to tell him they were leaving when a footman approached.

"My lord . . . Lord Tiverton's coach just arrived."

Kit raced toward the front door, but his relief plummeted into despair as a dark-skinned man leapt down from the coach, calling for help.

"What's happened?" Kit asked as he reached the man and grabbed his arm.

"Lord Tiverton is gravely injured. Some men took Miss Townsend. His Grace tried to fight them off, but there were too many. They took her."

The man flung the carriage door open. Darius's limp

body lay across the coach seat, blood dripping down his fingertips from a shoulder wound. His face was pale, lifeless.

Kit leaned against the side of the coach, fighting to breathe. Suddenly he was back on the transport ship, trapped between the bodies and the deep blue sea. Helpless. Broken. *Dying* on the inside.

"Oh God!" Vincent shouted as he jumped into the coach, grasping his friend by the shoulder. "Come on, old man, you can't do this. You hear me?"

"Not . . . dead . . ." Darius's voice broke through the agony that was squeezing Kit's heart like a vise. "Stop . . . *shouting.*"

"Bloody hell, Kit, we need a doctor!" Vincent's words snapped Kit out of a spiraling panic.

"You, what's your name?" he demanded of the dark-skinned man.

"Jude."

"Go to Wemple Street, house number seventeen, and fetch Dr. Jordan."

Jude nodded and then glanced at the coach. "Shouldn't I take Tiverton to him? I can drive the team."

In his panic, Kit had missed the obvious. "Yes, of course. Vincent, you must go with them. I must go after Suzannah." Kit turned back toward the house. Vincent called to him, and Kit turned back.

"Kill them, Kit," Vincent said. "Show *no* mercy." He tossed Kit his pistol.

"I have none to give." Walsh and Balfour would die for this, and if Suzannah was hurt, Kit would tear them to pieces with his bare hands. He'd tried not to be a monster, but now they'd created one by taking his wife and gravely wounding his dearest friend.

The next few minutes were a blur as Kit donned dark clothing and had a footman fetch every weapon in the house. Soon he had two pistols and two short daggers tucked away in his coat and boots. As he came down the stairs he found Warren, Felix, and Lionel all in the entryway arguing over what had happened.

"Kit, is it true? Darius is . . . ?" Felix began, but he didn't finish.

"He's wounded. Vincent is taking him to a doctor," Kit said. He didn't dare say more—they couldn't afford the distraction that Darius may at that moment be dying. Darius would want them to rescue Suzannah and deal with the bastards who'd caused all of this pain.

Lionel spoke up next. "Palmer said Suzannah has been kidnapped."

Kit only nodded. He couldn't bear to say the words aloud. It would make this nightmare too real.

Warren checked the pistol he held and frowned. "What's our plan?"

"We find the men who took my wife and *end* their lives. If we're found out, there is no guarantee the courts would look kindly on our actions. We may all be convicted of murder. If you aren't able to take that risk, I understand."

"We've always stayed by you, Kit," Felix said. "That's never changed."

Kit wished none of what was to come had to happen. Lives, even bad ones, were not easy to take, but Walsh and Balfour had left him no choice.

"Where do you think they would take her?" Lionel asked.

"I . . ." Kit realized he had no idea.

"My lord, if I may interject . . ." Palmer came toward him, holding a letter. "This was just delivered by messenger." Palmer passed the letter over to Kit, and Kit read its contents aloud.

"By now you know we have your prized possession. If you want her back, be on the deck of the Wind Sprite, *you know where, in one hour."*

It wasn't signed, but Kit recognized Balfour's handwriting.

"Where does the *Wind Sprite* dock?" Warren asked.

"Where it always has, at one of the wharves at the Thames, I presume. I didn't even know Walsh still had that ship after all these years."

"You know this is a trap," Felix warned.

Kit crumpled the letter in his hand. "Does it matter? I have to go. God knows what they're doing to my wife. She could be hurt or—"

"All I'm suggesting is that we come up with a plan of our own, rather than a headlong charge," Felix said. "And I may have an idea we can use."

"I'm listening," Kit said, and they all leaned in to hear Felix's plan.

~

SUZANNAH WOKE UP ON THE FLOOR OF A CELL, THE WORLD rocking gently beneath her. The sound of waves lapping against wood told her she was on a ship. Her body ached everywhere. She squinted around her in the darkness.

"This is a terrible idea!" someone hissed in the shadows.

"Shut up, you fool. You and I are committed to this now. You cannot back out," another voice growled. The two voices came closer, and a golden light illuminated the room as Maynard Walsh and Thomas Balfour stepped inside. Balfour clutched a lantern in one hand and raised it to shine on Suzannah.

"Good, she's awake," he said.

Suzannah scrambled to stand up and tried immediately to retreat from the male voices. Her legs collided with several large crates behind her, which forced her to stop. She was in some sort of storeroom rather than a cell. She knew little of ships, even though her father had worked more than twelve years as a shipping clerk.

"I can't believe you kidnapped her," Walsh muttered. "If he didn't want to kill us before, he certainly will now."

"All we need is for him to come for her." Balfour looked to Suzannah. "And he will, won't he?"

A chill slithered down her spine as she stared at the men who had ruined Kit's life, and hers.

"Why are you doing this? Why can't you leave Kit alone?" she demanded.

"Why?" Balfour stared at her as if she'd gone mad. "My dear, you simply cannot understand what he's done. The man's a criminal of the worst sort."

"He's no criminal. You used him, arranged for him to take the blame for your own crimes. And now he has proof. That's it, isn't it? He plans to send you both to Newgate."

Walsh's face paled. "You see—he told her."

"I never imagined he would tell a woman anything."

Suzannah stared at Balfour. This man had no understanding of love or why a man would trust a woman, or vice versa. Balfour was a coward and a bully.

"If you think I matter so little, then you can't think Kit would come for me," Suzannah said brazenly.

Balfour's lips curled up in a snarl. "Oh, he'll come for you. A man will do a lot for a pretty chit." His gaze raked down her body, coldly assessing her. She wanted to cover herself even though she was still fully clothed, but she didn't dare move an inch lest she betray any sign of weakness.

"Thomas, let's go," Walsh begged.

"Not yet. We have to set the scene for him, just like in one of those silly little plays you paint backdrops for. Yes, we'll give Kentwell quite the tableau . . ." He handed the lantern to Walsh, who set it down on a nearby crate. Balfour came toward her, his eyes gleaming dangerously.

Suzannah reached up into the coils of her hair, found a thin paintbrush that she usually used to keep her hair in place, and the moment Balfour lunged, she struck, plunging the sharp end of the paintbrush into his face. It sank into his cheek, blood spraying out, and he howled. But her victory was short-lived.

"I'll wring your little neck!" he snarled and grabbed her arm, flinging her toward the wall. She struck the wood paneling and lights dotted across her eyes, but she turned back to face Balfour, teeth bared, ready to fight them with all of her strength.

17

K it crept up the rope ladder that hung down the side of the *Wind Sprite*'s hull as it floated in the harbor. He left the small dinghy that he'd rowed up to the *Wind Sprite* and tied it to the ladder. The ship wasn't moored close to the docks, but was anchored farther out on the water and reachable only by boat.

Everything was quiet, but that was to be expected. It was a trap, after all. As he reached the quarterdeck, he checked the ship, searching for his enemies and his wife. No guards were present—it was as if the ship was deserted. He had commanded his friends to wait for him on the dock and watch for trouble. Felix was to fetch the nearest constable and lie in wait for Kit to signal when he'd found Suzannah and she was safe. No matter what happened aboard the ship, he didn't want Walsh, Balfour, or their hired men to flee, and the dock was the only avenue of escape.

He located the gangway down to the deck below and began searching room by room, one of the daggers ready in

273

his palm. He neither saw nor heard a single thing. Walsh must have sent the entire crew off the ship before Kit arrived. It wasn't until he went down another deck that he finally found Suzannah. She lay in a storeroom, her bright green gown trailing out from behind some crates. Someone had set a lantern on one of the crates nearby, illuminating the room.

He knew that if he entered that room he might never walk out of it again, but if he didn't . . . he would not have the chance to get his wife to safety. For the first time in seven years, revenge was not the most important thing on his mind. Love was. Love for Suzannah was the only thing that mattered.

"Suzannah!" He rushed toward her and rolled her onto her back. She was bleeding from her bottom lip, and a heavy red mark covered one side of her face. Someone had struck her. Her gown was in tatters with blood was splattered over her bodice. Other than her face, she seemed unharmed, so the blood was clearly someone else's, which meant Suzannah had put up quite a fight. She moaned as he cradled her in his arms and knelt on the floor. He could barely speak as Suzannah's lashes fluttered open.

"Please, be all right," he breathed. "Please," he murmured as he held her as the treasure she was to him. "I'll never let anyone hurt you ever again."

"Kit . . . you're here . . ." She started to smile, but the smile slipped into horror as the color drained from her face. "You must leave . . ."

"It's too late for that," Balfour said from behind Kit, who stiffened but didn't take his eyes off his wife. "Drop your weapon."

"Let me put Suzannah ashore and you can do what you wish with me," Kit said, his hand still clutching the dagger.

Suzannah grasped his arms, frantically shaking her head. "No," she begged. "We will face this together," she insisted as she tried to sit up.

"No, you must go," Kit whispered. "The others are waiting to take you to safety." He spoke the words so softly that only she could hear them.

"I'm afraid you're both staying," Balfour interrupted. "*Drop* the blade."

Kit slowly crouched and set the blade down upon the floor. Then he helped Suzannah stand and put her behind him as he faced Balfour. The man had a pistol aimed at Kit's chest. Walsh was hovering nearby. His gaze darted nervously around. Here they were, the men who had ruined his life, believing they had gotten the better of him.

For years, he'd thought they had succeeded in destroying him, but they had failed in the one way that mattered. He had someone to live for, not a cause to die for. So long as Suzannah was alive, Kit would fight to save her.

"She has no part in this. You have me. Let her go," Kit insisted.

Balfour ignored him. "Fetch the manacles," he said to Walsh, who produced a pair of iron shackles.

Balfour pointed at an iron bar half-embedded in the wood wall where crates were tied up to keep them from shifting. "Bind his hand to that railing."

Walsh approached Kit, forcing himself between Kit and Suzannah, who had to take a shaky few steps backward from them. Kit held still as the other man clicked one manacle around his wrist and the other to the iron bar.

Every instinct in him shouted that he should grab Walsh by the throat, but if he did, Balfour would shoot either him or Suzannah.

When Walsh finished securing one of Kit's hands to the wall, he retreated to stand behind Balfour.

"There, you have me. I cannot do anything against you, Balfour. Now let my wife go," Kit pressed. He hoped that by agreeing to Balfour's demands he could buy Suzannah's safety.

Balfour studied the pistol he held as if he was bored. "We had everything we wanted. The company, the money. You'd played your part. I don't fault you for surviving your time in Australia, you know. Not really. But you should have had the good sense to stay there. To come back to England on a foolish, pointless quest for vengeance. Such pride. I'd have thought the colonies would have beaten that out of you." His gaze moved from the gun to Kit, his eyes cold. Had Kit been alone with Balfour, he would have laughed at the challenge his gaze held, but Suzannah was in danger, and he could only think about doing what he must to protect her.

"You can still walk away, Balfour. You don't have to do this. You and Walsh can leave England."

Walsh started to nod as he agreed with Kit's suggestion.

"Me? Why should I have to go anywhere? You bankrupted Maynard, and as for me . . . Well, you've ruined everything. I'm being investigated for all of the cases where I sent people to the noose or had them transported. Do you know how hard it is to open an inquiry into a magistrate?" Balfour snapped. "We are like gods among men. And yet somehow you lined the right pockets with coin, and now everything I've built will be destroyed. I am owed all that I've taken."

"You sent innocent people to die," Kit replied.

"As if you care about anyone other than yourself. What are those poor pathetic creatures but dirt beneath one's feet? Even you, the son of an earl, didn't deserve the trappings of wealth. You were born into that life, yet you didn't deserve it."

Kit said nothing. He slowly reached a hand to Suzannah, hoping to pull her behind his body, but he couldn't quite reach her.

"Everything that happens now, Kentwell . . . is because of your insolence." That was Kit's only warning of the danger that was coming. Balfour raised the gun toward Kit, but then he swung his arm toward Suzannah.

"No!" Kit lunged for her, but the iron manacle stopped him. He jerked to an abrupt halt, his hand grasping Suzannah's arm. She cried out as the bullet struck her, and when she stumbled a step it was in his direction. He pulled her toward him, catching her.

"It will be such a *tragic* story for the papers," Balfour said. "A crazed convict kills his wife, then in a fit of grief ends his own life by burning the very ship he robbed all those years ago."

Suzannah struggled for breath as Kit held her against his chest. He could feel her blood sinking through his clothes from her body. He stared at Balfour, that old rage that had kept him alive in his darkest times rising to the surface once more. It raced through his blood like liquid fire.

"You will suffer for this," Kit growled. "You will beg for mercy and you will find *none*."

Balfour smiled. "That will be difficult if you're already dead." Then he and Walsh backed out of the room. The lantern on the crate sputtered, and the shadows closed in. Kit sank to the floor, holding Suzannah as she bled. So *much* blood coated her chest. It was just like his nightmare of the wedding all over again.

"Kit . . . I'm . . . sorry," Suzannah whispered, her voice wavering with pain.

He brushed her hair back from her face and tried to stay calm for her, but he could not hide the pain from his voice. "For what? You have nothing to apologize for."

"For . . . for everything. If my father hadn't spoke against you to protect me . . ."

Even facing her own death, she thought only of his life. That thought shattered him in a way nothing else could. His darling little painter.

"You have *nothing* to be sorry for, you hear me?" he said, his tone rough. "I would have done nothing differently. *You* are the only thing in my life that was ever worth saving."

Something wet rolled down his face and dripped onto Suzannah's cheek.

"Don't cry," she begged, her eyes dark with worry. "Please."

He was indeed crying, because his heart was breaking and nothing he could do could stop it. He couldn't save her . . .

"Don't lose yourself in the storm," she breathed. "Find your way back . . . to shore . . . no matter what happens." Her eyes closed as she slipped into unconsciousness.

Far away, he heard a distant crash and a sudden roar of flames. Walsh and Balfour had set the ship on fire. Numbly, he stared down at Suzannah, feeling that storm she'd warned about raging in his very soul.

"Don't lose yourself..."

Smoke crept down the corridor toward the storeroom where he and Suzannah were.

"Don't lose yourself in the storm..."

But he wasn't lost. He was not on a ship being battered about upon the seas in a storm. He *was* the storm.

Flames could be seen now down the hall, and he could hear the ship creaking and groaning like an old beast dying. They didn't have long before the ship would take on water and sink beneath the waves. He set Suzannah down and planted one of his feet on the wall while grasping the manacle's chain with both of his hands and pulled with all his might. Nothing. He tried again and again until the strength died within him.

He slumped, spent, and glanced at Suzannah's body. She'd blamed herself for all this, but she was wrong. It was his fault. If he hadn't sought revenge, she wouldn't be here now. If he hadn't fallen in love with her, she wouldn't be...

The rage came roaring back, but it was a rage born of love, not vengeance. He gave a wild, animalistic howl and pulled the chain with the biblical might of Sampson. The wood creaked and the iron bar bent just an instant before the wood holding it in place snapped. He stumbled away from the wall. Kit jerked the chain up the length of the pole and off of it. Panting, he knelt and picked Suzannah up in his arms before he left the storeroom.

The smoke and heat of the fire were almost overpowering as he stumbled up the gangway toward the next deck, but a wall of flames blocked his way before he could get to the quarterdeck above. The smoke began to blind him, forcing him to turn around and seek another way out. There *had* to be another way. He ran the length of the corridor and found another set of steps. His chest burned as though he were breathing in fire.

He stumbled upon the last few steps, but he reached the top. Clean air met his lungs as he landed on the quarterdeck, but everything around him was burning. The little boat he had rowed up to the ship was gone. The distant figures of Walsh and Balfour were rowing toward the docks on the dinghy.

Men ashore were screaming *"Fire!"* as the docks came alive with calls for help. Other nearby vessels were now at risk of being set ablaze. Frantic sailors rushed to move the ships as fast as they could away from the *Wind Sprite.*

Kit didn't have time to think of another way off the ship. If he and Suzannah didn't get off now, they would die. He didn't dare think that Suzannah might already be gone, because the moment he did, he would be gone too. There would be nothing left for him in a world without her.

"Hold on, my love," he whispered to Suzannah as he approached the railing.

There was only one way off the vessel. *Down.*

He held her tight and jumped into the dark water far below. The impact hit his body like stone. He and Suzannah plunged deep beneath the surface. In those inky depths, he struggled to hold on to his wife, one arm around her waist while he kicked desperately toward the surface. The fire's glow illuminated the air above the water, giving him a direction to swim toward until he broke through.

Kit began to swim on his back, keeping Suzannah's head above the water as he swam toward the distant docks nearly two hundred yards away. The tempest within him was still raging, the force of his love giving him the strength to keep going when he should have nothing left.

Every moment under the lash of a whip, every time he'd faced danger and death in Australia, those moments of pain and hardship had prepared him for this day when Suzannah would need him not to give up.

With every stroke he took, his heart beat hard and strong, each pulse saying one name. *Suzannah—Suzannah.* His heart was hers, had always been hers. Everything in the universe now spiraled into this single moment. He could not afford to fail her.

"Kit!" Warren shouted as he dove off the docks and swam toward them. When he reached them in the water, Kit felt his body give out.

"Take her. She's hurt—" Kit gasped. He sank briefly below the water as she was taken from him before kicking his way up again. Felix climbed down a ladder into the water and helped carry Suzannah up onto the dock.

"You must get the water out of her lungs!" Kit's words came out a husky, smoke-filled croak. When he finally reached the ladder, he no longer had the strength to pull himself up, so he clung to the bottom rung and floated below the dock. His body was shaking hard, and he had to focus on catching his breath.

Warren grasped Kit by the arm and pushed him up the

ladder while supporting him from below. "Come on. Up you go, old boy."

Others grasped Kit's waist as he reached the top of the ladder. He nearly collapsed twice, but they stayed with him until he'd reached Suzannah. Felix had Suzannah on her back and was breathing into her mouth while pinching her nose closed. Then he pressed on her chest with his palms in a rhythmic pattern. Her body seized and water flooded from her mouth. She coughed, then lay still, breathing steadily.

"She's bleeding," Felix said. "What happened?"

"Balfour shot her." Kit sank to his knees beside his wife, the weight of the world crushing down on him as he wished he could take her pain, her suffering, and carry it alone for her.

"It looks as though the bullet passed through her shoulder. She's lost a fair amount of blood," Felix said. "We need to get her to a doctor at once."

Kit watched the men around them running to help the other ships move away from the sinking *Wind Sprite*, and his eyes fell on Lionel who stood a short distance away. He had a pistol trained on Walsh and Balfour, who were trapped against the edge of the docks on their knees, hands slightly raised in the air.

"We've summoned the authorities," Felix said to Kit. "They should be here any minute."

Kit nodded and lifted Suzannah in his arms, and she stirred, her lashes fluttering open.

"Kit . . . ," she breathed, and her lips trembled upon a smile.

"Hold on, my darling," he whispered. "Just hold on."

Warren stayed close, taking a pistol from Felix as they left the docks.

Balfour suddenly screamed at Kit's back like a madman. "Why won't you die?!"

"Kit, look out!" Lionel shouted, and Kit spun. He had only an instant to shield his wife with his body before he heard the crack of a pistol. He flinched, expecting the bite of a bullet, but felt nothing.

Balfour was kneeling on the dock, a pistol in his hand as he stared at Kit. Blood blossomed on his chest as he fell face down on the deck.

"What . . . ?" Kit then realized that someone had shot Balfour before he could fire.

"That . . . was for our fathers," Suzannah said in a breathless voice. She held a spent pistol in her hand, which she had taken from Warren, who stood staring at her in shock.

Suzannah's fingers loosened and she slipped back into unconsciousness, and Warren took the gun from her. "I'll call for a hackney, Kit."

Kit held Suzannah the entire ride to Dr. Jordan's residence. Only then did he allow Warren to take her from him. A middle-aged woman acting as a nurse helped him into the medical room, and Kit collapsed into a chair beside the bed where his wife now lay.

"Do not fear, my lord, she will most likely live." The doctor's words were the last thing he remembered before he sank into a long-delayed oblivion.

～

Suzannah was beneath the surface of the sea, light shimmering above her. She struggled toward it, moving sluggishly, her limbs encumbered by the water all around her. At last, she broke the surface and sucked in a deep breath. Her lashes fluttered as she realized there was no water, no vast ocean, only sunlight and a comfortable bed.

Kit lay beside her, one arm loosely wrapped around her waist. It took her a moment to realize they were in Kit's bedchamber back in London. But how?

She moved to sit up, and pain lanced through her shoulder, then ripped through the rest of her. Her throat was too dry to make a sound, but she tried anyway.

"Kit . . . ," she rasped.

He shifted, sighed, and held on to her tighter, still asleep.

"Let him rest," a voice said from the shadows by the door. She saw Lionel sitting up in a chair, his face lined with worry. He stood, fetched a goblet of water for her, and then helped her drink. His hazel eyes were soft and his hair was untidy, as though he had dragged his hands through it repeatedly.

Grateful for the water, she lay back on the pillows. "Thank you," she whispered. Then after a moment, she found the strength to ask, "What happened?"

He set the empty goblet on the table beside her. "How much do you remember?"

"The ship . . . Balfour and Walsh were there. Then Kit found me . . ." Flashes of memories dug into her head like shards of glass.

"You were shot. Balfour set fire to the ship and nearly killed you and Kit. Kit leapt off the deck with you and landed in the water. Walsh is under arrest. Balfour had a pistol hidden on him. He tried to shoot Kit, but—"

"I shot him." She had killed a man who could only ever cause harm. She had no strength to care for taking that life. Balfour's death was already a hollow memory for her, one she sensed would fade almost completely with time.

"Is Kit all right?" she asked Lionel.

"Yes, he's just exhausted. You've been asleep for three days. He's kept a vigil at your side every minute. He refused to leave you, even though the magistrate handling the case for Walsh demanded he make a statement. In the end, he had to make his statement in here. I daresay having the magistrate see you like this helped Kit's testimony."

With a trembling hand, Suzannah stroked Kit's hair. Then she gasped. "Oh my God. Darius. He tried to save me. Balfour's men . . ." She couldn't finish.

"Darius is alive. If your friend hadn't found him, however, we would have lost him."

"My friend?" She couldn't think of who Lionel meant.

"That theater fellow. Jude something or other. He found Darius and got him to Dr. Jordan. He saved Darius's life."

Suzannah shut her eyes, whispering a thank-you to Jude for being there.

"What will happen now?" she asked Lionel.

Kit's friend grinned, despite his obvious weariness. "Now? Now you get to live, truly live, without looking over your shoulder or fearing the past. I imagine that at some point you have a portrait to finish, and we have a play to attend, as I believe you requested."

She shook her head, unconvinced. "But is this all *truly* over?"

"Yes, it is. Walsh's shipping company belongs to Ashton Lennox now, and Balfour's cases are being reexamined. Even though he's dead, it will certainly be proven that he was guilty of the crime of false imprisonment on more than one occasion. Others might now find their freedom or at least their good names and memories restored thanks to Kit."

Kit stirred, yawned, and opened his eyes. "Lionel, what are you—?" He then realized that Lionel was talking to Suzannah, not him. He sat up in shock.

"How long have you been awake?" he asked, leaning forward and placing a hand on her hip.

She covered his hand with one of her own. "Only a few minutes."

"Are you in pain? Lionel, fetch something for her pain—"

"I hurt, yes, but I don't need anything right now. Please, just rest here with me."

He seemed to understand what she was asking and leaned down to kiss the crown of her hair. "For as long as it takes," he said.

Lionel grunted as he stood with a weary sigh like he was a man twice his age. "I shall leave you alone for a while," he said with a twinkle in his eye, then quietly stepped outside the room and closed the door.

She sighed in relief. "It's over. *Finally.*"

"It is far from over," Kit said.

She tensed, fearing what new danger he might be referring to.

"But Lionel just said—"

Kit stroked a long, calloused fingertip over her cheek. "I meant the story isn't over."

"What story?" she asked, mesmerized by the light shining from his dark eyes.

"*Our* story."

"I do love stories," she admitted. "But how did ours begin?"

"Once upon a time . . . ," he said in a sonorous voice that made her giggle.

"That's how all fairy tales begin."

He traced her lips with the pad of his thumb. "Did I not mention our story is a fairy tale?"

"No, you didn't." She was delighted to see Kit so playful, even though he was clearly tired.

"Well, it is. Now, where was I?"

"Once upon a time . . ."

"Oh yes, once upon a time, there was a kindly old king and his young prince who ruled a distant land. And in that land, there was a crofter and his lovely young daughter. When she'd been born, the fairies had gifted her with the talent to paint the truth of anything she saw."

Suzannah carefully settled back on the pillows more. "Is that so?"

"Yes, and one day an evil sorcerer put a curse upon the prince, sending him so far away that he could not find his way home. But the crofter's daughter painted, and her art started to break the evil spell upon the prince.

"The prince journeyed for seven years to try to return home, a journey that was hard and dangerous. But the old king had died while the prince was away, and so had the crofter, but the little artist continued to paint and the prince continued his journey.

"One night the prince came upon the crofter's daughter painting the world with her magic, and just like that, the curse withered away like the vines on an old castle. The chains that had bound him crumbled to dust. She had set him free."

"What happened next? Did they live happily ever after?"

"Of course," Kit said. "She went on to paint kings and queens. Artists across the kingdom wanted to learn to paint the truth like she did."

Suzannah ran her fingertips over his bare forearm. "And what about the prince?"

"He realized he was a man *blessed*, not cursed. He had his home, his friends, and above all that he had love in his heart again because of her. Someday he would grow old, surrounded by children and grandchildren, but so long as he had his little painter to love and cherish, the soul inside him and the soul inside her were together always because . . . well, death cannot harm those who love, can it?

"So they lived on forever, even after their bodies had passed on. They lived in the air, in the soil, in the trees, and in the lives of those they loved. That is what happily ever after means, doesn't it?" Kit's words were heavy with emotion, and Suzannah grasped his shirt and drew him down to kiss her.

In that moment she glimpsed the shining future she knew they would have. She had rarely given thought to fairy tales or happily-ever-afters—those weren't normally part of the lives of women like her—yet somehow she had been running toward one all along, and so had Kit.

As their kiss deepened, she felt like a young girl again, running free through a meadow, feeling the sun on her skin and the breeze in her hair. Every bit of her life as a child had held wonder. There were infinite glories out there, from the distant stars above to the petals of the wildflowers beneath her feet. One had simply to see the beauty for what it was . . . and love it all with the same wonder as when they were young.

When they took a moment to catch their breath, he smiled down at her.

"And they lived . . . ," she began.

"*Happily* ever after," he finished.

Two months later

Kit was in the drawing room wearing his best evening clothes and doing his best to fight off a sudden rush of nerves. The room was full of his friends, all similarly dressed, and the staff of his London house, along with Henry, who was no longer on crutches and stood beside Jude. In the last few months, the lad had grown another two inches or so, Kit would swear, and he'd filled out to a size more appropriate for a boy his age. Mrs. Swanson's cooking had worked miracles on the lad.

Everyone in the drawing room held glasses of punch and talked excitedly until a hush finally descended on the room when the double doors of the large drawing room opened.

Suzannah floated inside. She wore a silvery Ankara pearl silk evening gown, which gave off a shimmering iridescent sparkle as she moved through the room. She removed her evening gloves, handing them to a waiting maid, as she came toward the room's focal point.

There stood a tall canvas in the center of the room with a white sheet draped over it. Suzannah had been fiercely protecting it for the last few months, allowing no one to see it. The train of her gown swept behind her as she turned to the crowd. A slender diadem of sapphires rested on the wild waves of her coiffure. She was his countess, and today she looked every bit of it. Kit could not deny the swell of pride he felt in that moment to call Suzannah his wife.

"I would like to thank all of you for coming tonight." Suzannah spoke clearly, but Kit heard the note of raw emotion in her voice. "We've had quite a change in our world these last few months, a shift toward a new future in this house. As you may know, I met my husband when he hired me to paint his portrait." Suzannah's gaze touched his, and her lovely eyes softened. Kit's hands shook as he set his glass of punch down. He barely dared to breathe.

"He asked for me to paint the truth. To show London the kind of man he was now, what society had made him after seven years of transportation to Australia for a crime he didn't commit."

Kit was dizzy now, his nerves running riot within him. He reminded himself that it was over. Balfour was dead and Walsh had been sentenced to transportation. One man was gone and the other was dead. There was nothing left to fear. Suzannah's portrait shouldn't frighten him, but somehow it did. He had demanded the truth from her, but now he found he was not ready for it. That old Kit, the man full of only rage and vengeance, was gone, and he never wanted to see that old version of himself again.

"It is my pleasure to unveil this portrait of my husband." Suzannah reached up to grasp the sheet with one hand and pulled it down. The white fabric billowed like a ship's sail a moment before settling at Suzannah's feet. Not daring to look, Kit heard the gasps of men and women around him. Dread squeezing his heart, Kit finally raised his gaze, prepared to face the truth.

Warren reached out and grasped his arm, holding him steady as his knees buckled. It was not a portrait of him brooding and shirtless with his scars on full display. It was of him seated at a breakfast table in lively conversation with his friends. He and Darius were laughing. Suzannah had captured Darius's gentle affection, Vincent's quiet charm, Warren and Felix's teasing banter, and Lionel's amusement.

The colors, the expressions, the emotions she had captured were so real that for a moment it was like staring into a mirror. On the mantel behind Kit she'd painted a ship, much like the one that had taken him to Australia, and on the table, next to a vase of colorful exotic flowers, was a small ivory elephant. She hadn't tried to hide what he'd been through, but she hadn't let those experiences define him. This was his new truth—the man who'd survived so much had now found joy again. She'd painted him with love, with compassion, with *truth*.

"What do you call your painting, my lady?" one of the guests asked.

Suzannah bit her lip, and then, unable to help herself, she broke into a wide smile.

"I call it *The Rogues of Devil's Square*."

Kit found he was smiling back, so full of love for her

that he couldn't think past the thought that he wanted to kiss her right there in front of everyone.

"The king will have to have a portrait made now," Vincent chuckled from Kit's side. "I hear he's craving to convey a more approachable image. He'll be mad with jealousy until she paints him like that."

"Then everyone in London will want her to paint them," added Darius.

Kit kept his gaze on his wife, his heart bursting. How could so much change so fast in such a short time? From darkness to light, from hopelessness to hope? A new sense of wonder filled him at how unpredictable life could be in the best of ways.

"She deserves to be seen for who she is," he replied. "To be recognized for the spark of genius and magic within her."

"Everyone deserves that," Vincent said and placed a hand on his shoulder. "Including you."

Magic was indeed in the room tonight. Magic born of love, loyalty, and trust. Kit couldn't have asked for anything more.

Suzannah passed through the crowd until she stood beside him.

"Well?" she asked.

"*Wellll . . .*" He drew out the word with a teasing, indecisive tone. "I think you've proven how brilliant you are, my darling."

"You truly like it?"

He pulled her into his arms, kissing her and wishing they were alone so he could do more than that. "You gave me my life back, my friends, my heart . . . my hope." His throat tightened. "You gave me *everything*, Suzannah. How can I ever repay that debt?"

His little painter smiled impishly. "I suppose by loving me until the end of everything."

"And beyond even that," he promised.

"Good." She locked her arm through his. "Now that's settled, we had better leave or we'll miss the play."

Kit kissed the top of her head and shouted to the room, "Do you hear that? Time to leave, everyone! The coaches are waiting outside. I expect it will be a packed house tonight."

Outside, the stars above glittered and the sounds of merriment echoed down the street. Soon, the curtain would rise in the theater on Drury Lane . . .

Darius excused himself from the crowd of friends outside Kit's home and quickly crossed the street, using his cane only sparingly now. He had recovered from his wounds but was still a bit stiff in the mornings and evenings. It turns out getting shot wasn't the best thing for a man's constitution. He walked up the steps to his home, and Mr. Chelsea opened the door.

"Your Grace?" His butler stared at him in open confusion. He was not expected to return until much later this evening.

"I forgot my gloves," he said in apology. The butler nodded and sent a footman upstairs to fetch them.

When the footman returned, Darius thanked the man and then went back outside so he wouldn't miss his ride to the theater, only to barrel into a figure that had been coming up the steps behind him.

"Oof!" a feminine voice gasped. Darius took hold of the woman by the arms just in time to prevent her from tumbling down the stairs.

"I beg your pardon," he said to her automatically, then blinked as he got a good look at the woman.

She was perhaps five and a half feet tall, with soft and classically beautiful features. Her mouth was perfect for kissing and one that gave him the most wicked fantasies. But it was her eyes . . . the kind of eyes that would haunt him forever. They were the most beautiful hazel eyes he'd ever seen. They held a hint more green than blue and had gold flecks shimmering in the irises.

Dark brown lashes fluttered as she seemed to take him in at the same time. Darius didn't miss the innocent flash of desire there. He knew when a woman wanted him, and this woman, innocent as she was, wanted him now. It was a response he was used to, but he tried not to get carried away with that when it came to the fairer sex.

With this woman, however, he was tempted to give in to his less-than-gentlemanly instincts. She couldn't have been more than nineteen, perhaps twenty. Darius had only one thought in his head as he stared at her.

I'm going to take her to bed and see those eyes light up with ecstasy . . .

"Are—are you Lord Tiverton?" The woman's voice was soft, yet he heard strength in it too. She was here with a purpose.

"Yes." He watched her break eye contact with him to dig

in her reticule to produce a letter. She held it out to him, and he took it from her in confusion.

His name was written upon it. The handwriting was one he recognized. He broke the seal and unfolded the letter.

Darius,

It has been a long time since we've spoken. I regret my last words to you the day we buried your father. Losing my brother broke my heart, and you reminded me so much of him that it hurt me to see you.

If you are reading this, it means I am gone. I have but one favor to ask of you. Take care of the young woman who bears this letter.

Her mother was someone I loved many years ago, but she chose to marry another. When that man died and left her both penniless and with a child, I took pity on her. I settled them in a little cottage by the sea. When she died, I took that child in to raise as my own when she was fourteen. Recently my health has been failing, and I fear my role in raising her has come to an end.

Please help her come out into society and provide for her what she will require as a *young lady. The entirety of my estate must go to my son, which means all of Meredith's needs must be met by someone else, and I am hoping that someone will be you. Please see that she is married well to a good man. I wish I'd been brave enough to say my apologies to you in person, nephew, but at least they are here now in this letter. I am sorry.*

Yours faithfully,
Benjamin St. John

DARIUS LOOKED UP AT THE YOUNG WOMAN WHO UNTIL MOMENTS ago had featured in his most wicked fantasies. Now he was supposed to take her as his ward?

Damn his uncle . . . damn him . . .

"What is your name, child?" Darius asked curtly. He knew she was called Meredith, but he wanted her full name.

"I'm not a child. I'm nineteen," she said quite proudly. "And it's Meredith Montague."

He held up the letter. "Have you read this?"

Meredith shook her head. "No, but Uncle Ben said I was to deliver it to you. He said that you would help me find . . . a husband?" She said this with adorable uncertainty.

"You traveled all the way from Yorkshire alone?" Darius asked. He saw no coach or servants with her. She looked so young and innocent, though certainly not a child. Behind her brave front lay a deep concern about her future. It made him want to pull her into his arms and kiss away the worries that hung upon her brow.

"Yes, I took stagecoaches and spent the night at a coaching inn. I had a little pin money saved up, but I'm thankful you were home this evening . . . I have no money to stay anywhere else."

Darius couldn't help but stare. This lovely urchin in an out-of-season frock was seeking refuge in his home, and he was going to have to behave himself. But something of her story confused him.

"My uncle was able to leave you no money at all?" he asked. Surely his uncle could have left her some travel money, if nothing else.

"He tried, but . . . you see, it was a bit complicated after he died. His will only left a wish for his son to provide me with travel money at his discretion. Harry said that I should remain at your uncle's estate, and . . . Well, he demanded I be his companion if I wished to stay. Naturally, I couldn't agree. No matter how insistent he was." She touched her arms as thought to hug herself, and Darius spied the hint of bruises upon her wrists. "He then refused to provide me with any money at all, since it was at his discretion."

Darius scowled. The next time he saw his cousin, he would throttle the bounder. Harry had always been prone to excess, with drinking and gambling occupying much of his time. Darius could only imagine what he had told this poor young woman she would have to do to keep a roof over her head. He'd been no better, he realized. Unlike Harry, however, he would protect Meredith, even from himself.

"Harry is a bastard," he said bluntly, and pushed the

door to his home open. "You will be safe with me." He studied the valise at her feet. "I don't suppose you have any decent evening gowns in that small travel case?"

"Only one, but it's a bit out of fashion—"

"That will do. Come inside and change quickly. I am off to a play that I simply cannot miss, and you shall come with me so we can discuss your situation further."

She opened her mouth, her eyes wide with worry.

"Fear not. You have a home here, Miss Montague. It is only the details that remain to be seen."

Her lashes fluttered as she exhaled in relief.

"I loved my uncle and will honor his wish to care for you and see you settled in marriage to a good man."

"Thank you, Your Grace."

In the meantime, he would figure out what he was going to do with her. Even if he called Meredith his ward, this would still create a stir in society. He would need to hire a chaperone and have a wardrobe purchased for her.

His entire life was about to be upended, all for a pretty pair of hazel eyes. Damn his uncle. How was he going to be a gentleman when he had to keep himself from seducing the most beautiful woman he'd ever seen?

THANK YOU SO MUCH FOR READING *THE SCOUNDREL OF DRURY LANE!* The Rogues of Devil's Square continues in The Duke's Carriage Window which is available now at all retailers!

www.laurensmithbooks.com

www.facebook.com/laurendianasmith/
www.instagram.com/laurensmithbooks

ABOUT THE AUTHOR

USA TODAY Bestselling Author Lauren Smith is an Oklahoma attorney by day, who pens adventurous and edgy romance stories by the light of her smart phone flashlight app. She knew she was destined to be a romance writer when she attempted to re-write the entire *Titanic* movie just to save Jack from drowning. Connecting with readers by writing emotionally moving, realistic and sexy romances no matter what time period is her passion. She's won multiple awards in several romance subgenres including: New England Reader's Choice Awards, Greater Detroit BookSeller's Best Awards, and a Semi-Finalist award for the Mary Wollstonecraft Shelley Award.

To connect with Lauren, visit her at:
www.laurensmithbooks.com
lauren@Laurensmithbooks.com

facebook.com/LaurenDianaSmith

x.com/LSmithAuthor

instagram.com/LaurenSmithbooks

amazon.com/stores/Lauren-Smith/author/B009L54KTC?
ref=ap_rdr&store_ref=ap_rdr&isDramIntegrated=true&shop-
pingPortalEnabled=true

bookbub.com/authors/lauren-smith

www.ingramcontent.com/pod-product-compliance
Lightning Source LLC
Chambersburg PA
CBHW021234310726

48971CB00006B/1823